THE LONG PAST

& OTHER STORIES

BY

GINN

HALE

BLIND EYE BOOKS
blindeyebooks.com

The Long Past
& Other Stories
by Ginn Hale

Published by:
Blind Eye Books
1141 Grant Street
Bellingham WA 98225
blindeyebooks.com

Edited by Nicole Kimberling
Copyedited by Anne Scott
Cover Illustration by Gwen Toevs
Interior Illustrations by Dawn Kimberling

The Hollow History of Professor Perfectus first appeared in the *Magic & Mayhem* anthology from GRNW Press 2016.

An earlier edit of *Get Lucky* first appeared in the *Once Upon a Time in the Weird West* anthology from Dreamspinner Press 2016.

First Edition October 2017
Copyrite © Ginn Hale 2017

Printed in the United States
Print ISBN: 978-1-935560-51-7
Digital ISBN: 978-1-935560-52-4

CONTENTS

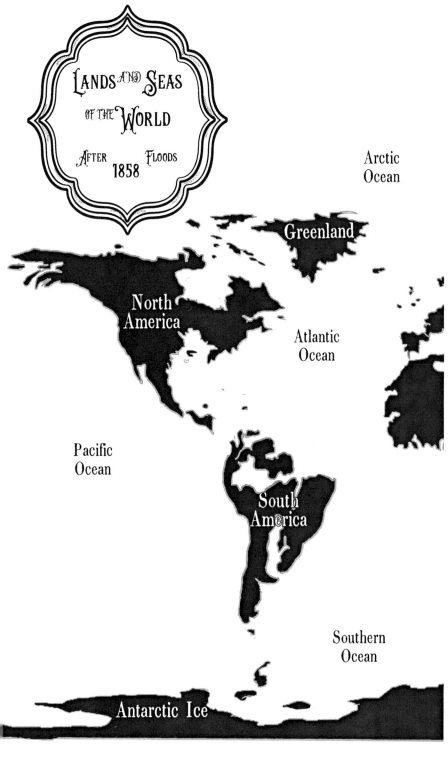

Arctic
Ocean

Europe

ASIA

Pacific
Ocean

AFRICA

Indian
Ocean

Australia

Southern
Ocean

Antarctic Ice

AFTER THE FLOODS OF 1858

CANADA

New Boston

New York

Chicago City

INLAND SEA

Fort Arvada City

San Francisco City

MEXICO

THE LONG PAST

Chapter One

Colorado Territory 1864

High up in the clear blue sky, a group of pterosaurs swept past the red-and-white-striped balloon of an approaching airship. The gull-sized creatures soared through the dirigible's wake and then dived towards dark waters far below.

Grover watched the wily green pterosaurs descend to snatch silver-sided fish from the waves of the Inland Sea then go flapping back towards their roosts in the sea-swept cliffs of the Rocky Mountains. His attention returned to the star-spangled airship with its brassy gondola. The ship hadn't yet crossed through the gray haze of the spell dome. It arched up from the alchemically fortified walls of the city and kept out most anything bigger than a songbird. Even across the distance and through the distortion, Grover thought he could make out the gold sun-shaped insignia of the US Office of Theurgy and Magicum on the gondola's prow.

Theurgist professors, soldiers and maybe even a mage floated up there. All of them coming here to investigate the big blue sea that had flooded the states and territories from Kansas to the Gulf of Mexico.

The High Plains had transformed into a seabed. The foothills of the Rocky Mountains had become a chain of islands dotting the blue water, while high peaks now stood like a vast, great levee. As the waters had spread, so had lush fern jungles and the strange, old creatures that inhabited both.

Land and lives had been lost, and Fort Arvada had been inundated with refugees. And yet after six years, this single airship was all the aid the federal government sent. Grover just hoped they'd brought plenty of powdered alchemic stone. The city's fortifications had been uprooted and stretched thin as paper to enclose as much farmland as possible, but the spells were old and growing weaker with every season.

Soon nothing would stand between the farmers of Fort Arvada and the old creatures.

Back on the bandstand, the musicians indulged in a final practice of their jubilant welcome to the visiting dignitaries while the gathered crowd peered up at the sky. Grover briefly spotted his cousin Frank, looking sharp despite having his nine-year-old daughter balanced on his shoulders. She waved her rag doll at the sky.

Up on the bandstand Mayor Wilder anxiously leafed through the pages of his speech. Mrs. Cora Cody and several other society women straightened their patchwork dresses and smiled at each other like they were about to attend their first dances. Then Cora turned to her husband, George, and straightened his beaver pelt top hat. Miss Xu Song shouted gleefully from the crowd that she could see the airship. Hundreds of men hooted and whooped.

From his post within the church steeple, Grover studied the expanse of cloud drifting across the blue sky. A ghostly pale wing dipped down from the white billows. Grover hefted his rifle and tracked the huge silvery pterosaur.

"Thunderbird," Toby Cody whispered from beside him. The spindly ginger youth worked the focus of his spyglass. "Holy Moses! It's a big'un, Grove."

Grover continued to follow the beast through the sight of his rifle. Its silver membranous wings stretched a good thirty feet across. Sunlight glinted along the saber-sharp beak. Squinting, Grover could just make out the jet-black eyes and that slight curve that lent all thunderbirds the appearance of smiling slyly down on the rest of the world.

It swooped into a killing dive and Toby gasped. A shot rang out from spiked turret on the roof of the bank and then two more. Sheriff Lee shooting, like some greenhorn, at a target too far to hit. The sheer size of thunderbirds always made them appear closer than they were. Grover kept watching the huge pterosaur—a female, he guessed from the muted gold color of her skull crest. Such grace and speed flowed through even the slightest flick of her wings.

"Grove." Toby's voice rose with nervous alarm. He didn't grasp Grover's arm, but he sounded like he wanted to. "Grove, she's close to the airship!"

"They got plenty of spells and guns of their own." Grover kept his eyes on the thunderbird's angle of descent. It was like watching an arrow in flight. "Anyhow that thunderbird ain't interested in them. She's after a mountain goat."

Sheriff Lee fired again, and this time managed to wing the airship's gondola.

"Oh Lord," Toby whispered as the airship's cannon ports swung open and cannon barrels angled down toward the welcoming crowd gathered in the city square.

The thunderbird snatched a white goat in her massive jaws and swooped up, soaring across the mountain face to claim a perch on a distant cliff. Likely she was young, and keeping out of her elders' territories by nesting along the city's fortifications. Come fall she might grow bolder. It would do to keep track of her, if she remained in the area.

Meanwhile, on the open ground of the square the hundreds of folk, all turned out in their Sunday best, stood frozen staring up at the airship's glinting long guns.

Toby's blonde aunt, Cora, rose to her feet on the bandstand. The blue ribbons festooning her yellow hat and dress wavered in the breeze as she started to sing "My Country, 'Tis of Thee". The band struck up after her, and soon the entire crowd joined in, belting out the anthem. In response the airship's cannons retracted and the gunports fell closed.

The massive dirigible descended, its alchemic engines droning over the gathered crowd. Blue light flared as it passed through the spell dome. Federal airmen dropped ropes and slithered down them to secure the lines to the ground. As they hauled the airship down, Toby looked to Grover and grinned.

"You read that thunderbird like the Bible, Grove."

Grover shrugged but indulged the youth with a smile.

At ten, Toby was still more in awe of Grover's sharp-shooting and tracking skills than he was aware of him as a Black man. Even that didn't mean what it would have once, not with slave states from Texas to Georgia and down to Florida underwater. Blacks, Whites, Indians, Mexicans, even Chinese—they were all refugees in the mountains now, and for six years the people of Fort Arvada had only had one another to trust in and rely upon.

"You figure them federals are gonna put everything back to how it was before?" Toby asked.

"Stranger things happen, I reckon," Grover replied. Though he wasn't sure how he felt about returning to an age of cotton fields and plantations. He'd take floods and dinosaurs any day if it meant an end to pattyrollers and slave catchers.

"You think they brought sacks of magic dust with 'em?"

"Sure they have." How much they'd charge for the ground alchemic stone was another matter, but Grover figured that if anyone could bluff, bluster and charm a load of federal bigwigs it would be Mayor Wilder.

"Do you suppose one of them's a real live mage?" Toby leaned against the steeple railing and studied the line of uniformed men descending the gold stairs of the airship gondola. Grover followed the boy's gaze. He took in the two slender white men both sporting blond mutton-chop sideburns and top hats. Not much of interest to see there, aside from the fact they appeared to be twins.

An emaciated, gray-haired woman wearing a mink jacket and a massive sapphire dress over a cage crinoline followed them. The mourning band sewn to her coat sleeve displayed the Union Jack often worn by the English diaspora. Grover wondered if she was one of those lady mages who'd forfeited her title to practice magic legally in the US. Or maybe she'd fled to escape the floods in England and France. She looked old as iron and hard enough to split flint with her glare.

A fourth figure stepped down from the stairs and started towards the bandstand where Mayor Wilder stood waiting. For an instant Grover felt like his eyes failed him. As the tall, lean man approached the bandstand, the mayor's composure faltered. His lined, pale face flushed, and he grinned like a joyous child. Cora Cody, on the other hand, paled noticeably, and her husband reached out to steady her.

Grover's grip on his rifle nearly slipped, and his heart began to beat so hard he felt it in his temples. He gaped down at that angular face and the wind-tousled auburn hair he'd never thought to see again in his life. Lawrence Wilder took the stairs of the bandstand quickly and embraced his father.

Grover couldn't pull his gaze from Lawrence. Every detail of the other man held him, from the supple, worn quality of his black boots and long army coat, to the string of medals decorating the chest of his blue uniform. He'd grown broader in the shoulder, but his face seemed hollowed and his smile appeared oddly fleeting. There was something slightly off about the motion of his right arm as well. He held it stiffly and moved it with deliberate care.

Grover wondered if his skin still smelled like ponderosa pine or if that boyish hitch caught in his low laugh when he was drunk. Did he even remember Grover or their secret adventures into the woods?

"Who's that?" Toby pointed as if Grover might have missed the spectacle.

"Mage Lawrence Wilder, the mayor's son." Grover hoped the boy didn't notice how his voice caught on the name. "He went off to fight the Arrow War over in China eight years ago. He died in battle—" The anguish of that loss tore through Grover even now. Unlike Cora who publically mourned her fiancé's demise, Grover had found solace only in the isolation of the wilderness. He still couldn't ride past the apple trees of the Wilder House without feeling as if someone had pushed a knife into his chest. "Or that's what was reported."

"But he's alive." Toby angled his spyglass down at Lawrence.

"That does appear to be the case." Eight years he'd been gone and six of those presumed dead. What in the blazes had happened?

On the bandstand, Lawrence and the mayor broke apart and welcomed the other officials from the Office of Theurgy and Magicum. Briefly, while the mayor read from his speech, Lawrence seemed to search through the gathered crowd. Grover fought the urge to shout or wave like a mad man—that sort of scene wouldn't do anybody any good, and that was assuming it was him Lawrence looked for.

Eight years without a single letter wasn't exactly an indication of fidelity.

Toby toyed with his spyglass and heaved a particularly dramatic sigh.

"You wanna go down and sing with Aunt Cora and Uncle George?"

"Nah, I ain't likely to recollect most the words." Grover hardly pulled his gaze from Lawrence. His pulse still pounded so hard that he felt certain his voice would quaver like some old auntie if he tried to sing. "I'm going to keep watch up here a while longer. The dome ain't quite healed up from where the airship burned through it."

Toby hesitated. But after Grover pointed out that Maria and Claudia Garcia were selling cochinito cookies one dozen for a nickel, Toby abandoned him right quick.

Grover watched and listened to the formal welcome but in such a shaken state that he wasn't certain he understood half of what was said. He couldn't stop staring at Lawrence or wondering what had happened to him.

The mutton-chop twins revealed themselves to be the brothers David and Nathaniel Tucker, both war veterans and professors of theurgy. While they grinned and offered assurances about advances in alchemic engines and expanding the fortification spells, the gray-haired woman, Lady Honora Astor, glowered at the crowd. When asked to offer a few words, she stated that justice would be had for all those thousands whose lives and homelands had been torn from them.

Her words inspired resounding cheers from the crowd, but made Grover feel uneasy. Lady Astor's ire reminded Grover of when he'd been six years old and Reverend Dodd had stormed into his family's cabin, red-faced and accusing Grover of feeding his parishioners' dairy cows locoweed and cursing their milk. Grover's ma had looked terrified, but she'd stepped right between the reverend and Grover and hefted her snakewood broom like she meant to lay Reverend Dodd out with it. A moment later Grover's pa had bounded in from the tanning shed with his fleshing knife still in his hand and sent the reverend running.

Grover had felt both awed by and proud of his parents that afternoon.

But a week later, Grover had woken, choking on smoke as his ma pulled him from his bed and flames climbed the walls of their cabin. He and his ma escaped, but his big, gentle pa had died fighting to save their home.

Instinctively, Grover glanced to Mayor Wilder. He'd been the one who'd given Grover's ma work at his mansion after the fire, and he'd seen to it that Reverend Dodd let them be. The mayor was a strong believer in abolition and also related by blood to too many genuine mages to confuse a little boy's capering with any sort of real curse.

Today the mayor beamed at his son and assured the officials that all the resources of Fort Arvada City would be at their disposal. Then Cora Cody and her friends in the Ladies' Christian Charity Union sang a hymn. Grover could sense Cora fighting not to stare at Lawrence the entire time. Lawrence offered her a curt smile but he didn't hold her gaze, nor did he sing along.

At last the public welcome ended. The party of federal officials and the city's most prominent citizens began dispersing to prepare for the private celebration to be held that evening at the mayor's residence. Though just as Lawrence reached the steps of the ribbon-festooned bandstand, he raised his head, and Grover thought that he stared straight up at him. But Lawrence's expression remained distant. He descended into the crowd flanked by ranks of blue-uniformed soldiers while all around excited throngs cheered and waved.

Long rays of setting sunlight shot between the jagged peaks of the surrounding mountains. Up in the cliffs a pack of coyotes howled high and long against the wails of a flock of pterosaurs.

Grover shifted in his saddle and tipped back his wide-brimmed hat.

He hadn't been down to the Wilder House in years, and in truth he had no right or reason to go now. If he possessed a drop of common sense, he'd turn around right now and ride back to his room in the Codys' boarding house. Because what the blazes was he going to do when he got there? Hitch Betty to a post with a bunch of nervous horses and stroll on in through the front door like he'd mistaken himself for a man of high society rather than the son of their former cook?

Beneath him, Betty ruffled her rust-speckled feathers and twisted her long neck back to cast him that eerie owl-like stare of hers. Grover reached out and stroked the warm blue skin between her huge amber eyes and her glossy bronze beak. In response she produced a sweet little chirp then picked up her pace, carrying Grover down the road at a breath-taking clip.

Betty was no more natural to this world than the hulking, toothy giants that stalked the mountains. Grover knew that. But he'd found Betty five years ago, still trapped in her egg at an abandoned nest, and something about her plaintive peeping had moved him. Maybe he'd just been too lonely out in the woods with no company but his memories of Lawrence—he didn't know.

Whatever the reason, he hadn't left her to die. Instead he'd carefully pried the shell open and kept the little beast fed and warm all through that fall and winter.

In spring when he brought her with him back into town, it had caused a stir. But Betty liked to show off, and that made it easy to demonstrate how well he'd trained her.

Both Robert Haim and Will Blackhill had offered to buy her off of him. Grover declined as politely as he knew how and sold them the hides and feathers of other dinosaurs instead. To stable her, he'd handed over an extra pound of salt alongside the pelts and dried meat that he normally traded George Cody for his own room and board.

Round the dinner table at the boarding house, George Cody reckoned Betty was some kind of early relation to an ostrich. (He was a firm believer in Mr. Darwin's evolution theory.) He'd shown around several lithographs from his fine volumes of natural-science books. But comparing an ostrich to Betty was like comparing a canary to an eagle. She stood hip to hip with most horses, and instead of tiny wings, she possessed feathered arms, ending in three-taloned fingers—which she was not shy of slashing at any stallion that came after her feed. Claws like Bowie knives tipped each of her long toes, and her plumed tail rippled with so much muscle that she could lash even the meanest dog ten feet in the air.

Though tonight, Grover hoped no one would be setting dogs on him and Betty.

Ahead, the Wilder House loomed up over the other tidy wood-trimmed homes lining both sides of the packed dirt street. The three-story house sported wide steps, carved pillars, big windows and a steep, sweeping roof. The setting sun lit the touches of gold that adorned the oversized front door and glimmered from the star-shaped weather vane.

The gnarled apple trees that Grover and Lawrence had climbed as children had grown taller than the wrought-iron front gate. Their white blossoms littered the brick drive like confetti. As he rode up the drive, Grover caught the long notes of a fiddle emanating from the house. Then the rest of a string band swung into a lively dance tune. The music sounded nearly as raucous as a flock of pterosaurs singing into the cool twilight. When he drew nearer, the low rumble of conversation drifted to him from behind the impressive white walls.

Silhouettes fluttered and danced across the white curtains of the big bay windows. Couples circled and promenaded while music and muffled laughter drifted on the evening wind.

To Grover, the flickering figures looked ghostly, like phantoms of the years past when he had so often peered between the kitchen doors, spying on all the high-society folk of Fort Arvada as they strutted in uniforms and gowns.

Before Lawrence had grown old enough to join his father's guests, he, too, had crept down the backstairs and crouched beside Grover. They'd sat and laughed at how clumsy the guests became after they guzzled too much of Ma's special punch. Lawrence always leaned into him like he couldn't keep warm without Grover's arm around him.

Though all too soon Lawrence had numbered among those cavorting in the ballroom. More than once, Grover had been called upon to carry out the silver trays laden with punch-filled crystal glasses—by then he'd been much more able to manage the weight then either his ma or the housekeeper.

He scowled at the grand porch, remembering the anger he'd felt, having to bite his tongue and drop his gaze like a beaten dog in front of Lawrence. Equal parts shame and frustration churned in him as he recalled how he'd alarmed his ailing ma by acting up—one night he'd even sassed Lawrence in front of a dozen white guests. Lawrence had been startled but then conceded the point to Grover. But Grover's ma had been furious. She'd tanned his backside like she'd caught him thieving.

That had been the first time Grover had run off to sulk in the woods. Back then he hadn't understood that his ma had witnessed and endured brutal reprisals for "uppity" behavior. She had borne horrific scars across her back and thighs, which Grover had never seen until after her death, when he'd washed her body. Before then, he'd simply felt aggrieved that she encouraged him to be proud and honest like his freeborn father but also expected that he'd keep his mouth shut and his head down.

For a time he'd tried to please her, particularly after she'd fallen so ill. He acted meek as a mouse those last three months. But after she passed on, he couldn't bring himself to go on simpering and scraping. He'd left the Wilder home and taken up his pa's trade of trapping.

Now he wasn't anyone's servant, and he'd never been anyone's slave. He walked straight into a place through the front doors or he didn't go in at all.

But the Wilder House wasn't a saloon, dry-goods store, music hall or boarding house—in those places Grover was a man, as good as any other, and he'd flatten any man who tried to say he was otherwise. But never in his life had Grover walked in through the front doors of the Wilder House. Studying the broad steps now, Grover felt like he'd shrunk back down into the scrawny scared six-year-old he'd been when he'd first arrived here.

He didn't want to go back to that past, and at the same time the ghost of his ma seemed to curl around him, whispering warning of where his pride would lead him.

You give them any cause, they will kill you just like they did your pa. They won't feel any more guilt for murdering you than they'd feel over throwing a flea in the fire.

The sound of a wagon rolling up the street behind him drew his attention, and Grover peered back into the twilight to see George and Cora Cody riding towards the house. No doubt they'd been invited—even through the gloom Grover could see that they were both dressed for a dance.

The last thing Grover wanted was to slink past them like he'd been thrown out on his ass. They'd both of them make too much of it and probably insist that he come along with them. They'd been among the few white citizens who'd stood up against Sheriff Lee and Reverend Dodd during the riots that followed the first floods. Still, Grover hated to be looked at all sad and sympathetic, like he was a runt puppy. They meant well, he knew that, but Grover didn't particularly enjoy others intervening on his behalf when he could damn well stand on his own if he felt like it.

So instead of turning around he nudged Betty towards the back of the house, past the tidy stables and the outbuildings, to the deep shadows of the garden. Grover glanced at the beds of peas, carrots, seedling cabbages, tomatoes and sweet peppers. He wondered if the new cook still tended the strawberry patch his ma had planted. But he didn't venture along the rows of vegetable beds. Instead he swung down from Betty and led her up the low hill where iris blossoms and daffodil flowers dotted the shadows beneath six apple trees.

Betty snapped several fat bugs from the air while Grover closed the distance to the largest apple tree.

Back when he'd only been twelve, he'd thought himself real clever, secretly carving his and Lawrence's initials on the underside of one of the lower branches. Of course the tree had been pruned a couple years later and his precious little spell had gone up in the wood stove. Just as well, cause if his ma had known he was trying to ensnare another boy in a love spell she would have beaten him like a dusty rug.

A figure suddenly loomed out from the shadows of the tree, and Grover had to stop himself from going for his gun out of reflex. He was the one trespassing here, after all. Faint gold light angled across Lawrence Wilder's sharp features and caught an unruly lock of his hair, making it look almost red. He held Grover's gaze only an instant before his left hand came up in the striking position for a killing spell. Blue light hissed up between Lawrence's long fingers.

"Hey now! No harm done." Grover stepped back fast and caught Betty's saddle. He didn't know that he could make it clear of the spell at such close range, but at least he could shove Betty aside.

Lawrence's expression turned to confusion.

"Is that thing yours?" He didn't drop his hand but nodded in Betty's direction.

"Betty? Sure. She carries me all around. She's quicker than any horse and don't need shoeing." As he spoke Grover realized why Lawrence had appeared so shocked. Though now his expression melted into something more like amusement.

"You domesticated an avemosaur?" The hint of an English accent lent Lawrence a disconcertingly foreign tone. He dropped his left hand to his side and peered at Betty, who paid him little mind as she pecked a plump spider from the trunk of an apple tree.

"Found her still in her egg and she took to me." Grover hadn't heard the term avemosaur before, but since the telegraph lines had flooded out, news reached them real slow across the Inland Sea. The bigwigs and college deans back east had probably christened the old creatures with fancy new monikers. Grover named the dinosaurs he encountered, but they weren't proper titles made up from Latin and Greek. George Cody delighted in explaining the meanings of various scientific names to him, but they didn't exactly roll off Grover's tongue.

If he'd been thinking at all straight, Grover would have asked what avemosaur meant and made himself sound a lick smarter than he'd been before Lawrence had left.

Instead Grover stood there staring, like he'd never seen another man in his life. He'd thought so often of Lawrence and held him in in his memory so dearly that it felt somehow strange to see him in the flesh and realize how much he'd gotten wrong—or maybe it was just how much Lawrence had grown up and changed. The years seemed to have carved all the softness from Lawrence's body and demeanor.

Deep angry lines etched his brow, and a series of sharp white scars cut across his right cheek. He held himself straight, and though his clothes looked slightly past their best, the neat, polished quality of them still stood out. Grover counted five medals pinned to his uniform.

By comparison, Grover knew he presented a dusty, rough figure. Normally he didn't think much of looking a bit shabby; with the cotton plantations gone and sea monsters sinking so many of the ships that attempted to cross the Inland Sea, even the wealthiest folks in Fort Arvada sported patches and made do with older cloth. At least hunting gave him easy access to the gold-patterned dinosaur hide that made up his chaps and Betty's saddle, as well as the black plumes that decorated his coat.

Still, he felt very aware of the fact that his shirtsleeves weren't quite long enough for his arms anymore and the buttons running down his shirtfront didn't match. A ragged tear marred the brim of his hat.

If he'd known he'd see Lawrence face to face today, he would have paid Mr. Chen to cut and slick back his wavy hair. But he'd shaved this morning and worn his clean shirt.

Lawrence appeared lost for anything to say as well. He glanced towards the house, and Grover expected him to announce that he needed to go back inside. He didn't want Lawrence to leave him, but at the same time he knew it would be better, probably for both of them. So he decided to make it easier for Lawrence.

"Well, I should probably move on." Grover managed to get the words out. "Betty will be wantin' her feed soon—"

"No, Grove, don't—" Lawrence caught his hand. "I just… Father has been talking a blue streak about how you know the rift lands better than anyone. He says you've hunted monstrirex and ichthyosaurs… I'd love to hear all about it. Don't go."

Lawrence flashed him that charming smile and met his gaze like they'd only been apart for a couple days. But it had been years—years Grover had mourned—and all this time Lawrence hadn't bothered to send even a postcard much less come back home.

His fingers felt warm against Grover's cool skin, and Grover imagined that if he leaned in close and took in a deep breath that rich scent of ponderosa and smoke would roll over him again. Only they weren't boys playing around. They were grown men who hardly knew each other anymore.

"I don't reckon I have half the stories to tell that you do." Grover drew his hand back with the pretense of scratching his own shoulder. "Eight years gone halfway across the world and mistaken for dead. Bet you could make a fortune selling that story to one of them fancy periodicals."

Lawrence's smile compressed to a flat line.

"That's a bet you'd lose, Grove." Again, he glanced over his shoulder to the house, his expression deeply troubled, almost angry. Golden candlelight glowed from the windows, throwing soft pools of light across the grounds. Moths flitted around the light, and Betty watched them with predatory excitement.

Grover caught the leather lead attached to her saddle before she could race to one of the windows and likely scare the blazes out of someone. Lawrence eyed Betty, then his expression softened a little.

"Will she let anyone but you touch her?" Lawrence asked.

Grover nodded. Bottom fact was that Betty took to folk too well. She didn't know what sons-of-bitches some could be or how bad they'd like hurting her. But Lawrence had always been tenderhearted about animals and so, changed as he might be, Grover couldn't imagine him doing Betty any harm.

"Go on, hold out your hand to her," Grover instructed him.

Lawrence extended his left hand like he might have to a horse. Betty cocked her head, giving him her owl-look, then she dropped her head down and stroked the side of her big beak and cheek against Lawrence's fingers. Lawrence smiled as Betty worked her beak back over his hand like a cat wrapping itself around a fellow's leg. He laughed when Betty nudged up beside him and started her little song and dance of scratching the dirt and crooning as she settled herself down on the ground.

The entire time Lawrence's right hand remained shoved deep in his coat pocket, his arm stiff at his side. Wasn't no question of whether he'd been hurt during the Arrow War, only of how badly.

Bad enough to be pronounced dead, Grover thought. Was it any wonder he didn't want to tell all?

Lawrence knelt beside Betty gently stroking the long feathers of her folded arms, then he dropped his hand and simply studied her as she settled and coiled her tail around her body so the long plumes covered the tip of her beak. For a few moments he continued to gaze at Betty with the same thoughtful expression Grover remembered him wearing when he was out in the woods sketching leaves and birds in his diaries. He looked up at Grover.

"In all this time fighting, I've never seen one of these old creatures so…" Lawrence didn't finish but just offered Grover a brief smile and turned his gaze back down to Betty. He ran his hand over her back like she was blown glass.

The reel floating from the house faded to be replaced by a more plaintive melody. One of the ladies sang something about her boy coming home across green fields. Grover leaned back against the apple tree and searched between the breaks in crooked branches for the stars overhead. Dark protective spells nearly blacked them all out from here in the city. He'd only been back under the dome a month but already he missed the sight of clear, bright stars. Though Grover thought he could just make out the constellation of the big bear where Lawrence's airship had burned through earlier.

"You back to stay?" Grover asked. "Or just blowing through with the Office of Theurgy and Magicum?"

Lawrence looked up at him.

"I don't know," Lawrence said. "It's not all up to me."

"No? The blathering Tucker brothers giving you orders now or is it Lady Honora Sour-Cherry?"

Lawrence snorted but his grin didn't last. He rose to his feet.

"Honora's not bad. She used to be a joy but…" Lawrence seemed like he was searching for the right words but only shook his head. "Beijing took a lot out of all of us."

"Sure," Grover said. Wasn't much else he could say. For him, Beijing was just a yellow star printed on a map in George Cody's seventh volume of *Parley's Cyclopaedia of Universal History*. He'd read all he could of the long, convoluted history that accompanied the map—knowing that Lawrence was there—but the author went out of his way to twist his sentences around and evade any clear conclusions.

What Grove had managed to work out was that the Chinese rulers despised the opium trade England had imposed upon them. It had reduced thousands of their citizens to impoverished addicts and also funded English, French and American acquisition of Chinese estates rich in alchemic stone. Since the emperor was embroiled in a civil war against Taiping rebels, foreign opium dealers felt secure that he couldn't afford to waste his resources fighting their nations as well. But in 1856 the seizure of an English ship loaded with contraband opium and alchemic stone set off a series of battles. The emperor declared war and withdrew to a gilded city populated entirely by eunuch-mages and tiny, ferocious courtesans.

Even now it wasn't clear who, if anyone, had won the war. If rumors were true, a quarter of China was underwater, though far more of England and France lay submerged beneath a sea of ichthyosaurs and ammonites. The United States had lost the south and been split in two.

"So all that about justice that Lady Astor was saying?" Grover asked.

"Honora wants compensations to be made to those who've lost extensive property," Lawrence replied. "Mostly she's thinking about her relatives in England and France being offered citizenship and sanctuary here in the US."

"Cora and George have got a couple rooms free in their boarding house," Grover responded, and that won him a grin from Lawrence. "It's a nice place if you don't mind all the books."

"I had wondered where you were living now."

"I still have the cabin outside the fortifications. Come fall when the weather turns, most of the old creatures—dinosaurs—migrate back through the rift and they're easy to pick off."

"You really do hunt them?" Lawrence stared at Grover. "On your own?"

"Betty comes along." Grover shrugged. "Anyhow it ain't as if I go after giants like bigtooths or thunderbirds or long-necks. I only once made the mistake of pulling a sea monster out of the water. What about you? You said something about fighting them."

"We're closing the rifts." Lawrence said it quietly like a secret.

"We had heard rumors that the rift in England sealed back up," Grover said, nodding.

"We managed to collapse it, as well as the one in China. No more water's getting out from either of them. Not that we'll see many great changes for years." Lawrence frowned, but Grover wasn't sure if it was work itself or talking about it that displeased him. "But it's not as if I'm on my own. I have support."

"Lady Astor and the Tucker brothers?" Grover asked.

"Honora, yes. She's incredibly experienced and particularly good with subtle spells." Lawrence's expression turned briefly fond, but then he scowled like he'd tasted something foul between his back teeth. "Tucker on the other hand, he—they're the worst kind of theurgic professors."

Lawrence had never been too keen on holier-than-thou types, and most theurgic professors were supposed to be real Bible-thumpers. All their spells came from the good book—at least if they were practicing legally in the US—and the ground-up alchemic stone that powered their charms and curses were said to be God's gift to the righteous. So if a theurgic professor's spell worked or failed, well, that was down to the Lord's will.

For mages like Lawrence, the spells and the power just came out of them alone. They didn't need magic dust or holy books to work wonders or knock a man dead.

Which was probably why folks tended to grow nervous about mages and why theurgic professors were supposed to always be in charge of them.

"They worse than Reverend Dodd?" Grover asked.

"Oh, they're just as abrasive in spirit," Lawrence replied. "But far more dangerous in scope."

"How do you mean?" Grover asked. "They got it in for you?"

"Not just me." Lawrence leaned back against the trunk of the apple tree, beside Grover. "They're brewing up something particularly nasty, and I suspect that they intend to catch me or Honora acting against their orders so that they can charge one or both of us with sedition or even treason."

Grover stared at Lawrence in disbelief. That sounded like the lowest, petty kind of purpose a man could have. Particularly when, as far as Grover understood it, Lawrence and Lady Astor were trying to close the rift and save the rest of them.

"Why?" he asked at last.

"Because we are in the way of what they want and because we're the last two who were in Beijing when the rifts opened and all this happened." Lawrence gestured offhandedly at Betty.

"You were there but so what? Everyone knows it was the work of the Imperial Consort Cixi."

Lawrence's troubled expression gave Grover an uneasy pause. He leaned a little nearer to Lawrence, watching his face intently.

"It was her doing, wasn't it?" Grover whispered.

Lawrence dropped his gaze, and the muscle in his jaw flexed like he was fighting to hold his mouth shut.

"Lawrence!" Mayor Wilder's call from the kitchen door startled the blazes out of Grover. He managed not to jump back guiltily as he would have done as a youth, but his pulse still quickened like he'd been caught with his arms around Lawrence. Lawrence straightened but didn't draw away from Grover's side. He squinted into the light pouring out through the open kitchen door.

"I'm catching up with Grover," Lawrence called back to his father.

Mayor Wilder appeared only briefly puzzled by that and then he waved.

"Well, bring him inside, son. It's hardly sociable to make the man chat with you out in the dark."

"Oh no, Mayor Wilder." Grover stepped closer to the stairs leading up to the kitchen porch. He touched the brim of his hat in respect. "I was just passing by, sir. I shouldn't intrude—"

"It's no imposition at all, Grover. Fact is I was bragging about you to the Professors Tucker and Lady Astor. They're all roaring to meet you. They hope you can help guide them right to the rift." Mayor Wilder smiled at Grover with such easy warmth that he likely could have told Grover his invitation had been lost in the post and Grover would have believed him—at least for a minute.

"I'd need to stable Betty," Grover pointed out.

"Well, sure." Mayor Wilder didn't miss a beat. "You settle that ridingbird of yours in one of my stalls then come join us in the house, straightaway. I won't hear otherwise, young man."

"Yes, sir." Grover responded out of ingrained reflex more than desire.

"Now, Lawrence"—Mayor Wilder's slick, professional charm softened and a little worry crept into his wide smile— "son, come inside. It's cold out there and our guests are asking after you."

Lawrence sighed and cast Grover a look that he didn't quite understand—conspiratorial but also tired.

"Alright, I'm on my way," Lawrence replied to his father. Then he marched up the stairs to the kitchen door. As Mayor Wilder fell back, Lawrence glanced over his shoulder to Grover.

"Don't leave me waiting too long, Grove," he said.

That seemed rich coming from a man who'd been gone eight years. Still the sentiment touched Grover. He offered Lawrence a lazy salute and went to settle Betty.

Chapter Two

Much as he would have liked to take this opportunity to enter the house by the front door, Grover couldn't make himself do it. It would be too much of a spectacle, he decided, and he wasn't here for that.

Truth be told he no longer knew why he'd come, exactly. But he now had a reason to stay—a job that paid gold dollars.

He came in through the back door. The warm, fragrant atmosphere of the large kitchen felt familiar. He stopped to greet the new cook (a Creole lady named Camille) and then to allow the plump whirlwind of a housekeeper, Mrs. Citlali, to hug him and chastise him for wearing a hat indoors like "some kind of ruffian, raised in a barn". Grover removed his hat and thanked Mrs. Citlali when she hung it and his coat up with the aprons. Seized by memories of the last time he'd entered the ballroom, Grover tried to linger in the familiar surroundings of the kitchen, offering to haul in firewood as he'd done as a boy, but Mrs. Citlali wouldn't hear of it.

"Don't you steal my work, Grover. You mosey out and let those rich folks hire you to guide them through the rift lands." Mrs. Citlali playfully pushed Grover towards the hall door. "I expect you to do your mama proud and demand twice what they first offer. Or three times, even. They can afford to pay, believe me."

"I'll do my best, ma'am." Grover strode through the hall and slowly pushed open the door to the big ballroom. The light blazing from chandeliers powered by ignited alchemic crystals seemed to gild the dancing couples. It limned the multitude of single men who lingered at the sideboard tables and warmed the complexions of elderly ladies who sat around the grand fireplace chatting.

Far over by the bay windows, the musicians from the Variety Music Hall rolled out the sweeping notes of a waltz. Grover recognized one of the fiddlers—a handsome Black man—as the fellow he'd spent a few pleasant hours with naked in the attic of the music hall last summer. That hadn't lasted long past Grover noticing his wedding ring.

Still, Grover's gaze lingered on the man as he reflexively searched for an ally in this big room brimming with white folk. The treacherous sensation that he didn't belong and wasn't safe in such company crawled up his spine like a chill. Grover straightened his back, resisting the reflex to hunch low. It wasn't that wariness wasn't warranted, but he prided himself on his dignity and courage—he'd earned a reputation for living fearlessly alongside mountain lions and making game of dinosaurs.

Yet none of those wild creatures made him so uneasy as this room of near strangers. Sure, Grover knew the names of half the better-dressed folks, but he certainly wasn't in a position to use those names in any but the most formal terms. The few uniformed men who hadn't just arrived with the airship worked for Sheriff Lee and weren't any of them keen on Grover, not the least because he did business with Arapaho and Ute out beyond the scope of their authority.

Grover craned his head, trying to catch a glimpse of Lawrence or even Mayor Wilder. Instead Cora Cody gave him a very bright, pretty smile, and all at once drew her tall dance partner away from the other couples. Even before the man turned, Grover knew he was Lawrence. He made himself smile, though it hurt seeing how handsome a couple the two of them made. He had no right to feel jealous. Bottom truth was Cora had been Lawrence's childhood friend even before Grover had come along. And a long time before George Cody arrived in town too.

Grover glanced through the crowd and picked out George's big frame beside the ornate punch bowl. He stood, laughing with the Tucker brothers. If Cora dancing in the arms of her one-time fiancé troubled him at all, it didn't show in his cheery expression. Grover guessed the Tuckers must have been discussing natural sciences. There wasn't much else—aside from Cora—that lit George's ruddy face up to such a pleased glow.

"Grove," Cora called as she drew Lawrence along to his side.

"Mrs. Cody." Grover bobbed his head and kept a good step clear of her. Men like Sheriff Lee all too readily took offense at even a hint of intimacy between any man of color and a white woman. It suited Grover to stand beside Lawrence in any case.

"Isn't it wonderful!" Cora declared. Before Grover could ask exactly what she meant, Cora turned her gaze on Lawrence. "It broke our hearts thinking you were dead, Lawry."

"I said I was sorry," Lawrence replied.

"To me." Cora released Lawrence's left arm. "But I'd bet my back teeth that you haven't said a thing to Grover."

"Grover and I were speaking just a while ago, in fact," Lawrence replied and then grinned. "Which of your teeth would you like to hand over?"

Cora laughed at that but cocked her head slightly. The blond curls bordering her face bounced, as if still dancing to the happy melody filling the air.

"So you two…" She raised a brow as she looked intently at Grover. "You're loving friends as ever?"

Grover wasn't certain whether his own incoherent choking noise or Lawrence's look of tongue-tied alarm was more awkward, but one or both inspired Cora to shake her head and set her curls swinging again.

"It astounds me how articulate you men can be at times," she commented.

"Not every fellow is as eloquent as your husband, Mrs. Cody," Grover responded.

"True." Cora's fond gaze went at once to George, though a moment later she sighed. "He will never remember to bring me my punch with those two chatting him up." Cora pointed to the sideboard where George stood looking delighted as one of the Tuckers puffed up his chest like a prairie grouse and the other held out something in the palm of his gloved hand. Lawrence frowned, but whether it was at the reminder that Cora had wed another man or at the sight of the Tucker twins, Grover didn't know.

No reason it couldn't be both, he supposed.

The punch looked good though. So did all the platters of fried fish, clams and giant red crawdads. Silver dishes brimmed with chips of butter and little braided rolls of wheat bread. Grover didn't think he'd tasted real bread or butter in four years—maybe five.

"Have you eaten anything?" Lawrence asked. After a moment of quiet he prompted, "Grove?"

"Sorry. I thought you were asking Mrs. Cody," Grover replied. "I ate this morning. Nothing like that spread, though."

"Let's avail ourselves of the refreshments, then," Lawrence suggested.

"We'll have to," Cora agreed. "Especially as my husband has forsaken us for the wiles of those doe-eyed professors."

"He'll come to his senses the moment he notices that you've claimed two dashing dandies as escorts," Lawrence responded.

Cora laughed and Grover smiled. Dashing dandies had fallen on hard times if Grover was being admitted to their company. The three of them crossed the room and folks watched. Most the locals, Grover guessed, gawked and gossiped about Lawrence, only hours back from the dead and already dancing with Cora. Some of the newcomers from the east, however, appeared wary of Grover. Eyeing him like dogs hankering to get their hackles up.

Grover felt too hungry and too pleased with Lawrence's company to let himself be cowed by newcomers going red-faced at the sight of a Black man eating from the same sideboard table as them. Of the few men in fresh blue uniforms who cast him evil glances, none had the grit to meet Grover's gaze when he looked them in the eyes.

If they planned to stay in Fort Arvada for any time, they'd just have to get used to mixing with folk who weren't white, because outside of this quaint little party, thousands of people of every color and creed filled the businesses, boarding houses, music hall and saloons of the city. By Grover's reckoning they made up more then half of the population, and they weren't going anywhere, anytime soon. Just pondering the matter, Grover felt irritated with himself for allowing a few sneering bigots to get under his skin and rattle him so bad.

Lawrence asked him about a fern dish and two platters of fish. Grover quickly forced himself to put the men surrounding them out of his mind. He'd been invited in here by the mayor, and he had as much right to stand in this ballroom as any one of them did.

"You'll like them big crawdads," Grover assured Lawrence. "I saw the Liu brothers net them just this morning. The meat's real sweet. Them ferns are good too, they taste like green beans."

Lawrence helped himself to an assortment of small fish, crawdads and spring fronds. Grover claimed a thick cut of shark, a fried pterosaur leg and a warm bread roll, which he slathered with butter. Cora packed four rolls and several cuts of turtle on her small plate as well as a heap of butter chips.

Grover tried not to stare at Lawrence's right hand as he held his plate. Lawrence moved it so smoothly that it took Grover a moment to recognize that the jointed fingers and smooth palm were carved from polished ivory. Tiny gold grommets glinted along the joints.

For an instant, sorrow for the pain and loss Lawrence must have endured swept over Grover, but he didn't let himself dwell on it. Instead he admired how masterfully Lawrence manipulated his artificial fingers. Then, knowing Lawrence wouldn't thank him for gawking, he applied himself to his serving of shark flesh. Cora too darted glances at Lawrence's hand, but when she spoke it was only to say, "Lord, have I missed butter!"

None of them took long to finish off their food. By the time they approached the punch bowl, they'd all three turned their empty dishes over to the parlor maid, who'd whisked the plates out of sight like she was smuggling alchemic stones out of the country.

At the punch bowl, Cora cleared her throat loudly. At once George looked from the Tucker brothers to Cora and grinned.

"Darling!" He gestured her nearer, and when she reached his side he took her extended hand and kissed her fingers like they were still newlyweds. "You must see this preserved bone that the Tucker professors discovered in China. It bears a remarkable resemblance to the fossil Grover brought us from the rift."

"Really?" Unsurprisingly Cora's concerns over punch evaporated at once. She beckoned both Grover and Lawrence nearer as well.

Grover followed, taking his time to look the Tucker brothers over. Since all he knew about either of them was that they meant trouble for Lawrence, he was strongly inclined to interpret their narrow faces and large dark eyes as weasel-like. But if he gave them a fair shake, he'd admit they were good-looking in that flaxen-haired, wan manner of the sensitive but brooding heroes in Cora's favorite novels (chapters of which she read aloud at the boarding house once a week). Their slim builds lent them the illusion of youth from a distance but, standing closer, Grover noted the gray at their temples and the lines worn into their faces. Both were certainly past forty.

Aside from their thick, perfectly coifed sideburns, the thing that struck Grover as most remarkable about them was the effort they'd put into perfecting their resemblance to one another, not merely in the cut of their hair and tailored suits, but to the extent of displaying the same thin white scar across both their chins.

Grover wondered which of them had cut himself to match his brother.

"Professor Tucker and Professor Tucker," George said. "May I present my lovely wife, Mrs. Cora Cody. This fine fellow is Mr. Grover Ahigbe, the famed Fort Arvada hunter you've been asking about."

The twins turned their heads in perfect unison and appraised Grover like a strange but costly curiosity.

"A pleasure," the Tuckers responded as one. The one on the right added, "I'm Nathaniel, this is my brother David." Both of them looked smug about the introduction but neither offered his hand to Grover. Something about their expressions made him wonder if the twins weren't having a joke on everyone, maybe switching their names just to amuse themselves. It didn't escape Grover that Lawrence hung back from them.

"So, let us have a look at the fossil that Grover found." George stuffed his hands into his coat pockets, and after withdrawing a few odd rocks and a very battered pocket watch, he fished out a small tin and opened it to reveal the opal snail shell that Grover had found at the edge of the rift.

Lawrence cast George an uncertain look, but Grover wasn't surprised in the least that George had brought a variety of his geological wonders to share with the professors.

"Now watch this." George lifted the shell up and angled it out towards the overhanging chandelier. All at once it lit up, glowing as brilliantly as the alchemic stones that illuminated the ballroom.

"It's resonating with the illumination spells in the chandelier!" Cora all but beamed at George in her delight. Then she raised her delicate brows. "Does that mean that it's an alchemic stone, as well?"

"One could be forgiven for assuming as much," David Tucker replied. "However my brother and I have tested samples from the rifts and discovered that these new reactive minerals are chemically different from true alchemic stones. It seems that they have absorbed and retained alchemic qualities. This rodent's jawbone, for example."

Nathaniel Tucker drew a white kerchief from his pocket as his brother spoke and opened it to expose a small toothy bone. The luster of opal suffused it and, like George's shell, when it was held up the jawbone threw off thin beams of light.

"It is our theory," David Tucker continued, "that the alchemic energy released by opening the rifts was so explosive that it radiated into the surrounding minerals, impregnating them with alchemic properties."

Grover glanced back to Lawrence and noted how his mouth tightened into a hard line. But he couldn't figure out why. As he understood it, alchemic stone was rare and hard to process into the dust that powered most spells. The Wilders could display these shining chandeliers, because their family fortune had been built upon the discovery of a vein of alchemic stone in the hills surrounding Fort Arvada. But even that had nearly played out, and now the city's fortifications needed alchemic stone more than ever.

This ought to be good news. So why did Lawrence look so unhappy?

"The rifts could be a treasure house of alchemic power." Cora gazed warmly at the shell in her husband's hand then smiled at Grover. "Grove, you could have started a bigger boom here than the one in '39 when the Wilders started panning for magic dust."

"Certainly. Magic dust could become a readily producible material." Nathaniel Tucker folded his kerchief closed around the jawbone and slipped it back into his coat pocket. "But that is just one opportunity that the open rift offers us."

Grover noticed that a good number of men in sharp suits had moved closer to their group. The low murmur of small talk faded so it seemed like the whole population of the ballroom hushed to hear more of what the Tuckers had to say.

The stocky banker, Mr. Haim, his scrawny cousin Reverend Dodd and the handsome sheriff, Gordon Lee, all edged up closer. The smells of their cigar smoke and pomade drifted over Grover like too much cologne. Just beyond them Grover glimpsed Mayor Wilder and Lady Astor standing near each other and casting worried glances past him. Lawrence bowed his head, hiding his face as he feigned interest in his watch fob.

"We would never go so far as to call the opening of these rifts a blessing." Nathaniel Tucker raised his voice to address the crowd. "Our nation and our allies have suffered too much loss to ever say that."

"But we Americans have a history of facing our tragedies and finding opportunity where others see only defeat." David Tucker glanced to Lady Astor with a sly sort of smile. For an instant the gray-haired woman pinned the Tuckers with so murderous a glower that Grover thought she might hurl her punch glass at one of them. But then, like a trick of the light, her furious expression melted into a bored yawn.

David Tucker shifted his attention to the sheriff and his companions. "We don't need to remind you that a surprising number of savage Indian tribes survived this calamity to lay claim to what are now numerous islands along the Inland Sea. And untold hundreds of thousands of slaves have exploited the destruction of our southern homes to insinuate themselves into northern cities where they have passed themselves as free—"

"We aren't implying that one or both these groups were behind the opening of the rifts." Nathaniel cut in like he was taking a stage cue.

"No one in this country opened the rifts," George stated with that curt tone he used when he felt anyone at the boarding house needed reminding of the latest scientific fact.

"Certainly not." David agreed so lightly that he sounded like he was making a joke. A good number of the men and women surrounding them exchanged the kind of knowing looks that no doubt delighted prosecutors. Taking them in, Grover's entire body went ice cold and then sickeningly hot as dread and anger welled up in him.

The Tuckers' insinuations too easily stirred up those terrible first weeks after the rift opened, when rumors of Arapaho collaborating with abolitionists to destroy settlements and slave plantations had spread like brushfire. In Fort Arvada houses had been burned and families threatened. Grover had been in a couple close scrapes himself and had spent four hungry days with a busted hand and a black eye in a jail cell. But he'd counted himself lucky. Elsewhere people deemed to be rootworkers or shamans had been beaten to death, hung, drowned and burned alive.

If news hadn't arrived that rifts had also opened in Europe and China—that they'd likely been summoned by the Chinese Imperial Consort Cixi—the murders might never have stopped.

Grover sure as hell didn't like blame being thrown out at him and his again, not even as some sort of bad joke.

"Please forgive my ignorance, professors." Cora crossed her arms over her chest, like she did when Toby had earned himself a switching. "But I fail to see any connection between people of color and your discoveries concerning the properties of minerals at the rift."

"We weren't implying a corollary, my dear girl," Nathaniel responded, though he hardly looked at her. His attention remained focused on the men gathered around him. "Only pointing out that there are social troubles this last remaining rift might help us address. If we are not too hasty in closing the rift we, as a nation, could benefit far beyond simply powering theurgic spells."

"Indeed." David took up the conversation from his brother. "We all know that there have been immense difficulties enforcing the Indian Removal Act since the flood."

Grover couldn't help but raise his brows. Nearly all the old Indian Territories lay half-a-mile under the waves now. The Tuckers weren't seriously trying to imply that people ought to have attempted to live in the Inland Sea, were they? Grover stole a glance back to Lawrence, half expecting him to assure him it was all a joke. Instead Lawrence just gave a small shake of his head.

"Several tribes have taken over islands and land along the new coasts and threaten the construction of Mr. Moreau's railroad and telegraph lines. Without those we have little hope of reuniting our country. Indians can't be allowed to run wild, burning down bridges and terrorizing work crews," David said.

Grover hadn't heard of any plan to span the Inland Sea with a rail line. Reading the expressions of most the other townsfolk in the room, he knew they hadn't either. The federal soldiers from the east, however, nodded and scowled as if the project was a familiar and sore subject.

"But what if," David Tucker went on in a breezy tone, "we could relocate these savages to lands not already occupied nor of use for development. What if we gifted them with the vast unclaimed territories beyond the rift."

Grover stared at the twins, unable to believe he'd understood them correctly. Were the Tuckers really suggesting that refugee Cherokee, Choctaw and Chickasaw be once again uprooted? Did they imagine the Arapaho and Ute who'd repelled Comanche raiders and stood toe-to-toe with dinosaurs would go meekly into the quicksand and jungles inside the rift?

Not only was that a cruel proposition, but it also struck Grover as likely to start a war that isolated cities like Fort Arvada wouldn't survive.

Reverend Dodd's approving smile at the Tucker brothers assured Grover that not only was exile being suggested, but these men considered it a fine idea indeed. Both Cora and George Cody appeared to feel the same revulsion Grover did at the notion.

They hadn't forgotten how Chief Niwot and his people had sheltered refugees displaced by the surging floodwaters. The chief's sister, MaHom, had nearly died from the strain of holding huge waves back long enough for hundreds of families to reach the high ground in the mountains.

"But isn't the land beyond the rift terribly wild? Not fit for human survival?" George looked to Grover. Nathaniel Tucker answered before Grover could offer a word to describe the humid, reeking swamps and dark, insect-infested fern jungles that lay beyond the jagged stone of the rift's opening.

"A savage land for proudly savage peoples, I'd say," Nathaniel replied. "Haven't some of their braves already accommodated themselves to hunting dinosaur herds?"

"They have. And they aren't the only wild things to have profited from this disaster." Sheriff Lee cast a long look in Grover's direction. "Certain black buzzards are having a right time in all this human misery."

That tore it! He'd already been on edge, but now his outrage blazed into fury. Grover balled his hands into fists. He was gonna knock that smirk right off the sheriff's face.

But as he turned towards the sheriff, a warm sensation rolled up his spine. His legs went sluggish and heavy; his arms felt soft as honey. He sagged, just slightly. In an instant he recognized the heat of Lawrence's left hand pressed against his back. The spell wasn't even as strong as the ones Lawrence used to toss at him when they'd wrestled as boys—Grover could have shaken it off—but it gave him pause.

This wasn't the time or place to cross the law. As good as it might feel to punch Sheriff Lee to the ground, Grover wasn't ready to give up his home and live the rest of his life on the run for that brief exhilaration. It wouldn't go one drop to proving himself a better man than Sheriff Lee either. If anything, laying the sheriff out during a dance would only make him look like the animal Lee implied he was.

Still, Grover shrugged off Lawrence's hot fingers. If he was so damn worried, Lawrence might put in a word to counter the Tuckers. But he remained silent, his gaze downcast. Used to be, he'd shout down a hurricane if he didn't like the way it blew. Now he'd gone so quiet he could have been a shadow at Grover's back.

"Of course, this is all merely speculation," David Tucker went on, as if the comment hadn't been made, though he did turn his attention to Grover, offering him the sort of thin-lipped smile only a rattlesnake would find reassuring. "We have yet to observe the rift ourselves, but if the area is indeed rich with alchemic minerals then we will certainly have to consider the difficulty in mining the lands, particularly since they are populated with so many dangerous creatures."

Concerned murmurs spread through the room, and unsurprisingly more people gathered around the Tuckers and turned their attention to Grover. Of all of them, only he had crossed the rift. Normally, Grover took pride in that, but noting the Tucker brothers' speculative expressions and Lady Astor's dour gaze, he felt like he'd just set his foot down in a snare. Any moment the slipknot would pull tight.

"That's where the strong backs and brute characters of so many of the Blacks currently overrunning our cities could be put to great use," Nathaniel Tucker said. "If any people can thrive in such a brutish landscape, it would certainly be hearty Blacks like Mr. Ahigbe."

Grover didn't knock the grinning twins' heads together, but it took some will to suppress the urge.

"You two think folks with half the sense God gave a flea are gonna haul themselves through wild country and across the Inland Sea to work a federal mine for government wages?" Grover demanded, because it almost sounded to him like the bastard Tuckers had forgotten about universal emancipation passing in the Senate and thought they could just ship Black folk out like cattle.

"Well…" David gave a shrug while his brother Nathaniel smiled. "The Proclamation of Emancipation hasn't cleared the House yet. The representatives are awaiting our report from the Office of Theurgy and Magicum. So, procuring a workforce may not prove as difficult as you presume, Mr. Ahigbe."

Grover's face flushed hot with anger, and for an instant his right hand dropped to his sidearm but he caught himself.

Beside him, Cora stared at the Tuckers in horror and George made a face like he'd discovered a slug in his punch glass. Mayor Wilder paled when Grover met his gaze. But those repulsed and sorrowful reactions weren't reflected by even half the folks gathered around. Some simply continued dancing and laughing—utterly unaware—while others wore sly, smug smiles like poker players with all four aces in hand.

"That's just…shameful!" Cora sounded almost too angry to speak. "I've never in my life—"

"It isn't as though free men like Mr. Ahigbe would lose their liberty. So long as they aren't criminals and have their papers, free Negroes would remain so," Nathaniel Tucker responded. "Not that there wouldn't be positions available to them. In point of fact right now Mr. Ahigbe stands to make a pretty penny."

Grover turned away, because if he stayed even a moment more he was going to knock those white teeth right out of the Tucker brothers' mouths. And then he'd keep pounding the sons-of-bitches till they didn't move anymore. As much as he hated them, he knew they weren't worth hanging for.

He headed for the kitchen door, ignoring the Tuckers' sudden protests. One of them called an offer for his services as a guide. Incredulity nearly did stop Grover then. Did they really imagine that any amount of money would convince him to help them? After everything they'd said, could they imagine any person of color wishing for anything but to see them dead?

"I'll talk to him." Lawrence's voice drifted from behind him, but Grover didn't look back.

Betty wasn't too pleased to be woke in the dark of night. When Grover called her name, she lifted her head from the heap of hay where she'd bedded down. Through the deep gloom, Grover recognized the shine of her eyes. After a couple chirps she plopped her head right back down.

"Damn it, Betty."

"Grove, wait." Lawrence paused at the stable door. The faint glow of light from the house outlined his gaunt form.

"Hell no," Grover snapped. He glared at Betty. "C'mon you. We're leaving."

Betty pushed her head farther beneath her feathered arm, pretending not to hear him. Lawrence closed in behind him.

"Grove." Lawrence's left hand lighted upon Grover's shoulder.

"Don't." He knocked Lawrence's hand away hard. "I ain't in the mood to hear anything you or those sons-of-bitches have to say."

Lawrence stepped back. Grover stomped into the horse stall and frowned at Betty while she feigned sleep. He glowered over his shoulder to the far wall where his saddle and tack faded into darkness. He needed a lamp. If he'd had any sense, he would have brought one from the kitchen, but he was in no temper to go back and ask anyone for anything.

Lawrence cupped his hand to his mouth like he was warming it with his breath, but then he spread his fingers and small orbs of gold light drifted from his lips like he was blowing luminous soap bubbles. They rose and drifted through the stable, throwing a soft golden glow across the weathered wood and bales of alfalfa.

Betty, as well as several horses, took note. Though the horses, being shy creatures, pricked up their ears and went tense. Betty hopped up and snapped after one of the filmy lights like she thought it was a spicy firefly.

"She gonna get sick if she eats one of those things?" Grover heard the surliness in his voice but couldn't help it. He felt too angry to offer thanks. He hadn't asked for this. If Lawrence hadn't been here, he would have worked his own way through the gloom. He hadn't needed Lawrence's help for eight years now.

Lawrence met his glare. He looked damn tired, but didn't say a word.

It wasn't like him to keep so quiet, Grover thought, but reminded himself that he had no idea what Lawrence was like anymore. If he'd changed so greatly that he could support the Tuckers' plans, the man Grover had known might as well have died six years ago. Grover would almost have preferred that than to think Lawrence had so completely betrayed the ideals he'd once shared with Grover.

The notion cut deep, pricking at old resentments far down in Grover's core—remnants of his earliest sense of the injustice in the different circumstances of their lives. He'd always had to work twice as hard for anyone to think him even half as good as Lawrence.

But it didn't do any good to dwell on how Lawrence had been rich and white and able to command the magic of the earth while Grover had been forced into the role of a servant just because of the color of his skin. He was grown now and had to put away childish tantrums about the unfairness of the world. Moaning and railing didn't change nothing.

Deeds, not words, showed the true worth of a man.

Grover knew he was better than the Tuckers, better even than this stranger who'd come home answering to Lawrence's name. They and Lawrence could go to Hell if they thought he'd aid them in any way. Not for money or even long-lost love.

Though Grover reckoned his refusal would require exiting Fort Arvada right away before they realized they couldn't buy him. Because as soon as they did, he didn't doubt the Tuckers would find a reason that Grover should lose his liberty—with Sheriff Lee on their side it wouldn't take long to fit him up as an outlaw—and decide that Grover would work for them whether he wanted to or not.

No, he'd go up the mountain. And if they followed him…

Well, there were a lot of ways men—even trained soldiers and mages—could disappear. Especially near the rift.

Feeling better for having a plan, Grover fetched his saddle, bags and lead.

When he turned back he discovered Betty standing up and extending her long neck over the stall door for Lawrence to stroke her beak. Very slowly Lawrence lifted his ivory and gold right hand and held it out for Betty to inspect. Betty gave the hinged plates of the palm her owl-eyed look but then went ahead and ran her beak across the ivory fingers.

The relief in Lawrence's expression was so easy to read that Grover felt a pang of deep sympathy. It took a heap of rejection to make a man look that thankful for the acceptance of a critter like Betty. The thought tempered a little of Grover's rage but not enough to let him forget all that the Tuckers had said. Or Lawrence's silence in the wake of their suggestions.

"You might as well go back to the dance." Grover walked past him and into the stall. He threaded the leather lead under Betty's arms and buckled it across her back. "I'm not helping you to find the rift. I don't care if you offer to make me king of California."

"That's not why I followed you out here."

"Why, then?" Grover turned on him. "Cause if it's for my rollicking company, I've got to warn you I'm in something of a foul temper."

Lawrence simply nodded and Grover scowled at him.

"God's sake, Lawrence, can't you damn well say anything? Did you lose your tongue as well as your arm?" Grover regretted his words the moment they escaped his mouth. And seeing the brief flicker of pain in Lawrence's expression, he realized how low a blow he'd dealt the other man.

"I didn't mean—" Grover began, but Lawrence cut him off.

"That doesn't matter," he said. "What's important is that you understand how necessary it is for me to get to the rift before the Tuckers."

Grove paused with Betty's saddle in his arms.

"What do you mean?" Grover asked. "You work with them. You ain't thinking you can undercut the feds and stake a private claim like your granddaddy did, are you?"

"No." Lawrence stole a glance back over his shoulder to the stable door then lowered his voice. "I told you. I'm working to close the rifts. That's why I must reach the last one before they do. But I need your help to get there."

Grover stared at him. Lawrence's allegiance and obedience to the Office of Theurgy and Magicum glittered across his chest in an array of bright medals, but what he suggested sounded like insubordination—or worse if the Tuckers were reporting to the House of Representatives.

"Are we talking about an act of treason here?" Grover asked in a whisper.

Lawrence's expression turned particularly grim. "Please help me, Grove. I don't know that I can do this without you."

Grover silently absorbed the enormity that simple request belied.

A mage flouting the orders of his theurgist superiors might as well be defying God. Wasn't that the law? Grover couldn't imagine that either of the Tuckers would take such insubordination lightly. And it wasn't as if an accomplice would get off easy either. If he and Lawrence got caught at this then likely they'd share a gallows.

Only minutes before Grover had been thinking that assaulting the Tucker brothers wasn't worth hanging for. But stopping them? That might be. Grover felt sick at the thought of being strung up—he'd seen too many men kick and jerk at the end of a rope not to—but he forced his fear down.

"How soon can you get packed up and ready to ride?" Grover asked.

"First light tomorrow morning."

"They're going to notice you missing." Grover belatedly realized that he still gripped Betty's saddle. He set it down and spread a blanket over the downy feathers of her back.

"They won't," Lawrence replied.

Grover waited for Lawrence to explaining his certainty and got nothing for his patience.

"Won't they?" Grover prompted as he buckled Betty's saddle in place over the blanket and secured it to the lead as well. When Lawrence still hadn't responded, Grover turned to him. "You're asking for my help on this venture, so you might want to get back in the habit of being straight with me. Now, why shouldn't I expect the Tuckers to light out on our trail right away?"

Lawrence considered the question for a moment.

"Honora is familiar with a huge variety of spells, not all of which are...legal." Lawrence leaned into the stall and again lowered his voice to a whisper. "I've provided her with my hair and blood. She should be able to assume my form for at least the next month. She and her maid have already made arrangements for her to claim to retire to her sickbed tonight if she's needed to take my place."

Grover raised his brows. He'd heard tall tales of wicked witches, doppelgangers and boo hags stealing people's shapes, but he'd never thought it could really happen. Most spells, as far as he'd seen, were simple and elemental, like the shining spheres of light floating through the stable.

"If she's discovered she'll face beheading, so you can't tell anyone about any of this." Lawrence added, "Not even George or Cora."

"I'm not the one who got himself engaged to Cora," Grover replied, then he realized the response wasn't much of an assurance. He wasn't even quite certain why he'd said it. "You know full well I can keep a secret."

Lawrence nodded. "What about you? Will anyone remark on your absence from the boarding house?"

"No. I keep to myself for the most part. If folks don't see me around for a few weeks, they'll just think I've taken myself off to sulk in the woods."

"Brood off into the wilderness often these days?" Lawrence asked, though his expression was friendly, teasing.

Still it rankled. After he'd learned of Lawrence's death, Grover had gone out and lost himself in the wilds. No one had seen him for the better part of a year, and he couldn't rightly remember where he'd been himself. But that wasn't something he wanted to share, so he just offered Lawrence one of those shrugs he seemed so fond of.

Lawrence drew back from the stall, allowing Grover to lead Betty out of the paddock. He walked alongside Grover until they reached the stable doors. When he touched Grover's forearm, they both stilled. Grover felt the heat of his fingers even through his coat.

"I can't say how glad I am to see you again, Grove." Despite his words Lawrence's expression remained downcast. "But I'm also sorry as hell to have to drag you into this mess."

"I'm a grown man. Ain't no one can drag me into anything I don't want."

That won him one of Lawrence's wide smiles, though it didn't last so long as Grover would have liked. Nor did

Lawrence's warm hand remain on him. Instead he stepped back.

"Ride safe," Lawrence told him.

"Always do. Betty's the reckless one." Grover swung up into Betty's saddle and started out across the grounds, but he couldn't resist one glimpse back. Lawrence remained in the doorway, his eyes closed and his head bowed. Then he suddenly swung his ivory hand up and through the air as if raking aside a curtain. At once the lights all around him burst, and the night swallowed Lawrence completely.

Chapter Three

Early-morning light filtered through the dense branches of fir and spruce trees, burning the dew scattered across the needles to a white mist. Warm gusts buffeted Grover's hat and wound the perfume of sage blossoms around him. Lark buntings and a couple warblers sang out from their roosts in trees. Then came the rising caws of a little bluefoot dinosaur proclaiming its dominion over a patch of scrub oak.

Betty raised the crest of feathers atop her head and let out a proud crow in response. Some critter in the shrubs skittered away. To his credit, the spotted Palouse stallion carrying Lawrence took the noise—and Betty's company—in stride.

"Is she always so vocal?" Lawrence asked. He'd forgone his blue federal uniform for simple civilian clothes, a wide-brimmed hat and an old hunting coat that Grover remembered from years ago. Noting the slack fit of the coat, Grover couldn't help but recognize just how spare Lawrence had grown.

"No. Most of the year she just chirps and coos. But for a week or so in spring, she likes to let all the world know she's here." Betty getting her blood up was one of the reasons Grover preferred not to be out in the wilds with her in May. Last year she'd slipped away from him for nearly a week. She'd come prancing back to him one evening just when he was about to give up on searching for her.

Grover hoped she'd learned her lesson.

"She only crows in the morning," Grover added. "The rest of the day she'll be quiet as a shadow. If there's a bigtooth or a thunderbird anywhere near, she won't make a peep, don't worry."

"Bigtooth?" Lawrence asked.

"One of them dinosaurs." Grover tried to think of just how to describe the giant beast. He pointed to a slender poplar. "Stands on two legs about as tall as that sapling there. About forty feet from its nose to the tip of its tail. Great big head full of long teeth, huge hind legs but with weird, stunted arms."

Lawrence eyed the tree as they rode past it. "Is the tail remarkably muscular? Fuzzy speckled plumes growing down the neck and back?"

"Yep. You've run across one, yourself?"

"Maybe not the exact same species, but something similar. Tyrannusdente." He reaching into the pocket of one of his saddlebags and drew out a slim, leather-bound journal. It reminded Grover of the sketchbooks Lawrence had used to fill up with drawings and watercolor studies when they'd been boys. Lawrence held the journal out and Grover took it from him. Dark stains as well as singe marks speckled the aged cover. The thick pages within felt soft from wear.

"Ignore the first six pages," Lawrence said quickly. "They're a mess—I hadn't gotten used to using my left hand."

Seeing how self-conscious Lawrence looked, Grover flipped past the crimson-spattered watercolor studies of disfigured human bodies, ragged teeth and grotesquely distorted faces. Though in one corner, at odds with the horror surrounding it, Grover recognized the blue profile of the mountains rising in the distance ahead of them.

Lawrence must have been able to draw the landscape in his sleep for the number of times the two of them had passed beneath the shadows of the towering peaks.

Beyond that page he found detailed drawings of animals and plants. Some—like the tusked deer or plump black-and-white bears—Grover had never seen before, but many others he recognized.

If they weren't exactly the same breeds of dinosaurs he had encountered in the mountain valleys, they were very close. Three-horns with brilliant red crests shared pages with four-winged beasts and several long-legged creatures that resembled Betty—though they sported darker feathers. Pterosaurs of all sizes and colors filled a spread of two pages. On the twelfth page Grover found the painting of a bigtooth as well as several smaller animals, sporting jagged maws and large sickles for talons.

"That's a bigtooth, alright. Ones around here grow more olive plumage, but otherwise it looks the same." Grover considered the overgrown trail ahead of them. Betty knew the way, and this close to Fort Arvada they weren't likely to encounter much dangerous wildlife. Still the sight of the bigtooth, even in a drawing, set Grover on edge.

He glanced to Lawrence. "How did you get close enough to draw it?"

"I didn't unpack my sketchbook until it was dead. They're called liè lóng in China. The hunting dragon." Lawrence too studied the surrounding stands of fir and spruce warily. "Get many in this area?"

"Only three regularly venture far from the rift," Grover replied as casually as he could. Used to be none of them ranged beyond Mirror Lake, but each year more edged farther into populated territory. "Mostly they trail herds of big game. Three-horns and whiptails like you've drawn here." Grover lifted the sketchbook and Lawrence nodded.

"Triceratops and tenontosaurus," Lawrence informed him. "Though three-horn and whiptail strike me as much better names."

"Well, however you call them, they aren't the only game bigtooths are getting used to hunting. Late last fall I saw one tearing after a herd of elk."

"Did it catch any?" Lawrence asked.

"It didn't strike me as wise to linger and find out what it might do if it didn't," Grover admitted.

Lawrence laughed and Grover passed his sketchbook back to him.

After riding farther west, the close stands of fir opened to a spring meadow. Small pterosaurs and hawks circled and swooped through the open blue sky. Grover searched the horizon for any sign of thunderbirds. One of them could spear a man and his horse with a stroke of its enormous beak. Grover guessed that it was too early in the year for many of the cloud-white giants to be hunting near Fort Arvada. Still, he'd feel more at ease when he and Lawrence could travel under tree cover.

Though now, gazing at the vast expanse of sky, Grover remembered the Tuckers' airship. They'd make better time flying above the craggy land instead of riding across it.

"How long before they're going to start looking for the rift without a guide?" Grover asked.

"I expect that Honora may be able to delay them a week or two, but not much beyond that." Lawrence paused a moment, watching a speckled green pterosaur roll in the sky and snap up a butterfly. Grover could almost see the desire to stop and sketch flicker across Lawrence's sharp face. Then he returned his attention to Grover. "How long do you think it will take to reach the rift?"

"If the weather holds and we don't have to take a long way round to avoid a three-horn herd, it should be about sixteen days." Grover pointed northwest to where the diamond-sharp ridges of two mountain peaks rose over the rolling hills. "We'll swing under Two Guides and track north and follow the riverbank southwest."

"River?" Lawrence asked.

"The new one that the rift floods tore open. The waters swallowed up all of the Grand Lake valley and swept south and overflowed the entire Arkansas River." He and Lawrence had often hunted around the lake when they'd been boys. All those secret places where they'd lain down together now lay far beneath fast-moving waters. "For lack of much creativity, I call it the Rift River."

"Sensible, that. So sixteen days to Fire Springs?"

Grover nodded and continued riding. It wasn't until they'd crossed the meadow and returned to the shadows of dark pines that it struck Grover he hadn't told Lawrence the rift had opened at Fire Springs. An uneasiness began to gnaw at his gut. He thought back over their few conversations. But no, he hadn't once given away the exact location of the rift opening.

At last Grover wheeled Betty around, blocking Lawrence and his horse.

"If you already know the rift opened at Fire Springs then what the hell is going on here?" Grover demanded. "Why am I playing guide?"

Lawrence flinched like Grover had hit him with a hot poker. Surprise alone couldn't account for how the color drained from his face. He looked gray and sick as he met Grover's gaze.

"I don't know where it is exactly. The terrain has all changed." If he was lying, it didn't show.

"But of all the hills and valleys, you just figured it was the one where you and me used to fool around?" Grover asked.

Lawrence shrugged.

"That ain't no kind of answer, Lawrence." Grover paused, hearing a sharp squawk drift through the trees. The call of a wild ridingbird, like Betty, but a good distance off. He returned his attention to Lawrence, though he lowered his voice. "You know a lot more than you're telling me about all of this."

"Yes." Lawrence looked none too happy but didn't offer anything up to make either of them feel better.

"Just sayin' 'yes' ain't gonna cut it." If Grover'd had any tobacco, he'd have spit it. "Either you start being forthcoming or I'll turn right around here and now and ride back to Fort Arvada."

"You wouldn't let the Tuckers get to the rift first."

Grover wasn't certain if Lawrence was calling his bluff or expressing alarm at the thought of the Tuckers reaching the rift before him. Either way, Grover wasn't going to back down. Too much danger surrounded them in just the lay of the land. Grover didn't need other surprises springing up when Lawrence could have warned him.

"All I have is your word that you're planning to close the rift once we reach it. But these silences and shifty looks of yours make me worry you aren't up to anything better than the bullshit the Tuckers have planned."

"Grover, I wouldn't... You know me—"

"No! I *knew* you. Then you signed up to fight a war halfway across the world and left me!" Grover clamped his mouth shut and drew in a deep breath. He hadn't meant for so much of his hurt to come rushing out. This wasn't about what was behind them but what lay ahead, he reminded himself. He continued in a calmer tone. "It's been eight years and most everything has changed. So if you want me to trust you then you better give me a reason to. Tell me the truth."

Lawrence brought his ivory right hand up to his face and clenched his brow as if trying to keep his head from bursting apart. With a heavy sigh he dropped his hand back to his reins and looked to Grover.

"I'm not keeping things from you because I want to lie to you, Grove. I'm trying to do what little I can to protect you..."

"From?" Grover asked, and when Lawrence offered him a pained expression he added, "Telling me who I need to watch out for would sure as shit make it easier for me not to walk into anything, don't you think?"

"The Tuckers first and foremost. But also sycophants like Sheriff Lee. There's an army of immoral sons-of-bitches who'd like to blame anyone else for the consequences of their politics and greed." Lawrence scowled. "If they catch us, or if I can't make it… You'll be on your own against them, and the less you know, the less they can blame you for."

"You really think men like Sheriff Lee need anything other than the color of my skin to blame me for anything?" Grover snorted at the thought.

"No, but the Director of Theurgy and Magicum will. And in this case having them underestimate you might just save your neck. So long as Nate Tucker doesn't suspect that you've learned his secrets, he may assume you're too insignificant to bother hunting down and killing."

"Yeah, what about his brother David?"

Lawrence shrugged but he dropped his gaze to the ground. There was something there, Grover realized. But was it worth going after if Lawrence really was just trying to safeguard him from Theurgy and Magicum politics? Grover studied Lawrence, considering the situation. Then he shook his head.

He hadn't been sheltered from the world since his ma's death had left him to earn a living for himself at fifteen. Lawrence hadn't been able to defend him then, and Grover sure as hell didn't need him to now.

"I appreciate you trying to protecting me," he said. "But I'm not the little boy you knew back in the day. I ain't been that for a long, long time. I'm man enough to hunt whiptails alongside bigtooth dinosaurs. And I'm tough enough to knock Sheriff Lee on his ass if I need to." Grover held Lawrence's gaze. "Bet you a silver dollar I could even lick *you* in a fight if it came to it. Mage or not."

Lawrence laughed but not unkindly. He lifted his head and gazed up into the dark branches of the pines surrounding them, as if seeking an answer there. His horse stamped, growing impatient just standing. Absently, Lawrence stroked the animal's neck.

"I haven't ever, in all my life, thought you weren't tough. That's the one—maybe the only—mistake I haven't made," Lawrence said. "I wish to God I had possessed even half your grit back when we were boys. Instead, I let Reverend Dodd and Mr. Haim's insinuations rattle me so badly that I panicked and abandoned everything that mattered... Now it's too late."

"It ain't so late as all that," Grover replied as offhandedly as he could. "It's not even midday."

It wasn't as if he'd been fearless back then—he felt scared sometimes even now. But Lawrence's friendship and company had meant more to him than the safety of solitude. These days most everyone had more to worry about than who kept each other company.

"Even if it's dangerous, sometimes a man has to obey his own heart," Grover said, and Lawrence nodded.

"I do know that now. But it took getting engaged and running off into the middle of a war for me to realize just how stupid I'd been and how much I'd ruined... I made so many terrible mistakes." Lawrence's eyes flicked down briefly to his ivory hand. He looked to Grover with a resigned expression. "I know I can't put anything back the way it was. But I have to try to make it as right as I can."

Grover frowned, recognizing that Lawrence was talking about far more than just their broken romance. A notion, not quite formed but still disquieting, fluttered through Grover's mind.

"So if you have to have the truth then this is it." Lawrence paused and seemed to struggle to make himself speak. "I suspected that the rift opened at Fire Springs because I was involved in creating it…in creating them all."

"You?" The enormity of Lawrence's confession stunned Grover so completely that he hardly registered the second much-closer crow from a ridingbird. Beneath him Betty stiffened and swiveled her head towards the call.

"Creating the rifts wasn't our intention," Lawrence said quickly. "We were trying to manufacture new seams of alchemic stone."

"Like the Tuckers are after now?"

"Yes." Fatigue and desolation resonated through Lawrence's voice. He stared past Grover in the direction of Fire Springs. "Tucker designed the spell and picked three of us from the mage corps to ground and power it outside the Beijing Palace. We didn't know he'd already failed once himself, and none of us understood what it would do when we pitted ourselves against an earth mage as powerful as Cixi."

Suddenly a third ridingbird call rang out loud and sharp. Much too close.

Lawrence's hands came up fast, ready to unleash deadly curses. Grover lifted his rifle but could hardly hold it steady for Betty prancing back and forth as she let out a string of high-pitched whistles.

"What on earth is she—" Lawrence began to ask.

A flashy male ridingbird strutted out from between two lodgepole pines some fifty feet ahead of them. He fluffed up his brilliant gold-and-blue plumes and flashed his tail like some exotic fan dancer as he turned in a slow circle. Then he spread his arms to reveal the iridescent feathers cascading down his chest. He strutted round and round, pausing only briefly to waggle his head and tail.

Betty gawked at him with the slack-jawed appreciation of a prospector just down from the hills and taking in a dancing girl. She crooned and gave a low whistle, while the bright-colored male batted his lashes and shimmied his gaudy tail back and forth.

Grover attempted to retain his dignity when Betty began dancing from foot to foot. But then she wheeled around to flash the male a full view of her ass and hiked her tail up over Grover's head.

"Betty," Grover groaned. "You don't even know who that yahoo is. For God's sake, have some pride!"

Lawrence burst into laughter while his stallion appeared about as mortified by the display as a horse could look.

"You could scare him off," Grover suggested, as Betty's gyrations swung him back and forth. "Flash some lights or some such, like you did that night with the bear."

"Aw, but Grove, how could I come between two lovers?" Lawrence wiped his eyes but kept on grinning. "They're clearly taken with each other."

"They just met!" Grover shot the male bird a disapproving glance, which only seemed to amuse Lawrence all the more. "He's a flashy showman on the make. Betty could do better than Mr. Burlesque here!"

Thankfully the huge shadow of a thunderbird swept over them. Though the pterosaur likely glided a mile above, it was enough to spook Betty's suitor, and in an instant he disappeared back into the dark green shadows of the forest. Betty crooned after him a couple times but then heaved a sigh and settled down to preening her breast feathers.

"I told you he was fickle," Grover murmured.

"Me or Betty?" Lawrence asked.

"Both of you." Grover tugged lightly at the leather lead, and Betty started along the trail. Lawrence fell in beside them. Grover wasn't certain of what exactly had changed, but as they continued riding, Lawrence seemed to relax. He grinned boyishly when Grover pointed out the obscene profile of the stone outcropping that the two of them had dubbed "cock rock" nearly a decade ago.

"Well, it seems someone's happy to see me again." Lawrence gave the stones an absurdly flirtatious smile and Grover laughed.

As they rode higher up the mountain ridge, the tree cover thinned and wide breaks of spring grass, horsemint and columbine covered the ground.

"Not so much cactus as there used to be," Lawrence commented.

"More ferns though. We get a lot more rain now," Grover replied. High up overhead he caught the glint of gold and red that colored the head crests of big male thunderbirds. Grover stilled Betty and narrowed his gaze up into the drifts of white clouds. Lawrence drew his horse to a halt as well.

After a moment Grover picked out a single huge wing-beat. He made out the profile of the silver-white thunderbird. From the crooked tear in its left wing and that crest—bright as a monarch butterfly—Grover knew him at once.

"Up there," he pointed. "That's King Douglass."

"Douglass?" Peering skyward, Lawrence appeared suitably impressed by the immense wingspan of the pterosaur. "After Frederick Douglass?"

"That's right." The Christmas before he left, Lawrence had gifted Grover with a handsomely bound copy of *My Bondage and My Freedom*. They'd spent winter afternoons with a blanket wrapped around them, reading the book together. The prose hadn't been sensational—nothing like the poems in *Leaves of Grass*—but several times Lawrence had wept while Grover had pretended that his eyes weren't too glassy with unshed tears to go on reading. When he finally reached the end—that powerful, heartbreaking letter from the author to his former master—Grover had felt almost overcome. So much of Douglass's character roused old memories of his father. So much of his history reminded Grover of his departed mother's desperate flight for her freedom. He hadn't been able to summon words to express to Lawrence how moved he'd felt. But after that day he'd been more determined than ever to live his life as courageously as Frederick Douglass had.

"He's completely free and the whole sky is his kingdom," Grover said. "King Douglass, I mean."

Lawrence nodded but tensed as the thunderbird drifted closer. Sunlight played through the vast expanses of his membranous wings as if it were shining through cloud breaks.

"I've seen one of those creatures kill a whole team of horses," Lawrence commented. "Shouldn't we get to cover?"

Grover didn't answer at once but continued to watch King Douglass as he wheeled slowly overhead. He shifted a wingtip, arched his long fingers against the swift, cold wind and turned a perfect loop. Grover almost felt the thunderbird's pleasure in simply flying. He'd eaten recently—his belly full and fat with mutton—and now as he winged back to his roost, he enjoyed the liberty of the skies and the warmth of the sun spreading across his long wings. For a moment Grover thought King Douglass cocked his head, taking note of him. Grover offered the thunderbird a smile and indulged himself in thinking that the huge creature acknowledged him with the faintest nod of his crested head.

"He's just looking us over as he passes," Grover assured Lawrence. "Bet he's already filled up on bighorn sheep from the El Dorado Ridge."

"He told you as much, did he?" Lawrence raised his brows and continued to watch the thunderbird with suspicion.

"No, but..." Grover shrugged. "Sometimes I just know... Sort of like how you can look at a book and read the title without having to sound it out or nothing. It's like that."

Lawrence glanced between Grover and King Douglass with a puzzled expression. "You read him like a book?"

"I don't know how else to describe it. I think he can read me as well, so we understand each other, in a way," Grover replied, though putting his experience of the thunderbird into words made it sound strange. "He knows I don't mean him any harm, and right now I know he won't cause us any trouble. He's on his way back up west. He's got flaplings to feed." As if to prove Grover's words, King Douglass angled his body upward and suddenly rose, winging fast into the cloudy west. Lawrence watched the thunderbird for several moments then turned to Grover and glanced to Betty.

"In all my travels across China, France and England, I haven't ever met anyone who could understand a giant pterosaur at a glance much less charm an avemosaur into carrying him about."

"Maybe none of them ever tried," Grover answered, because it was surprising how timid some folk could be even in desperate times. He nudged Betty and they continued across the rocky meadow. Small lizards scattered from the tops of sunbaked rocks, and Betty eyed them but didn't snap after them.

"Perhaps," Lawrence agreed. "Or maybe you're just the most charming man alive."

Grover laughed. He had his ways with animals but when it came to people he usually grew self-conscious and awkward.

"I wouldn't bet money on that being the case, if I were you."

"Well, Cora seems to think you've won the heart of at least one girl. Susan?" Lawrence's tone sounded off. Grover peered over, but Lawrence bowed his head into the deep shadow of his hat, seemingly studying little sprays of buttercups surrounding them.

"She mentioned that you'd even met with the girl's father. So something must be going right," Lawrence added.

"Land sakes." Grover couldn't keep from laughing at the thought of asking Frank for little Susan's hand in marriage. The fact that she was nine was only one of a multitude of reasons he found the idea absurd. "Cora was having you on. Susan and her pa are my ma's people. My cousins. They escaped from Bynum when the floods came. I helped Frank find a house and work as a carpenter."

"Oh." Lawrence said nothing more for a few moments, though glancing at him Grover could see there was still something on his mind. "So, there isn't anyone you're… keeping company with just now?"

"Not just now," Grover replied calmly, though his pulse kicked up at the thought of Lawrence wondering. "You?"

"There was someone, but it wasn't—" Lawrence shook his head and gave the stand of white fir ahead of them a glower. "He was married. And from France, so…"

Recollecting how often Lawrence had abandoned his French lessons for their wanders, he suspected that conversation hadn't likely been the attraction.

"Doux mais brève?" Grover had learned the phrase from a Creole fellow he'd spent a few hours with. When Lawrence looked at him with puzzlement, Grover translated, "Sweet but brief?"

"Near enough." Lawrence gave a short laugh. "I suppose I could have fought a little harder to make the arrangement work, but my heart wasn't really in it."

Grover almost asked where Lawrence's heart might have really been, but he wasn't certain he wanted to hear an honest answer. If it had been with him, Lawrence wouldn't have left in the first place. He wouldn't have let him go on thinking he was dead for years.

"Well, sometimes a bit of distraction is a fine thing. It can't all be for better or worse and until death do we part." Grover knew that well enough, himself.

Lawrence nodded, and they continued riding between the stands of trees and breaks of meadows that made up the ridge. The quiet between them felt peaceable and comfortable. The sun rose high above them, and their shadows burned away to tiny pools of blue shade.

After they passed the first of the Two Guides—Long's Peak as Lawrence called it—they stopped at Mirror Lake to allow the animals to drink and graze while they shared a portion of Grover's dried three-horn pemmican. To Grover's surprise Lawrence didn't complain about having to eat the hunk of meat, fat and berries cold. Eight years ago he'd have groused after each mouthful. Instead he thanked Grover and wolfed his portion down, only pausing once to ask if it was chokecherry that Grover had added to the mix.

"That and wild strawberries I dried last summer." Grover tried not to be too obvious in watching Lawrence suck the grease from his fingers. A little oil lent a sheen to his lips and reminded Grover of all the lovely things Lawrence had done for him with that handsome mouth of his.

Eight years back, they'd been easy and playful, turning wrestling matches, foot races and card games into friendly sex without either of them ever saying much about it before or after. But now, Grover realized, they'd both grown up, fucked other men, and learned that it wasn't all sloppy grins and harmless fun.

Bottom truth was that until Lawrence left him, Grover couldn't have imagined what it would do to him to mourn so deeply while hiding his loss from every single soul around him. Even after his ma died he hadn't felt so utterly isolated and estranged. He'd had a right and a reason to grieve as far as other folks knew. Friends and family had been able to understand. But when he lost Lawrence there'd been no comfort offered, no understanding, no sympathy. Little surprise that he'd withdrawn to the wilds, he supposed. Despite the years that had passed, the awareness that he didn't truly belong among other people—that he wasn't quite one of them—still haunted Grover.

He turned his gaze from Lawrence to the rolling hills ahead. They'd made good time, and if they kept up this pace they might even reach the shelter of the temple rocks before sundown. Far off he could just discern the dark forms of a small herd of buffalo. Four juvenile whiptails stood grazing in their midst along with five red-crested three-horns. Wolves and cougars would certainly think twice before taking on that bunch.

"Looks like Romeo isn't dissuaded as easily as you thought." Lawrence pointed across the meadow. Sashaying out from the pines came the male ridingbird that had fled earlier. He flashed his bright tail like an overgrown peacock, and Betty pranced closer to him. Lawrence's horse edged away from them both.

"Betty." Grover pinned her with a hard stare when she looked to him. He pushed all of his determination into his voice. "Come here. Now."

Betty hunched her feathered arms like a sullen youth and pecked at a clump of chickweed. Grover drew in a breath to call again but she immediately slunk to him, making the same little chirps she'd uttered as a chick. He caught her lead and petted her head gently. She leaned into him, and Grover braced himself. She weighed as much as Lawrence's stallion but seemed to think she was still light as a bundle of feathers.

"It's for your own good, Betty," Grover told her softly. "You don't want no part of that philanderer, I promise you."

"Who'd suspect you'd make such a parochial guardian."

Lawrence laughed as he strolled to his own mount and caught the horse's reins. "You aren't going to make her hold out until her Romeo asks your permission, are you?"

Grover didn't know why but the question annoyed him. He didn't expect wild animals to put on the airs of romance and marriage. But Romeo—as Lawrence called him—was a big beast, and Betty was in Grover's care. He wanted to keep her safe. Though saying as much would probably only make Lawrence laugh all the harder.

"We don't have time to waste on a ridingbird romance." Grover swung up into his saddle. "Unless you aren't serious about reaching the rift before the Tuckers."

"Of course I am." Lawrence's expression turned grim at the mention of the rift. He tipped his hat to Grover. "Lead on. I and Romeo will follow."

Chapter Four

Lawrence wasn't wrong about Romeo. The ridingbird stuck with them like a burr in a wool sock—easy to feel but hard to pick out. Just the way Betty trotted and held her head, Grover could tell when the male ridingbird edged alongside them through the pine forest. But his presence worried Grover less than did the markings high up on the trunks of the blue spruce. Branches and bark had been scraped away, and deep three-toed furrows gaped open at the base of each tree.

Riding near, Grover caught a faint musky, sweet smell. Sap sealed the deepest gouges, and pinecones littered the ruts in the ground. The bigtooth that had marked the territory last summer hadn't yet returned. But chances were good it would head back to its hunting ground after wintering on the other side of the rift.

"Liè lóng?" Lawrence asked with a gesture to the nearest spruce.

Grover nodded and signaled Lawrence to silence.

They rode on in a hush. Grover studied the ground and brush for tracks or fresh markings, while Lawrence kept his head up, watching farther ahead. Soon enough they left behind the last of the buffeted spruce and took to higher ground.

As sunset colors spilled across the sky, they reached a rise where three huge rust-red boulders leaned into each other, creating a natural alcove. Over the last few years, Grover had further dug out and reinforced the shelter. To his pleasure he found the cords of wood he'd stashed there largely undisturbed. A few weeds poked up between the stones of his fire pit, but those were easily cleared.

Lawrence built a fire for them while Grover unloaded their saddles and hitched their mounts to nearby trees, where they could graze in sight of the fire. By the time he dropped his and Lawrence's bedrolls to the ground, bright orange flames blazed from the pit. Just the sight and scent of their shabby hearth put Grover more at ease. Most wild animals didn't like fire, but the old ones like bigtooth were particularly fearful. Even the smell of smoke could sometimes clear one off.

Lawrence crouched by the fire. The warm light softened the hard lines of his face and erased his jagged white scars. His ivory hand gleamed like gold, though he tucked it into his coat pocket the moment he noticed Grover coming near.

He glanced to their bedrolls. He looked like he might say something, but he turned back to the fire to add another branch to the burning logs. Grover kept his peace as well, busying himself digging his iron pan out from a saddlebag and filling it with pemmican and cornmeal. He found a good spot to rest the pan, and he let the flickering tongues of flame begin to fry up the corn, fat and meat.

Then he settled back on his heels next to Lawrence and set his rifle down on the other side. Lawrence left his own rifle with his saddlebags. Grover wondered if that was because he knew how little harm most gunshot could do a big dinosaur, or if it reflected a mage's confidence in his own power. An earth mage on his home turf was supposed to be nigh invulnerable.

"Supposing we come across a bigtooth," Grover said. "You got a spell that can knock it on its ass or do we have to improvise?"

It no longer surprised Grover that Lawrence didn't answer at once. He picked up a dry pinecone, turned it over in his hand and tossed it into the fire where it popped and crackled.

"I've recovered enough that I could probably put one down for good. But I'd only do that as a very last resort."

"Really?" Grover asked. "You got a fondness for the bastards?"

"Not hardly. But I have my reasons." After Lawrence met Grover's gaze, he went on, "First, I have to conserve all the strength I can to deal with the rift. Second, Tucker's equipment will pick up a burst of powerful magic. He'll come running. That's how he found us in England."

"So you went all the way from China to England. Why in all that time didn't you send word? How could you let us go on thinking you were dead? You just about broke your daddy's heart, you know."

"I wanted to contact you. I even wrote letters to you and him. But I never posted any of them. I couldn't risk Tucker discovering that I was still alive, not before we'd closed the rifts."

"So it's not just this one? You weren't supposed to close any of the rifts?" Grover asked. "How'd you explain the other two?"

"Officially troops weren't ordered *not* to close the rifts but simply to wait until Tucker and his men had assessed the worth of them. But Gaston, Honora and I already knew they had to be shut down. We'd seen firsthand what they were doing."

"Gaston?" Grover asked. "French and married?"

A slight flush colored Lawrence's face. He tossed a twig into the fire.

"That was him. Gaston Jacquard." Lawrence glanced sidelong to Grover. "It wasn't a great romance. We were both lonely for other people and kept each other company—"

"Sure. I understand." Grover didn't think he wanted to hear too many of the details. Lawrence returned his gaze to the flames while Grover watched the shadows beyond the firelight. Betty and Lawrence's stallion had both settled down to sleep.

"He died closing the rift in England," Lawrence said quietly. "I wasn't near enough and Honora didn't have the strength to pull him out."

The petty jealous thoughts winging around in Grover's head turned all at once regretful. He wasn't above rivalry but couldn't bring himself to feel anything but sorrow at the thought of the man giving his life to stop the floods.

"I'm sorry," he said.

Lawrence simply nodded then threw another pinecone into the flames.

"Everything dies eventually," Lawrence said. "At least Gaston didn't die for nothing. I don't know if any of us can hope for better than that, these days."

Now there was a bleak perspective, Grover thought. It didn't suit him and he didn't want it to suit Lawrence.

"As far as I see it," Grover answered. "Ain't a man's death that's so important as how he lives. Dying is just once and not too many of us have much say about it, but every day we're alive we choose what we do. How much joy we find and how we treat other folk, that's all up to us while we're living. That's what we leave behind when we die."

Lawrence scowled, but when he glanced to Grover his expression softened.

"God, Grove, you're still so…decent." He pulled a brief smile. "I'm glad, you know. It gives me hope for humanity."

"Yep, that's what I am," Grover said, laughing. "The hope for all humanity." The savory perfume of fried corn and sizzling meat drifted from the fire.

"Well, the only hope for my supper, at least."

"That's more the size of it." Grover used the sleeve of his coat as a mitt to pull the pan out from the flames. He set it down between himself and Lawrence.

They'd both packed their own cutlery, but they shared the frying pan instead of bothering with separate servings. Lawrence's spoon and fork gleamed like silver. Grover's were cast tin. Between them they cleared every speck from the pan. Grover set it aside. He'd scrub it out in the morning when the light was better.

Now he watched stars wink to life as the last of the sun's light sank below the mountain horizon. The constellation of the Big Bear shone bright overhead, while the Little Bear edged up from the east and the Swan soared above the ragged peaks in the northwest.

"The stars are different in China. The spring sky is a blue dragon and the winter is a black turtle." Lawrence lifted his ivory hand up as if to blot out the shining North Star. "Though now the protective spells raised over the cities block it all out. It's just black."

They were both silent for a few moments.

"Will you tell me what really happened in China?" Grover asked. "When you were supposed to have died?"

Lawrence studied him for a moment, and Grover half expected him to refuse but instead he reached out, pulled both their bedrolls over and leaned back on his own.

"It's a long story. You might as well get comfortable."

Chapter Five

Grover took his bundled blankets and settled cross-legged. He gazed at Lawrence's face as an old memory stirred—laying sated and sweaty against Lawrence's bare body and realizing that the firelight lit his gray eyes to gold. But Grover resisted the lure of nostalgia.

Lawrence didn't return his gaze but instead stared up at the constellations overhead.

"The problem started when we marched north towards the emperor's palace in Beijing." The hard English edge returned to Lawrence's voice as he spoke. "In the south we'd raided whole quarries of alchemic stone and shipped tons back to England, France and the US. Our theurgist commanders assumed we'd continue exploiting local stores as we pushed north. But they ignored reconnaissance reports that hinted at how completely the Chinese emperor had hoarded his alchemic stone there. Soon enough we realized that there wasn't a speck left in the ground. By the time we reached the Yellow River, our theurgists couldn't power even the simplest spells and our forces were facing ice curses with nothing but prayers and Baker Rifles. Our infantry died on their feet, and their Wuxia tore through our cavalry like all those riders and horses were tissue paper..." Lawrence paused, glaring at the emptiness above him.

Grover knew he couldn't imagine what Lawrence must have seen—must have felt. He'd had no idea how badly the campaign had gone. What little the papers had reported had amounted to lists of unfamiliar city names claimed as victories. Though even that trickle of information had dried up in the first year.

"We never heard much of anything back home," Grover admitted.

"No, you wouldn't have." Lawrence shook his head. "Nate Tucker sent reporters packing as soon as things started to look bad. Then he took, let's say, *liberties* with his reports back to Washington."

"Just the one Tucker?" Grover asked.

Lawrence got that uneasy expression.

"David didn't join us until August. God knows, Nate alone was bad enough. Ordering our infantry into villages to ransack shrines, temples even digging up graves searching for alchemic stone. What the bastard should have done was let us fall back to the southern ports where we could've resupplied—" Lawrence cut himself off with a rueful laugh. "No. Honestly, we should have hauled our asses out of China. We had no damn right to be there in the first place. We sure as hell weren't bringing them liberty and civilization with all that opium we forced on them."

"I thought that only the English were pushing opium." Grover recalled George and Cora debating the matter a few years back.

"Sure, we love to claim that we weren't any part of it. But the bottom fact was that our country gladly sent men to fight and die to defend opium interests in exchange for a first pick of Chinese alchemic stone. We were up to our necks in it."

Lawrence lapsed into silence and Grover didn't disturb him. Lawrence had always been so upstanding and righteous. Realizing what he'd really been fighting for in China must have cost him some pride.

"Of course the generals were all happily housed down in the south and not about to order a retreat. But we had to have protective spells for our infantry and cavalry or we would have all been dead in days. So our theurgists turned to older techniques. They started tapping us in the mage corps to power the spells." The muscles in Lawrence's jaw flexed and twitched like he was grinding nails between his teeth. "They wired us up like we were alchemic rocks and let us burn."

"They what?" The alarm in Grover's voice seemed to boom through the dark night. Shackling mages to spell forges and searing them to charred bones was supposed to have been outlawed hundreds of years back, along with sacrificing children to river gods and such.

"It wasn't—I'm making it sound dramatic, aren't I?" Lawrence pulled a self-conscious smile. "Most of us actually volunteered—how could we not? And they obviously didn't turn us to ash in the spell forges. They just wore us out. Most of us joked that we could disguise ourselves as bundles of firewood if we sat still." He gave a dry laugh. But seeing how bone-lean Lawrence appeared even now, Grover couldn't bring himself to laugh along.

"How long did that go on?" Grover asked.

"Only three months. August third we finally reached the outskirts of Beijing. Though by then only five of us could still report for active duty." Lawrence frowned. "Then David Tucker appeared out of the blue, and Honora knew right away that something was badly wrong. She was sure Tucker had gone from wiring up spells that weren't strictly by the book to building one that had been outrightly banned—"

Grover frowned at that.

"Doesn't them having to ban certain theurgic spells cast a little shade on all the claims that theurgists couldn't do wrong because they're working from God's word and with the Lord's consent?" Grover couldn't help make the comment.

"You'd think, wouldn't you?" Lawrence laughed but dryly. "It turns out to be a little different in practice than in theory. See, a mage like me might use his power to break a common law, but unless I trained in theurgy—which I haven't—I couldn't create a spell that draws on enough different sources of power to break any of the Laws of Divine Order. And I wouldn't know enough about the workings of the Divine Order to even figure out how to undermine the laws."

"You mean doing things like pulling the stars out of the sky or something?" Grover asked.

"Sort of. It's less about exactly what they do than how they do it." Lawrence looked thoughtful. "Suppose a theurgist wants to move a boulder. He's allowed to create a spell that shatters it or even shoves it out of the way, but he's not allowed to build a spell that makes it just float off, because that breaks the Divine Law of Gravity. And if gravity were to come undone then the whole world and all the stars could fall apart. It's those kinds of laws they can't break— the ones we imagine God set in place when he created the universe."

Grover hadn't ever thought of gravity as a law that could be broken. He considered it.

"So they can make spells to power the engines of an airship, but they aren't allowed to just make the airship itself lighter than it ought to be?" Grover asked.

"Yep. " Lawrence replied. "I guess there's a whole list of ways that theurgists aren't supposed to cast spells. Lots of esoteric rules that you wouldn't imagine would need making. In particular, they aren't supposed to build a spell that manifests in a time before it was created."

Lawrence gazed at him meaningfully as Grover let the thought sink in.

Time.
Of course that would be a Divine Law.

"So a spell cast now shouldn't affect an age back when dinosaurs were alive and wandering the earth?" Grover raised his brows.

"Exactly." Lawrence nodded. "There's more as well but I don't know it all. Honora could tell you, of course. Before the war she received special dispensation to study under the Master Theurgist, Michael Faraday."

Grover vaguely recalled George mentioning the man. A wind mage who'd trained in theurgy and gone on to create cages that could trap lightning. George owned a bound transcript of some Christmas lecture he'd given off in England. More to the point, that meant Lady Astor wasn't just a mage but like Faraday was also a theurgist.

"Anyway most theurgists don't break Divine Laws—not just because it's illegal and dangerous, but because doing so requires vast amounts of power," Lawrence went on. "But Tucker had concocted a pet spell that he figured could cheat Divine Law by creating a source of even more power than he expended."

"By creating alchemic stone?" Grover asked just to be certain.

Lawrence nodded. "He'd worked out that the explosive energy released by breaking the Divine Law of Time would charge surrounding minerals. They'd become so alchemically potent that they'd actually radiate more power into the minerals around them and those in turn would do the same to minerals all around, creating a sort of chain of reactions. In theory entire mountains and valleys could be transformed into magic dust."

Grover frowned. Turning whole mountains to dust struck him as something along the lines of blotting out the sun or changing the ocean to blood. It was hard to imagine the mind of a man who would delight in the prospect, much less work towards it as a goal.

"But it was you and Honora and Gaston who actually powered the spell and manifested it?" Grover asked.

Lawrence turned away from Grover to pick up a stick and shift the wood in the fire. Red sparks flared up over the flames and burned out in the cool night air.

"Yes. We knew it was dangerous and that it might not be strictly legal. But we'd spent three months burning in spell forges, and the prospect of being able to somehow create alchemic stone from thin air was so relieving of an idea. We—I—didn't ask exactly how the spell worked or if there might be complications. I was so tired and I just wanted the war to be over."

Somewhere, out in the dark, one of them long-clawed, kicking dinosaurs gave a screech.

"The idea was that Honora would disguise herself, Gaston and me so that we could slip into Beijing city—"

"Neither of the Tuckers came along?" Grover asked.

"No, and that alone should have told me something. But I was past thinking by then. Like I said, I just wanted it to be over. By then I knew what a mistake I'd made in running away to join the mage corps. I wanted to come back home so much..." Lawrence glanced to Grover with such a longing expression that Grover felt his chest sort of flutter. But then Lawrence shook his head and went on. "So I took my section of the spell and went with Gaston and Honora. We made it into the city by the skin of our teeth and positioned ourselves outside the emperor's palace, near where the alchemic stone was stored—"

Lawrence paused again to shift the wood and embers of the fire. His expression turned distant, and he seemed, for a long while, like he couldn't bring himself to look up from the smoldering coals at the heart of the blaze. Then he sighed and leaned back again on his bedroll.

"I know that Nate Tucker had attempted the spell himself and failed. Gaston thought it had been because he couldn't endure the pain of it, but Honora thinks being a wind mage not an earth mage, he simply wasn't anchored strongly enough to a single physical place to command the force and mass necessary to complete the spell."

"But you could since you're an earth mage," Grover said.

"Yes, and so was Gaston. And so was the Imperial Consort Cixi. About halfway through the spell, she must have sensed us starting to power it. From inside the palace she began fighting us. She dug deep into the strength of her home ground, attempting to wrench the spell—and us—apart. In response Gaston and I reached out to our own strong grounds."

"And yours is Fire Springs," Grover realized.

Lawrence nodded slowly and with such sorrow in his expression that he could have been confessing to murder. In a way he was, Grover realized. Thousands of people had died. There wasn't anything Grover could think of to ease the burden of that. He just let Lawrence finish.

"Gaston grounded himself in the *Îles d'la Manche*—islands in the English Channel where is wife and daughter were living. I held firm to Fire Springs where you and I had spent so much time. Cixi kept pounding at us until it felt like I was being pulled in two. And then all of a sudden there was this godawful roar. Louder than anything I've ever heard—like the mountains were crumbling. The entire side of the palace collapsed down into the ground, and geysers of fire split up into the sky. It was the dead of night, but I saw sunlight shining up out from the rift we'd torn in the ground.

The water came surging up over me, and I realized that my right arm was badly broken. Gaston's ribs were shattered. I could hear him calling for help, but I couldn't do anything to stop the water. I barely managed to reach him and keep both our heads above the waves." Lawrence's voice sounded rough. He cleared his throat. "Honora got us out and away somehow. She had contacts among the Taiping revolutionaries. I don't remember much about the journey except that we were in the hills overlooking the Yellow River when they took most of my arm off. I remember the murky river cascading down to the clear floodwaters and pterosaurs soaring overhead while they sawed… I suppose I was glad enough for the opium then."

Grover recalled the quick glimpses he'd caught of terrible and tortured forms in Lawrence's sketchbook. It must have been hell.

"After that we traveled with a party of merchants, gathering information. That's when we learned the full extent of the damage we'd done and that Tucker had placed all the blame on Cixi."

"But you all knew he'd been behind it," Grover commented. "Didn't you try to tell anyone?"

"We were the ones who actually cast the spell. We were as much to blame as Tucker. And it wasn't as if Tucker wasn't on the lookout for us. He sure as hell didn't want any of the three of us showing up alive to implicate him. There were still plenty of mercenaries and warlords more than happy to hunt us down for him." Lawrence stared up at the sky. "Exposing Tucker didn't matter nearly as much to any of us as closing the rifts did. So we decided to remain dead to the world and out of Tucker's grasp. We sailed north and thankfully Cixi found us—"

"The enemy rescued you?" Grover's mind boggled at the notion.

"Well, it wasn't pleasant at first, but eventually Honora convinced her of our good intentions. We are all mages after all. And we all knew the rifts had to be closed. After we sealed the rift in China, Cixi provided us with funds and supplies to get us back to Europe where we closed the second rift. That was when Tucker found us. He was with a party of dignitaries and generals, so he couldn't just have us shot and kicked into anonymous graves.

"Honora and I played dumb, as if we really believed that the rifts had been Cixi's doing and not part of the spell he'd concocted. Considering the state of communications, it wasn't unreasonable to claim that we hadn't known the fate of our regiment and had simply taken it upon ourselves to undo Cixi's spell. After that we were guests of Emperor Napoleon III, and he handed us off to President Lincoln."

"That's when you got all them medals?" Grover asked.

Lawrence nodded, his expression ashamed.

"There are thousands of other people more deserving of them than me," Lawrence replied. "But I couldn't refuse them without causing an outrage or rousing Tucker's suspicion. So…"

Both of them remained quiet for a little time. The fire crackled and bats flitted through the darkness.

"I don't think many folks would have gone back to put it right, though," Grover said at last. "Takes real courage to face up to something like that."

"It isn't courage. I just couldn't live with myself any other way." Lawrence drew in a slow deep breath and released it. "No matter what, I have to do everything I can to close this last rift. That's all there is to it."

Grover leaned back, resting his head on the bedroll. His hand brushed against Lawrence's cool, ivory fingers. He wondered if Lawrence could feel his touch through the spells, clockwork and gold.

Above them stars blazed bright and clear while the crescent moon hung back, faint and wan as a wallflower.

"I was so afraid that I had killed you," Lawrence whispered. "I can't even tell you how overjoyed I felt when father told me you were fine. And when I finally saw you alive and well standing under that apple tree last night I... You looked so different. And you were wearing dinosaur leather. I've been all over the world and never seen another man like you."

"You think I'm a sight now, you should have seen me six years back. Pine needles in my hair and mud caked about everywhere." Grover said it teasingly but Lawrence shook his head.

"I'm not joking, Grove. You're the most handsome, upstanding man I've ever known."

"I...I wasn't..." Grover felt the flush rising across his face like a sudden fever. "I suppose I'm just trying to tell you that six years back, when they sent word that you'd died. Well, it knocked me down pretty hard."

"I'm sorry, Grove. Truly." Lawrence turned on his side to face him. "But I didn't know that I would survive closing the remaining rifts. How cruel would it have been to put you through thinking me dead, then discovering I was alive only to learn that I'd actually died in England? Only a heartless bastard would play with someone like that. So, I didn't contact you or my father, not even after Tucker discovered us. I just assured myself that you were both still safe and well and that I would see you again. That kept up my courage to close the rifts."

Far in the distance, the calls of coyotes rang out in dissonant quavering notes. Strange harmonies rose and fell. Grover supposed each member of the pack knew their own, recognized their voices calling out in the darkness. They didn't croon a pretty song, but he reckoned it wasn't meant for him. Maybe to the ones it was for, it was the most beautiful melody they could hear—one they couldn't keep from answering to.

Lawrence closed his ivory fingers around Grover's, and Grover thought he could feel the whir of tiny gears fluttering like an excited pulse.

"Well, we're both alive and here together now." Grover spoke quietly, though there was no one to overhear them for miles. "I don't see any reason we shouldn't unroll these blankets and make ourselves more comfortable, do you?"

Lawrence's hand tightened around his, and for an instant silence hung between them. The firelight lent his skin a golden sheen and lit his eyes like polished silver.

"None at all," Lawrence replied. Then he leaned closer. Grover reached out and pulled him into a deep kiss.

It wasn't quick and easy like it had been.

They kissed long and deep, tasting and teasing each other, then parting, breathless. Grover toyed with the buttons of Lawrence's shirt, but Lawrence stilled his hands before he unfastened the second button. Grover wanted to assure him that it didn't matter what scars he bore, that he was still the one man Grover wanted more than any other. But so much tension played in Lawrence's expression that Grover relented, simply stroking the hard warm bulk of Lawrence's left shoulder and tracing the wiry muscles of his left arm.

"The sky's beautiful tonight. The stars, so bright and clear." Lawrence slid his hand up Grover's stomach and chest. As Grover allowed Lawrence to push him onto his back, he easily read Lawrence's relief.

"It's a lovely view," Grover murmured. And it wasn't any hardship, running his hands through Lawrence's hair or caressing his head while Lawrence opened up the front of his trousers and sucked him like he'd been starving for this all his life. Grover gave himself over to the glory and joy of that hot mouth and slick tongue. If it was better than he remembered, he didn't trouble himself just now, worrying who Lawrence had learned those lovely tricks from.

After he'd arched and spilled out his pleasure, Grover took his turn showing off the fancy and flattering lip service he'd picked up himself. Hearing Lawrence moan his name as he bucked and groaned went a great way to soothing Grover's hurt over the eight years he'd felt so alone and abandoned. The way Lawrence gazed at him afterwards, it made Grover feel like his heart had become a wild, fluttering thing, beating at the cage of his ribs.

Grover settled down alongside Lawrence, and for a brief time they watched the stars shining against the black night sky. Studying the vast milky spill, with the taste of Lawrence on his lips, Grover couldn't suppress a grin. He didn't say anything, but Lawrence gave him a sleepy, conspiratorial smile. Then he laid his head on Grover's chest and Grover pulled a blanket over them both.

"If only things could stay just like this," Lawrence whispered.

"You don't reckon you'd get bored of laying on the ground after a few days?" Grover teased him.

"I don't know, I might just be happy to have that long to rest." Lawrence shifted slightly, and Grover wondered if his arm didn't pain him a little.

"But it's enough, isn't it?" Lawrence asked. "Snatching this little bit of pleasure even if it can't last?"

"Sure it is," Grover replied, and it was for now. Tomorrow he could wonder why Lawrence seemed so certain that they would not share a future together. Tonight, he felt too contented to disturb this fleeting bliss with questions.

Chapter Six

Over the next five days they traveled quickly and grew more at ease in each other's company. Their conversation and quiet times began to feel like they had years ago. At first the sight of Lawrence's ivory arm and the leather harness that held it in place disturbed Grover. It struck him as a symbol of all that Lawrence had endured and suffered—all they had lost—over the last eight years. But observing how naturally Lawrence moved the limb when he relaxed and the care he took in maintaining and exercising it, Grover began to realize that for Lawrence the prosthetic represented accomplishments—both his survival and his capacity to recover something of the life he'd left behind. Looking at it in that light, Grover found himself appreciating the feel of those polished fingers and even admiring the beauty of all the fine gears and spells. He welcomed that faintest of hums that passed from the ivory palm to his bare skin when they lay naked together.

In response Lawrence shed enough of his self-consciousness to allow Grover to see him without his shirt in the morning sunlight. Grover suspected they might have laid in late and indulged in some fun if it hadn't been for Romeo attempting to sneak into their camp and causing a wild commotion when he stepped on a hot coal in the fire pit.

While screeching and fleeing, the ridingbird managed to overturn and scatter just about everything. Grover and Lawrence's sleepy, sultry morning turned into several hours of repacking while playfully bantering about Betty's taste in males.

Despite himself, Grover felt a secret sort of relief when he sighted Romeo trailing them with his normal spry step.

The embers hadn't done him any real harm aside from making him hotfoot it when he wanted to be courtin'.

He'd never admit it, but the ridingbird's determination sparked sympathy within him. After all, here he was traipsing through the wilds at Lawrence's side hoping, silently, that somehow this time Lawrence would stay here with him.

Sometimes, Lawrence's smiles and affection offered him hope, but other times he'd glance over when Lawrence wasn't looking and catch that forlorn countenance. He'd only seen one other man wear so desolate and despairing an expression, and he'd been standing on the gallows, with his hands already tied behind his back and a rope around his neck.

The moment Lawrence noticed Grover watching him he instantly hid his stark sorrow, but the thought of it troubled Grover more deeply than he wanted to admit.

Their sixth evening riding, the air remained still and nearly cloudless. Miles of forest spread behind them, looking clear and precise as a picture. Grover spied no sign of the Tuckers' airship. Though far in the distance, thin trails of campfire smoke rose in straight lines, completely undisturbed by wind. Grover guessed that Weeminuche Utes hunted in the hills south of them. The smoke of so many fires made him wonder if they hadn't located a large herd of surviving buffalo. Calves would be plentiful this time of year and hunting easy.

"The smoke looks like streaks of rain," Lawrence commented. "Only rising up into the clouds, instead of falling down." Grover nodded, liking the idea. Smoke rising, rain falling, the earth and the sky reaching out to each other.

They rode a little farther into a protected valley and made their camp on a rise overlooking a meadow. All around them spikes of purple lupin and gold sunflowers shot up over a patchwork of wildflowers. Lawrence's horse grazed on verdant oatgrass and ricegrass while Betty snapped up the little critters the stallion startled from the ground cover. Grover pretended not to notice Romeo creeping up between mounds of sagebrush and wild rose bushes, though it took some doing. Between the ridingbird's brilliant plumage and hulking size, he might as well have been a bejeweled stage-coach slinking through the meadow.

Quite a sight actually.

Lawrence sketched the scene while the light lasted. As the moon began to climb through the brilliant colors of the setting sun, Grover secured Betty for the night. Lawrence hobbled and picketed his stallion then he joined Grover in preparing dinner—a grouse Grover had caught earlier. While they worked they sang their own randy versions of "The Old Bachelor".

"I'm an old bachelor, of twenty and three
And nary a maid has lain with me
I know little of women, little at all
Still, I and the lads have us a ball.
I am an old bachelor, of twenty and six
Carousing with men, I've learned some tricks.
I can ride any horse and drive a hack
Found many warm welcome round the back."

They went on, improvising lyrics and laughing between bites of their supper.

After they'd eaten, they cleaned up and made their bed, still laughing and singing to each other. Lawrence allowed Grover to help him with the buckles of the harness that held his ivory arm in place. Free of the harness, Lawrence drew in a deep breath and rolled his shoulders as though they ached. Then he placed his prosthetic arm atop his folded coat with great care and lay down beside Grover.

They were both tired. Still, they made the short time before they fell asleep pleasurable.

"This is what I want to remember," Lawrence whispered, sounding on the edge of sleep. "When it's all ended, just this…"

Grover stroked a damp lock of hair back from Lawrence's face, and for a few moments he studied his gaunt, scarred beloved in the faint glow of the moonlight. He wished he had the words to express the tenderness, fear and longing that churned through him. Or at least some way to temper the sorrow that haunted Lawrence. Grover just shook his head. He wasn't a man of great words, and in any case, he could tell from Lawrence's breathing that he was past hearing him. Already fast asleep. Moments later Grover joined him.

He dreamed of the night that surrounded them. Its darkness was like the surface of a still lake, hiding countless hungry, restless bodies. They flitted and prowled through Grover's mind. Some scampered and played. But one presence steadily grew in Grover's dream. A belly raw from hunger, and a spirit seething with the frustration of aching joints and old, dull teeth drifted over Grover like a warm wind.

It hated the smoke in the air but also smelled freshly spilled blood and flesh. Through the darkness, its eyes picked out soft, warm bodies lying exposed and asleep. Excitement surged through aged muscles, making it feel almost young again. Its heart raced as it stalked closer through the grass, muscles trembling with tension.

Close now, so close.

The disconcerting image of two men lying under a blanket washed through Grover's mind. He felt predatory hunger even as he recognized his own hat balanced on a stone and Lawrence's ivory arm draped over a folded coat.

Grover jerked awake, throwing his blanket back just as Betty let loose with a wild crow. He caught up his rifle. Next to him, Lawrence gave an inarticulate groan and rolled to his knees. Grover fired. The boom of the rifle rang through a mountain lion's grating, furious snarl.

Then all at once orbs of golden light rose from Lawrence's lips, illuminating the meadow. Hardly five feet from Grover, a big tawny mountain lion swayed on its feet. A dark stain of blood colored the pale fur of its throat, but its gaze remained locked on Grover. He gripped his rifle ready to swing the butt hard when the big cat pounced. A blue light crackled from Lawrence's right hand.

The mountain lion staggered.

Suddenly, Betty lunged from the shadows with a wild cry. She kicked the huge talons of her right leg into the mountain lion's side and sent the cat sprawling sideways. Its body just missed the smoldering embers of the campfire. A second powerful kick tore open a huge gash in the mountain lion's belly. Its body flopped across the ground like a sack of rags. Betty kicked and pecked at the creature farther out into the gloom of the meadow.

Grover recognized that the mountain lion was far past feeling any hurt. It had already been dead when it stood staring into Grover's face, with a bullet hole punched through its neck. It just hadn't known as much.

Lawrence clenched his hand around the spark of blue light, and it died out. The gold orbs floating over them continued to glow but not so brightly. Standing at the picket line, Lawrence's horse appeared to have only awakened at the tail end of the commotion. The stallion stamped a few times but settled enough to sample a mouthful of flowers.

"What the hell just happened?" Lawrence stared after Betty then turned his attention back to Grover. He looked as shaken as Grover felt. His eyes wide and his hair sticking out at unkempt angles.

"A mountain lion. I reckon he was old and relied on hunting newborns calves. But with the Weeminuche so close to the buffalo herd, I think he hadn't had much luck. So he took a chance on the nearest thing that seemed easy." Grover frowned at the embers of the campfire. "The smell of our fresh grouse probably drew him. He must have been desperate, near starving, to chance coming so near Betty. Wolves and mountain lions both tend to keep clear of her now that she's full grown."

"But how did you know it was there?" Lawrence asked.

"I heard Betty crow." Grover sat back down amidst the bedding but didn't set aside his rifle. He doubted that he'd be able to return to sleep anytime soon. Briefly he wondered if he ought to attempt to hitch Betty back to the picket that she'd broken free from. Probably wiser to let her be for a little time. She was still worked up and tearing at her dead foe.

"That was a hell of a shot." Lawrence too knelt back down on their bedding. His shoulder brushed Grover's, and Grover leaned into him just a little. Three of the gold orbs dimmed and went out, leaving only two still shining. "How did you see where to aim through the dark?" Lawrence asked.

"I don't rightly know that I did, so much as I just snatched up the rifle and fired." Grover considered for a moment, remembering fragments of his strange dream. "I just sort of knew it was creeping up on us from the left."

Lawrence studied him a moment.

"The same way that you just knew that King Douglass didn't mean us any harm that first day we set out?" Lawrence asked.

"That's right." Grover replied. "My ma used say that if folk just learned to listen, they could hear every living creature around them. My pa thought so too, that was how he taught me to hunt."

Lawrence nodded, his expression thoughtful but not quite so strained as it had been earlier.

A thin seam of pale light was seeping along the jagged line of the eastern horizon. It would be dawn soon. There wouldn't be any point in trying to go back to sleep, at the same time it was a little too dark to begin the day's work.

"Do you think there are any more mountain lions out in the dark about to attack us?" Lawrence asked.

"Not just now, no." Grover decided after a moment. "I think it's mostly songbirds, little blue-footed dinosaurs that are waking up to begin their dawn choruses." First thing, the birds and dinosaurs could make quite a racket, all of them calling and chirping to each other.

"I don't suppose you'd be interested in putting down your rifle? Perhaps we could bide out time until the sun's up?" Lawrence leaned into Grover and almost shyly stroked Grover's back with his left hand.

That struck Grove as about the best thing he could think of doing. Lawrence let the last of the gold lights go out, and the two of them lay back together.

By noon, they reached a narrow pass Grover called the Needle's Eye. There they turned west, descending towards the brackish waters of the Rift River. The terrain grew wet and warm. Lush vines, dense stands of magnolia and giant ferns invaded groves of native aspen. Veils of mist filled the gullies and rain showers fell most evenings. The ground turned to mud and creeks that Grover easily jumped across in winter now spread into bogs. The signs of bigtooths grew more fresh and common.

That afternoon they came upon a gargantuan longneck carcass sprawled across several uprooted willows. The smell of it filled the air like a fog, and its prone body rose like a hill of bloody bone and overripe meat. Pterosaurs, vultures, eagles and vast flocks of crows blanketed the heights of the mountainous corpse, while coyotes, foxes and even a bear fed on the hunks of flesh and bone that the bigtooth had left after it fed.

"Wolves have already been here." Grover noted the tracks in the soft mud. "And a momma cougar with two kittens it looks like."

"You reckon the liè lóng—bigtooth—will come back for seconds anytime soon?" Lawrence inquired.

"This time of year there might be a whole brood of 'em." Grover touched his rifle like a talisman but didn't free it from his saddle. "But from the look of things they ain't going hungry just now."

"Still…" Lawrence said, as a second bear ambled out from between two magnolia trees.

Grover nodded. A carcass like this would pull every hungry predator for miles and miles away. He felt no inclination to repeat their earlier encounter with the mountain lion. Only a fool would make camp anywhere near here.

"We should keep a move on," Grover finished for him.

They forwent their lunch, riding till twilight to get well clear of the rank, rotting scent of the remains.

That evening, Grover hiked a little distance to refill their canteens from a fresh water spring. He nearly jumped out of his skin when a form burst through the underbrush. Grover whipped up his rifle only to find Romeo gawking at him with disappointment. Clearly he'd picked up Betty's scent off of Grover's leathers and gotten his plumage all glossy and proud for their assignation.

"I'm already spoken for," Grover muttered.

Romeo quickly scuttled away, and Grover won a good laugh out of Lawrence when he related the story over dinner that night.

Frogs sang Lawrence and Grover to sleep as they lay in each other's arms. In the mornings the hum of mosquitoes woke them. It should have made for a miserable slog, but Lawrence maintained an amused attitude and at times seemed genuinely fascinated by the strange world that their once-familiar stomping grounds had become. When he pointed out a vibrant flower, Grover couldn't fail to see the beauty in it. He didn't gripe when Lawrence took a few moments to sketch, particularly not after Lawrence took to showing his drawings when they settled down for supper by their fire.

"Are those farts you've drawn puffing up from the back ends of them three-horns?" Grover asked.

Lawrence grinned at him. Wasn't as if both of them hadn't coughed and choked on the pungent fumes the herd had left behind. In spite of that Grover found the drawings fascinating. As much as the rift had destroyed the lands, it had also filled Grover's life with wonder and created opportunities for folks like him to succeed. But when he told Lawrence as much, Lawrence just shook his head.

"That's because you're an exceptional man, Grove. But I don't think one in a hundred people would thank me if they knew what I'd done to them."

Grover frowned at the flurry of pen lines that so perfectly captured the motion and power of three-horns running and rutting. Of course the rifts had been terrible, but not everything that came of them was bad. Lawrence had to see that, otherwise how would he ever manage to live in this world?

"You know, sometimes the world needs to get shook up so the people on the bottom have a chance of going any place else. My cousin Frank only managed to free his daughter because of the floods. If they hadn't come when they did, she would have been sold on to a bordello owner," Grover said at last.

Lawrence considered that silently and offered Grover a faint smile. "I'm glad for that, then."

Grover supposed it would be best to let it go for the night. There were other ways to show Lawrence that life right here and now still promised pleasure and joy enough.

❖ ❖ ❖

Early on their ninth day riding, they reached the huge canyon that the Rift River had plowed through Grand Lake Valley. The track they followed narrowed and they rode single file along the cliff's edge. Below them dead and decaying trees lined the riverbanks, while beds of sedges, salt rushes and agave grew up in their places. The waters roared past, far too wild and deep to ford. But fish leapt and splashed through the torrents, while an enormous crocodile basked beside the salt pools and ponds that edged the river. On the far side of the canyon, some fifty jade-green turtles the size of prize pigs slowly dragged themselves into the river, leaving behind sandy mounds and clutches of buried eggs.

As they rode lower Grover pointed out the white salt crystals that limned tree trunks and rocks like frost. Thick crusts edged pools nearer the river. Grover spotted a herd of bighorn sheep licking up the salt while nervously eyeing a lounging crocodile.

If he'd been on his own Grover might have worked his way down to harvest several pounds of salt himself. The stuff was as valuable as gold dust back in Fort Arvada. But he could sense Lawrence's anxiousness to keep moving and reach the rift. By now the Tuckers were likely searching it out for themselves and—unless they were dolts—they'd start by attempting to follow the Rift River to its source. That meant they'd be closing in on him and Lawrence soon.

"On our way back after this is all done, you think you'll have time to spend a few hours scraping salt?" Grover gestured to the white blooms encrusting a pool some thirty feet below them.

"I'm not—" Lawrence cut himself off short as Grover looked back at him. Then he shrugged. "I can't make any promises. Not before I've closed the last rift."

"Fair enough," Grover replied, but Lawrence's refusal made him uneasy. Not just because he wouldn't commit to something so small as a couple hours, but because of the desolation in his expression when he spoke of the rift.

Though once they rounded the curve of the raging river and rode out of earshot of the torrents, Lawrence's easygoing temperament seemed to return to him. He made light of the ticks and biting bugs that bedeviled him through the lush brush of ferns, oaks and cycads, referring to himself as a three-ring flea-circus. When their path opened up, Lawrence rode alongside Grover.

"Don't suppose there's something you can do about my little army of hangers-on?" Lawrence inquired.

"How do you mean?" Grover asked.

"Well, you don't seem much bothered by the blood-suckers." Lawrence scratched at his chest and then scowled as he flicked a fly away. "The entire time we've been riding through these swamps, you've hardly been bitten. Whereas I and my horse are being eaten alive."

It was true that Lawrence sported a number of bites and welts while Grover remained largely untouched. He'd never noticed the absence of the little torments when traveling on his own, but now it did strike him as odd.

"Maybe I taste bad," Grover suggested.

"Now I know for a fact that that ain't the case, Grove. You are sweet as honey and intoxicating as calvados." Lawrence favored him with a sultry smile which made Grover's cheeks flush with the hot memory of Lawrence's lips on him.

"There is something that you do though, isn't there?" Lawrence's expression turned more serious. "When you get a bite. I bet you curse the little critters silently or some such, don't you?"

"Well, I don't hardly wish them a hearty meal and a happy stay with me."

They reached a small waterfall of meltwater and Grover stopped to refresh their canteens. Lawrence rinsed his face and hands. Both Betty and Lawrence's horse drank from the pools surrounding the fall. Larks and tiny, fuzzy pterosaurs flitted between the water and the flower-laden magnolias surrounding them. While their mounts drank, Lawrence drew in his sketchbook and in a matter of moments produced copies of several of the orchid blossoms that sprang up from the mossy stones as well as overhanging tree branches.

Then they both mounted once more, and Lawrence returned to their previous conversation.

"There was a girl I met in China who could drive off lice with a wave of her hands," Lawrence said. "She also called wild horses to her and tamed them with a touch."

"Oh?" That sounded like something from the stories his ma used to tell him. It put him a little in mind of Queen Adiaha Umo judging for the fly wronged by a cow. "Did she make good trade out of it?"

"She did well by me. But my point is that in my travels I've come to realize there are many more types of mages than just the elemental trinity that theurgists recognize. I think you might have something in common with Jingfei— the Chinese girl who sold us horses."

"I don't know about that." Grover couldn't imagine calling himself a mage, and he didn't want to even think about the hell Reverend Dodd would give him if he had to register himself and take an oath, as Lawrence had back when he'd turned sixteen.

"I suspected that you wouldn't take to the idea, but you have to admit there aren't any fleas or flies on you and it isn't just anyone who can understand a dinosaur at a glance, or feel a mountain lion through the dark—"

"But that's nothing," Grover protested. "None of that's a sign of being a mage. Not like that one night when you pulled light right up out of the ground and lit up the Fire Springs all around us."

"Well, how else was I going to witness the glory of you swimming in the buff under the stars?" Lawrence gave a soft laugh and Grover smiled at the memory of the evening. He'd been real shy at first, all lit up like that, but Lawrence had joined him in the warm spring water and made him feel handsome as anything.

"There's so much that theurgists don't know, and so much more that they just won't acknowledge because it falls outside the Holy Book," Lawrence went on. "But believe me, there's more power in this world than just earth, water and wind. There's the life itself coursing through all of us, from fleas and flowers up to presidents and popes."

Grover nodded. He'd seen enough of the living and the dead to know that something subtle and yet integral separated one from the other, and it could be lost in a single breath. That still didn't make him a mage.

"In China they called it qi. In India the Hindus whisper of it as prana despite a veritable army of English theurgists banning practices of controlling such power." Lawrence's tone alone conveyed his annoyance at that. "A Hebrew trader I met in Salonica described living energy as Ruah. Even one of the theurgist missionaries Honora introduced me to admitted that the ancient Hellenes knew the concept and that the people of Oceania believe in a vital force that flows through every living thing."

"You're just telling me this as an excuse to brag about all the places you've been, ain't you?" Grover teased. Frankly, he hadn't thought about how far and how long Lawrence must have been making his way secretly from China to England. Nearly six years he'd have been journeying alongside Gaston and Honora.

Grover wondered how early on Lawrence and Gaston had become lovers, then wished that he hadn't because knowing either way, it wouldn't do him any good.

"God's own truth, I am not," Lawrence replied. "I honestly believe that you're a kind of mage, Grove. I've thought so for a long time, but it didn't seem like my place to push it on you."

Grover watched a dragonfly dart past him and felt its papery wings hum across his skin.

"But now it is?" Grover asked.

"Now…things are different. Knowing what abilities you have to call upon could make all the difference if matters turn bad."

"You think I ain't seen my share of hard times already?" Grover raised his brows but then he laughed and shook his head, because he didn't really want to argue with Lawrence. "Even if I am some half-assed mage, I don't reckon it would change much. Except I suppose I'll give it a go running any biting bugs off you and your horse tonight. Or was that all you were after?"

"Well, I wouldn't object by any means, but no that wasn't my purpose in initiating the conversation."

"So?" Grover prompted.

"So, I think that if you are a qi mage, it couldn't hurt you to actively practice your talent." Lawrence paused, and he bowed low to his stallion's neck, ducking below an overhanging willow branch. "What you've managed, just on intuition, is astounding. Think what you might be able to do if you honed your skill."

"Send an army of fleas and bedbugs to harass Sheriff Lee?" Grover suggested.

"Or dissuade a bigtooth from hunting you." Lawrence raised his brows. "That might come in handy, don't you think?"

That would indeed, Grover thought.

"Am I even going to have to worry about that once you've closed the rift?" Grover asked.

"What's on this side of the rift will be trapped here and vice versa." Lawrence glanced down the cliff's edge to the river now far below them. "The floodwater may dry up over time. Dinosaurs could adapt and keep breeding."

Grover wasn't certain if he ought to feel happy or disappointed about that. On one hand it would slow communications as well as farming and ranching. On the other hand all those plantations would remain under saltwater and worthless to the bastards who'd profited from making slaves of their fellow human beings.

Also, Grover wouldn't lose Betty and King Douglass. Admitting how close he felt to the two critters, he supposed there might be something to Lawrence's speculation…maybe.

"I don't rightly know how I'd practice," Grover admitted at last.

"If you'd like I can show you a couple exercises I learned in the corps."

Grover didn't know why, but the suggestion delighted him far more than it ought to have. Then he realized Lawrence wasn't only promising to improve his chances against a bigtooth, this was the first time Lawrence had so much as hinted at the two of them being together beyond the present moment. Through all the days and nights they'd spent together so far, he hadn't once mentioned a future beyond the closing of the rift.

Grover didn't want to push Lawrence, but he hated how the uncertainty gnawed at him. Every day he rediscovered more of what he'd adored and cherished in Lawrence's company. At the same time, he fought his own happiness back down, because he didn't think he could stand to care so damn much for the man and lose him all over again.

"I'd like that." Grover didn't dare say more.

And fortunately he didn't have to since all at once the ground began to shudder beneath them. Flocks of birds in the trees ahead of them took to the skies in streaming clouds.

Grover and Lawrence both stilled their mounts, and Grover thought he noticed Romeo stop off to his left near a thicket of hackberries.

"Was that—" Lawrence began, but Grover silenced him with a finger to his own lips.

The earth shook again—leaves and blossoms tumbled down from trees—as a deep, lowing moan rolled through the air like thunder. Another call followed it.

"Longnecks," Grover told Lawrence.

"Not a bigtooth?"

Grover shook his head. Heavy as they looked, bigtooths moved as stealthily as cougars. In fact, it had been the sudden terrified silence of every bird and little chattering beast that had alerted Grover to the presence of a hunting bigtooth on several occasions.

They rode on, and about an hour later when they reached high ground, they found themselves treated to the sight of two gigantic golden longnecks humping and lumbering across a flowery meadow. Their massive tails swept across yards of ground, sending leaves, blossoms and several shrubs sailing through the air. The gleaming behemoths united, both of them bellowing and snorting like two steam engines suddenly endowed with the anatomy and desire for amorous congress. Tremors rocked through the soil, and a family of voles dashed from their nest and raced past Grover.

A small herd of buffalo looked on from the far edge of the meadow. Grover wasn't sure if they seemed more awed or horrified witnessing the awkward climax of these two giants.

"It's like watching landslides copulate," Lawrence commented. Then he added with a crooked smile, "And here I thought I'd seen it all."

"It's a world of wonders when you're traveling with me, that's for certain," Grover replied.

While the two longnecks disengaged and returned to the more subdued activity of grazing, Lawrence and he rode along the edge of the meadow and crossed back under the cover of trees. They made the Rabbit Hills before sundown and ate a meal of clams that Grover gathered from one of the distributary streams that splintered off from the Rift River. Lawrence contributed some of the rice he'd brought along, and that combined with a few sprigs of wild sage made for quite a repast, in Grover's opinion.

"Could do with a beer though." Lawrence scratched at the thick stubble covering his jaw. Grover had forgotten how red Lawrence's beard came in. The hairs looked like copper in the glow of the fire.

"I built a still at the cabin and hauled up my ma's old oak barrels," Grover informed him as he stretched out and warmed his damp feet by the fire.

"Don't tell me you're distilling your mama's applejack?" Lawrence's face lit up with delight. Grover might as well have told him he had hot taps, a flushing toilet and a solid gold bed; he still wouldn't have impressed Lawrence more.

"Yep. I had to do something with my time at the height of winter. Only so many hours a man can hunt." Grover indulged himself in a satisfied smile. "I've got two barrels aged five years now. I figure it couldn't hurt to sample some. If you ain't too busy with other things."

"Now you're just teasing me!" Lawrence laughed then

he sighed. "The whole time I was traveling through India, I kept having this dream that you brought me a bottle of that sweet applejack…"

"Is that all I did?" Grover expected not, knowing the sorts of dreams he'd indulged in while missing Lawrence. Most involved fucking and laughing and the immense relief of knowing that Lawrence wasn't lost to him.

Those dreams had been worse to rise from than nightmares because they left his waking days desolate.

"In the dreams you would always put your arms around me and let me rest my head on your chest. Then you told me that I had to keep going and make things right," Lawrence said, and Grover didn't like the sadness in his tone, but then Lawrence caught himself and pulled a smile. "Speaking of not shirking my duties. Wasn't I supposed to show you a little mage training?"

"Well, the suggestion was made. But am I gonna have to put my boots back on?" Grover scowled at the slumped piles of marsh-soaked leather sitting next to Lawrence's riding boots beside the fire. "My toes are just starting to warm up."

"No. You don't even have to stand up if you don't want to." Lawrence quickly closed the distance between them, sitting down beside Grover. He held out his left hand. "Just take my hand in yours."

Grover took his warm hand. Lawrence interlaced their fingers and very lightly traced a circle over the back of Grover's hand with the ivory fingers of his right hand. Grover felt the slightest tickle and only heard a murmur as Lawrence whispered foreign-sounding words.

"What's that supposed to do?" Grover asked.

"Keep your feet warm," Lawrence replied, and Grover wasn't sure if he was serious or not. He almost asked but Lawrence gave him a serious look.

"Close your eyes and let yourself relax," Lawrence instructed him. "Whatever might be bothering you, forget about it for the time being. Relax."

Grover closed his eyes and took in a few deep breaths—breathing the way his ma had taught him to when he needed to cool his temper. Not that he felt angry now, just a mite too excited and nervous. Over and over he drew a slow breath in and blew it out, along with the tension in his muscles. Until he felt like he could almost drift off to sleep.

"Now listen to your surroundings," Lawrence said quietly. "Not just the sounds but the silence. Feel the waves moving through the air and the deep stillness of the surrounding stones."

How in the blazes he was supposed to accomplish that Grover had no idea, but he went ahead and tried, listening intently to the noises of the twilight night. Bats peeped and fluttered between distant stands of trees. Lawrence's horse snored softly while Betty scratched grass and earth into a bed for herself. Way off he could just make out the rumble of the Rift River.

But as for waves moving through the air or the stillness of stones, no. Grover focused hard, attempting to pick out the faintest trace of either, but only his awareness of the warmth of Lawrence's fingers seemed to grow. Where their skin pressed, Grover sensed a hum of excitement but also steady waves of heat, pulsing like a heartbeat. The steadfastness of that rhythm struck him as deeply comforting and drew him closer to Lawrence. As he focused he realized that Lawrence blazed like a brilliant fire pored into the shape of a man. Though his right arm flared with tiny blue sparks.

A strange sensation came over Grover, as if he were floating over his own relaxed body and curling around Lawrence in a plume of smoke. He caught the exhalation of Lawrence's breath and rose with it into the cool evening air. All around him he felt tiny pulses flicker like starlight as moths winged past him and bats pursued them. As Grover took it in, he realized that each of them shone with a warm glow that lit their flesh like light streaming through stained glass.

Farther out, the lush forest radiated luminous green while countless creatures—some huge others miniscule, some stalking others sleeping—gleamed like a million scattered candle flames. He felt almost as if he could reach out and catch even the largest ones—that sleeping bigtooth only a few miles west, or the two sated longnecks that lay curled around each other—with just a flick of his hand. The warmth of them pulled at him, though the longer he focused on any one of them, the more it seemed to stretch towards him. Briefly he wondered if he couldn't draw a light all the way from the flesh it inhabited into the palm of his hand, but he resisted. That seemed, somehow, wrong to him.

Instead he turned his attention to the weird blue haze that bobbed far off on the horizon. A grating, mechanical beat reverberated from it, and Grover could see the golden lights of night birds, bats and insects whirling away from its slow path across the sky.

Could that be the Tuckers' airship, he wondered?

Without thinking, he curled himself around the swift soft body of a bat and winged after the airship. It floated a great distance away, and when the little bat's strength flagged, Grover pushed some of his own warmth and light into the bat's weary body. A feeling of shared exhilaration flooded him. As one he and the bat snapped up several fat mosquitoes and tore through the night to swoop alongside the sleek airship's long gondola.

Dozens of shining human forms crowded the deck as he passed. Though three of them struck him as very strange.

Up at the bow on the bridge stood two forms, both faint compared to the others surrounding them. But stranger still was the fact that when one moved away from the other, a stream of light stretched out between them like an umbilical cord. As Grover watched he saw the light flare up in one of the figures—growing almost as bright as it blazed in the surrounding people—but then it seemed to drain into the second body.

Back near the quarterdeck, the third figure sat near five others. But unlike the others this body seemed swathed in an immense ribbon of sparkling blue letters, while a tiny, intense gold light shone between and beneath them. Grover suspected that he knew who these people were but he wished he could be certain. If only he could actually see them instead of sensing the brilliance their lives threw off.

If he could somehow use other eyes…then he cursed himself for choosing to ride along on a bat. The moment the thought occurred to him, he was surprised to find he really could see the figures of the uniformed men on the deck of the gondola.

On the quarterdeck, a group sat near and on artillery cases, placing bets as they studied their hands of cards. Recognizing Lawrence's countenance in their midst gave him a little jolt. He'd suspected as much but hadn't realized how perfect Lady Astor's impersonation would appear. She grinned, Lawrence's crooked grin, and laid out a royal flush. The guards and crewmen groaned and coins changed hands. One of the men complained that the naked women drawn on the cards had distracted him.

"At least you claimed a lovely view from a losing hand," Honora replied. "My girl on the king of diamonds nearly made my eyes water." That won her guffaws and a slap on the back.

Grover swept over them and circled one of the hanging lamps, snapping up a moth.

Suddenly one of the Tucker twins came pelting towards the gathered men. The second twin followed right behind—and now Grover suspected he knew why they stayed so very close to each other.

"There's a spy on board!" the first Tucker shouted.

"There." The second lifted a pistol towards Grover. Terror raced through the tiny body he inhabited.

Honora instantly stood, blocking the shot.

"Are you mad?" Honora's words boomed out in Lawrence's voice. Even the Tuckers froze in response to the authoritative tone. "We're surrounded by cases of explosives, alchemic dust and black powder. And you're aiming at a lamp!"

Grover took advantage of the Tuckers' hesitation to flit back into the darkening sky.

"It set off an alarm," one of the Tuckers snapped. "Likely another bird or bat possessed by another of those filthy redskins to spy, and you've let it escape."

The rest of his words faded from Grover's hearing as he raced from the airship and soared back towards the camp where his body lay slumped across Lawrence's lap. The sight of that gave him another shock. What if he'd died somehow? Was he going to have to live out the rest of his life eating mosquitoes and hearing shapes all around him?

"Come on, Grove," Lawrence said softly, and he traced the circle around the back of Grover's hand again. "Come back to me, darling."

Grover felt a slight tug and let himself be pulled free of the bat. At once he sank back to his own body, and then rushed in like a deep breath. He felt cold and oddly stiff. Lawrence's hand seemed hot as an ember.

Grover opened his own eyes to gaze up into Lawrence's strained face.

"Did you know that bats aren't actually blind?" Grover asked.

"I didn't." Lawrence laughed, looking relieved. Then he stroked Grover's cheek and leaned down and kissed him.

Chapter Seven

The next morning, after Grover took a few minutes to drive off the bugs that bedeviled Lawrence and his stallion, they shared a quick breakfast. Over pemmican and whiptail eggs, Grover described the airship's distance and how he'd reached it. Lawrence gazed at him with an expression near reverence.

"You could see all that?" Lawrence asked. "And you took possession of a bat?"

"I guess you could call it that. Isn't that what you meant for me to see and do?" Grover scraped up the last of his egg and downed it. Discovering the clutch of eggs had been a rare treat though the absence of a parent guarding the nest implied that a bigtooth hunted very near their current location. Still Betty hadn't been half-overjoyed to indulge in her share.

Out of the corner of his eye, he glimpsed her rolling one of the eggs into a bush, which barely disguised Romeo's brilliant blue plumes. Grover returned his attention to Lawrence.

"I suspected that you were sensitive to qi, but I had no idea that you'd go so far the very first time." Lawrence reached out and touched the back of Grover's hand lightly. "Thank God the holdfast between us held."

"Don't look so serious, Lawry. Ain't no way you could lose me so easy." Grover grinned at him with a shade more bravado than he honestly felt. "I'd find my way back to you no matter what."

"I'll hold you to that," Lawrence replied.

Grover just nodded. After all he wasn't the one who'd left. He wasn't the one who couldn't say if he'd stay.

For an earth mage Lawrence sure was prone to wandering.

But then, Grover reminded himself, Lawrence wasn't the only mage who didn't seem like what he was. There was Lady Astor all fitted out like a man and looking so at ease with a deck of dirty cards in her hand that Grover felt certain this wasn't the first time she'd played that part. Hell, she could probably piss standing up.

And there were the Tuckers, too.

"You mentioned earlier that Nathaniel Tucker was a wind mage as well as a theurgist. But he isn't a mage anymore, is he? He lost his power when David Tucker showed up, didn't he?" Grover caught and held Lawrence's suddenly fearful gaze. "They aren't anything like twins."

No surprise that Lawrence hesitated in responding. He'd made it plain days ago that he didn't want Grover finding out anything about Nathaniel Tucker that could make him a threat. But that had been before Grover had seen into him.

"Yes, he lost much of his strength. And no he wasn't born a twin," Lawrence replied. "But you can't ever let him even suspect you know as much."

"Because the two of them are living proof that they—he—broke a Divine Law." Grover felt certain of it now.

Lawrence nodded.

"Honora suspects that he somehow pulled himself in two when he first attempted to create alchemic stone. He did have a younger brother, David, who served with us in China, but he died of flux early in the summer."

"The man certainly put that tragedy to good use." Grover studied Lawrence and thought again of what he'd witnessed on the airship. Two men sharing one life. That odd flow of their living force, almost as if one of them constantly fed into the life of the other. For the first time he considered what it would mean for a man to break through time, not to an ancient age but to his own past…

"I think I know how Nathaniel created David," Grover said at last.

"Oh?" Lawrence appeared only a little amused at the presumption of him making sweeping pronouncements after just one whirl out there with the lights and darkness of magic.

"If you were gonna violate a Divine Law and open a rift in time for the very first time you'd do it real careful," Grover speculated. "Try to make it such a little difference that maybe no one would notice. You wouldn't pick an age full of floods and dinosaurs. The first time, I'd bet my back teeth, you'd aim for a time when you knew exactly what to expect."

"Sure," Lawrence agreed.

"So what happens if you open a rift that reaches back, say, five minutes? And you do it hidden inside your own tent where you've been all alone scheming for the last couple hours?" Grover flashed a grin. "Who might just step through from the past?"

All at once realization lit Lawrence's lean face.

"You think David isn't half of Nathaniel but actually the exact same man brought forward in time just a few minutes?" Lawrence asked.

Grover nodded.

"We've both seen a body pulled in two—Nathaniel Tucker ain't a heap of blood and meat. What he is, is the past and the present forced to share every moment. They have to split the life that was meant for just the one of them. Maybe if he hadn't been a mage Nathaniel wouldn't have survived at all."

"That is such a strange idea." For a moment Lawrence frowned intently at the ground like he was working out a tough riddle. Grover understood. He'd spent at least an hour lying awake in the predawn gloom contemplating the exact timing required for Tucker to have opened a rift and transported an earlier version of himself without changing history so that he hadn't opened the rift in the first place. The earlier Tucker—David—must have crossed through after he'd opened his own rift back in time. Which meant that maybe another Tucker had crossed over into David's place… And maybe that pattern repeated on and on.

It made his head hurt to think about it too much.

"Just strange," Lawrence repeated.

"I know." Grover nodded. "But it explains why the next time he designed the spell he created rifts so far back in the past. He didn't want to risk giving his game away by doubling anyone else or himself again."

"Thank god for that small mercy, I suppose." Lawrence pulled one of his wry grins. "I'd likely throttle my younger self if I could get my hands on him."

"I don't know." Grover laughed. "He was awful charming last night."

But the thought lingered with Grover the rest of the day. If the past altered—a man killed his younger self or thousands of miles of seawater drained away—wouldn't that alter the future? If it did, was the world around him and his very life actually the outcome of things that had happened so long ago, but been triggered by the Tuckers, only six years past?

At last he gave up thinking about it. A fellow could drive himself mad chasing those sorts of thoughts.

The next three days they covered more ground and much faster than Grover had expected. In large part because they didn't have to fight deep drifts of winter snow when they crossed the high passes. But the awareness of the

Tuckers close behind them added to their sense urgency. Despite the abundance of opportunities, they didn't linger in any one place—except to sleep at night. Their afternoon meals were comprised of lumps of pemmican they wolfed down while riding. When their mounts flagged, they walked and allowed the animals to graze and feed while still gaining what ground they could.

Though they both paused after they came over a ridge to see a beaver pond and a vast alpine meadow spread out below them. A huge herd of snow-white mountain goats grazed on brush and explosions of wild flowers, while a pairs of ridingbirds cooed and preened from mounded nests. Betty watched them and then peered back over her shoulder to where Grover knew Romeo trailed them. Two days past Grover had allowed him to sleep curled up in sight of their campfire; since then the male ridingbird had grown steadily less shy.

But it wasn't the mountain goats, riding birds or even the clouds of butterflies descending upon the flowers that captured Grover's attention. Some one hundred yards from them, King Douglass stood, his wings folded, watching over four fuzzy, speckled flaplings as they speared and poked after marmots, snakes and hares. Between catches, they scampered on all fours, like gigantic bats, squealing and chirping and then playfully fencing one another with their glinting beaks.

Grover felt King Douglass's pride as he watched the young thunderbirds. They already stood taller than full-grown men and sported dots of fiery color across their growing crests. In a year's time they would be magnificent.

"You really adore that fella, don't you?" Lawrence asked.

"I…" Grover flushed, realizing how absurd he must look grinning happily at the big old thunderbird. "But just look at him. You can tell he's been through tough times.

That rip in his wing, the scrapes across his beak and all those scars on his back legs. But he's still got his dignity and his pride. He ain't been beat for all the hard knocks he's taken."

"I suppose," Lawrence allowed, and they rode on.

Though that night just before they went to sleep, Lawrence took out his sketchbook and showed Grover a little cartoon he'd made of King Douglass wearing a battered crown and a heart-shaped locket. The tiny portrait inside the locket looked suspiciously like Grover himself. It was silly but it made Grover strangely happy.

The next day they at last reached Grover's cabin, which he'd built back into a hill on the high ground overlooking the rift lands. Before this, he'd thought it had been a miracle that his place hadn't been destroyed when the rift had opened up. But now he wondered if somehow Lawrence hadn't protected the cabin, even while he'd battled against Cixi.

"It's even prettier than I remembered," Lawrence said softly.

Grover nodded.

The sod roof sported so many flowers it reminded Grover of his ma's Sunday hat. A family of squirrels had moved into the outhouse, but the rest of the place Grover had sealed up tighter than a crypt when he'd left. His little treasury of smoked meat, tanned hides and applejack remained undisturbed. Lawrence helped him set up the A-frame that served as a stable and pull off the heavy shutters to air out the stuffy interior of the cabin itself. Grover hauled water from the nearby creak while Lawrence fed and penned his horse. Betty and Romeo settled themselves down to flapping and flirting near the sapling apple trees Grover had planted two years back.

The cabin's single room wasn't so nice as the place Grover rented from the Codys, but he took great pride in it. The table and three chairs had belonged to his parents, as had the few dishes and the simple tablecloth. He'd built the two cabinets and the bed himself, and he'd worked himself almost to death the first year he'd been on his own to save enough money to buy the cast-iron potbelly stove.

Watching Lawrence build a fire in the stove, while he made-up the wood-framed bed with furs and his prized quilt, Grover felt nostalgia creep over him. Though in the past Lawrence might have grumbled and pouted about doing woman's work and, of course, there wouldn't have been a tiny green pterosaur peering in the newly opened window.

"You've done a lot with this place since I was last here." Lawrence closed the fire door.

"Not that much." Grover glanced around, trying to remember what he'd added or refined since Lawrence had left. The fact that he'd thought so often of Lawrence while he'd worked—at least in those first two years before he'd learned of Lawrence's death—made it difficult to recall his absence as much as the longing for his return.

"I remember helping to haul parts of this blasted stove out with you," Lawrence said. "But there was only one window back then. And the walls weren't anywhere near as thick as these are now. The second cabinet is new too."

"Stick around and you might get to sample a three-horn haunch from the new smokehouse I'm planning." Grover made the remark lightly, and Lawrence did smile, but only for a moment. Then he picked his hat back up off the table.

"You said the rift is just west of here." Lawrence started for the door. "I should probably go have a look."

"You'll have better luck finding it if I go with you."

"I figured I'd just follow the old path down to the springs," Lawrence replied, but he stopped in the doorway. He cast Grover a sheepish smile. "Which I can tell from your expression isn't there anymore, is it?"

"The place thereof knows it no more. To misquote the Good Book. The whole hollow where the Fire Springs were isn't anything like it used to be. But I know a couple shortcuts I might be willing to share with you. If you asked nice."

"All right. Nice as you like." Lawrence pulled off his hat and bowed low like he was some old-time knight. "Will you do me the kindness of showing me the way, good sir?"

"Certainly." Grover tossed the last blanket across the bed and swept up his own hat.

"There's no need to look quite so smug." Lawrence commented.

"Just wait, you'll see," Grover replied.

As soon as they reached the great cavernous tunnels that the explosive opening of the rift had torn through the surrounding hills, Lawrence agreed that Grover had every right to look smug.

Ferns, cycads and young ginko trees hid many of the openings, and others had long ago become homes to a few bears, and several skunks. But one of the tunnels rose up like a black mouth in the side of the hill.

"Takes a little time for your eyes to adjust, but once they do it's easier to find your way," Grover assured Lawrence.

He nodded and stared at the surfaces of the immense cavern they strode through.

Big white-and-blue crystals as well as huge shards of obsidian studded every surface of the tunnels, catching light and reflecting it across the dozens of tiny streams that ran down the walls and pooled across the floors. Bats veered overhead and disappeared into a dark crack in one wall.

"This is like walking through an immense geode," Lawrence marveled. His voice soft as it was, bounced and echoed all around them. He glanced sidelong at Grover.

"How did you ever learn to find your way through this place, Grove?"

"I followed a mother whiptail leading her young back across the rift and then marked the path." Grover pointed to the tattered remains of cord that he'd first tied around the base of a gleaming white crystal. Though now he could have found his way blindfolded.

"You never fail to astound me." Lawrence smiled at him with such open admiration that Grover felt almost giddy. He had to look away, and it was good that he did because he nearly missed a turn in his delighted state. That would have made for a nice bit of irony, he supposed.

After that near miss he quickly led Lawrence out from the tunnels. They emerged on one of several promontories that ringed a deep ravine. A multitude of ferns and orchids clung tenaciously to the slick, wet stone walls, and a strange variety of bees buzzed between them.

Across the ravine, some three hundred feet away, a huge waterfall gushed from the jagged rift in the mountain wall. Red splinters of the mountain itself bridged the distance between the gaping rift and the surrounding cliffs like fallen trees spanning a stream. Some of the stone bridges were too fragile to support anything above the weight of the eagles that nested on them. But only a short hop down from where he and Lawrence stood was a bridge that jutted out wide as a city road and sturdy enough for two longnecks to stroll across.

Thankfully today it stood empty except for a couple of hawks.

Six years ago, all of this had only been a little gully where a hot spring bubbled away.

Now, walls of salt mist rose up from the river far below and blanketed Grover in the scent of the ancient ocean that poured improbably from the tear in the mountain's stone face.

While overhead the sun had only risen an hour or so past noon, rays of twilight sun streamed out from the breech in time, throwing odd shadows across the stone bridges.

Grover crouched down and contemplated the chasm ahead of him. The rift wasn't a neat straight line but crooked as a lightning bolt and much wider at the far end where floodwaters roared out.

"How did you ever get through there?" Lawrence asked.

"I walked across like everything else." He'd only crossed over once and had been all too happy to turn right back around once he took in the miles and miles of swamp and jungle that surrounded the heaving sea. Not that he needed to tell Lawrence that right now.

"But how did you get through all the water?"

"Only part of the rift opens underwater. See up there." He pointed to the top end of the lightning bolt. "Higher up, at the end of that stone bridge, there's land. You can just make out the beach and the forest beyond that."

Lawrence continued to survey the chasm of the rift then he grimaced.

"Neither of the other two rifts opened on such a steep angle. I'd hoped…" He drifted off as he swung down onto the big stone bridge. He strode several feet farther and then obviously sized up the distance to another far more fragile-looking one. It angled high into the far wall of the mountain. Lawrence started to lean out to it and alarm lit through Grover.

"Stop!" Grover shouted. "It won't hold you! There's a huge crack in it farther along."

Lawrence nodded and sauntered back to rejoin Grover, standing at the edge of the promontory.

Grover tried to hide how jumpy Lawrence's recklessness made him by casually asking, "So we're here now. How do we close this thing?"

"If you look closely at the edge of the rift," Lawrence said, "you can see white flecks in the midst of all the burnt and blasted stone."

Grover scrutinized the dark edge and spied the opalescent rock Lawrence pointed at.

"It's a hunk of alchemic stone, isn't it?" Grover asked.

Lawrence nodded, his expression grim.

Once Grover recognized the first alchemic stone, he quickly picked out another five, studding the chasm's gape. He squinted and felt sure he could just make out tiny symbols flashing from the stones' surfaces.

"They're the lynchpins that I focused on when I was manifesting Nate Tucker's spell and fighting Cixi. Now they continue to radiate the spell and hold the rift open. What I have to do is get close enough to burn at least half of them out. Once they fail then the entire rift will collapse."

"How close do you need to be?" Grover asked. After all he'd opened the rift from half a world away.

"Touching them would work best," Lawrence replied, his gaze still pinned to the chasm. "Farther than three feet away and I risk the lynchpins radiating the spell to all the other alchemic stones surrounding them and just making the rift stronger. I have to be close enough to isolate them. Honora worked the distances all out."

Grover had heard enough of Lady Astor—and seen enough of her skill—to take it on faith that she was right. But the distance between the top and the bottom of the rift opening was easily ninety feet at the narrowest spots. It would be a hell of a trick to get up that high to reach the alchemic stones ringing the opening.

He and Lawrence both stared at the sheer face of the mountain ahead of them. Something large and dark plunged over the edge of the waterfall and disappeared into the clouds of white mist below. It was such a long way down, Grover wondered how anything survived such a fall, even into the deep, deep water of the Rift River. But creatures of all kinds did. He'd seen them basking on the riverbanks and swimming in lakes.

Just because a thing seemed impossible didn't mean it couldn't be done.

"Are you thinking of scaling the side of the mountain?" Grover asked. If so, they'd need ropes and pitons. If they had a month or two, that wouldn't be any concern at all. As it was, they likely had mere days before Tucker found the rift. Maybe they could construct ladders of some kind—they had more than enough wood in the surrounding spruce. And if they only needed to reach half the lynchpin stones, maybe they could manage it.

"It's too steep and too wet to climb, but I can bring the stones down to me," Lawrence said. "That's what Gaston had to do to reach his."

"Didn't he die?" Grover asked.

Lawrence said nothing but just continued to glower at the scattered alchemic stones glinting across the rift's gaping mouth. Inside the rift, the sky darkened and a strange scattering of stars gleamed from the black.

"Look, I ain't a mage or a theurgist but even I know that pulling a heap of boulders down on top of yourself is a terrible plan," Grover announced.

"Sometimes bad choices are all you have—"

"But it *isn't* all you have!" Grover grabbed Lawrence's arm and jerked him around to face him, instead of the yawning pit of the rift. "You have me and we still have time to think this through. Unless what you're really after is a way to kill yourself!"

Lawrence flinched slightly at the accusation but then shook his head.

"I don't want to die," he said quietly. "After I lost my arm I did think about it. But I realized that what I truly wanted was to come back here, to see you again and tell you how sorry I was that I ran away and left you."

Grover wrapped his arms around Lawrence. The two of them held each other.

"I have to put things right, Grove," Lawrence whispered. "I don't know how but I have to find a way."

"I know," Grover told him. "But you don't have to do it this minute. Come back to the cabin with me. We'll make our selves some supper and think about how we can get this done. Tucker and his airship are probably still a few days behind us."

Lawrence nodded and turned with Grover. They walked through the tunnel with their arms linked.

"If only I had stolen the damn airship," Lawrence murmured, and he gave a soft laugh at his own suggestion. "Well, most likely if I tried I'd have been riddled full of bullets before I could even work out how to fly the bloody thing."

Grover paused as something in Lawrence's words sparked a thought. Flying...if only he could fly.

Perhaps it was a mad idea but all at once Grove felt his entire body humming with excitement.

"You could fly!" Grover's voice echoed wildly through the cavernous tunnel. A bat flitted away.

"What are you talking about?" Lawrence asked.

"King Douglass, Lawry." Grover had to fight to lower his voice. "I could do like I did with the bat and get him to carry you."

Lawrence went very quiet for several moments as they left the tunnel and started through the woods towards Grover's cabin.

"I find the idea of being *carried* by a giant pterosaur terrifying. However…" Lawrence paused like he had to work out a math problem before he could go on. "If you really could control it, your plan might just work."

"Sure it could." Grover's thoughts raced forward. "We could build you a sling out of tanned skins, and King Douglass could pick that up and fly with you. We'd have to practice first of course, but it could work, Lawry. It could. I could do this for you."

"As if you haven't done enough for me already." Lawrence shook his head but he was smiling.

Chapter Eight

After they returned to the cabin, Grover decided to break out his best smoked meat and tap his aged applejack, by way of a small celebration and maybe to show off a little. After all, it was Lawrence's first night back with him at the cabin, and they'd completed the journey with days to spare.

When he returned from his dry cellar with the haunch and jug, he found that Lawrence had not only set the table but shaved and put some effort into gussying himself up. The shirt he wore looked cleaner than what he'd been sporting for the last week, and he'd combed his auburn hair back in a stylish sweep.

"Well, howdy-do, handsome stranger," Grover greeted him. "You ain't seen my dusty traveling companion anywhere about, have you?"

To Grover's surprise Lawrence flushed slightly at the passing compliment. Lord knew why—the man was a looker, always had been.

"I took the liberty of acquainting myself with your bare spice cupboard and reckoned that now might be a good time to break out the masala powder I won gambling in India. I'm thinking of making you a curry like I had there." Lawrence took the smoked haunch from him and laid it down on Grover's cutting board. "I don't suppose you have any potatoes or onions in the root cellar?"

"There should be a few." Grover watched as Lawrence drew an ornately decorated box from his saddlebag. It looked like a miniature treasure chest. "I ain't never heard of masala powder. Is that it?"

Lawrence flipped open the lid of the box and held it out to him. Grover took a sniff and about a thousand perfumes rolled up over him. Pungent, hot and sweet. Christmas cake, Chinese tea and mole poblano all floating through his senses.

"That's amazing." Grover couldn't help but take a second sniff of the complex aromas.

"I know," Lawrence replied. "The variety of spices in India was astounding. If things had been different, I would have brought more back home for you. The food there was—well, hot as Hell, but also delicious in ways I would never have imagined."

"Wish I could have tasted it," Grover sighed.

"The best I'm likely to manage is a poor imitation, but it's not too bad, if I do say so myself."

Grover nodded. No doubt it would be like nothing else he'd tasted, and he looked forward to that. Though he found himself thinking of all the other fascinating and exotic things he might have experienced if he'd traveled across the world as Lawrence had. For the first time it occurred to him that he could have done so. Nothing but his own fear of the larger world had kept him from following after Lawrence when he'd left.

"Something wrong?" Lawrence inquired.

"No. I was just pondering how hard it might have been to hunt you down all those years ago," Grover admitted. "I should have tried."

Lawrence frowned like Grover had suggested something almost unbearable. He set the spice box aside and met Grover's curious gaze directly.

"As much as I missed you, Grove. As much as I know you would have fought better and harder than anyone I could have had with me—I'm glad that you weren't there."

Lawrence reached out and stroked Grover's shoulder almost as if assuring himself of the solidity of Grover's body.

"I'm not proud of this." Lawrence's stare faltered and he bowed his head. "But there were weeks when I lost all hope… I stopped carrying my pistol because I kept imagining myself putting it to my head and pulling the trigger. Up in the mountains, I fantasized of just stepping off a cliff's edge. But the idea of getting back here to you, that kept me moving on the path in front of me. In the worst days, you were the only goal—the only future I could keep fighting to reach. You kept me alive."

"I…I'm glad I stayed here, then." Grover drew Lawrence into an embrace, and for a few moments they held each other close. Then Grover drew back just a little and offered Lawrence his best smile. "But from now on I'm not leaving you on your own to face trouble. I'm with you, Lawry. For better or worse."

Grover kissed Lawrence's freshly shaven cheek once, before drawing away. It would only embarrass Lawrence if he made too much of Lawrence's confession or his own promise. "I'd better fetch those onions and potatoes if we're ever gonna have our supper."

Lawrence nodded then turned away to wipe something from his eyes.

Grover found a good number of decent potatoes and a nice plump, golden onion out back in the root cellar. When he climbed out of the dark, cramped space, he only absently noticed how quiet the afternoon seemed. Wind sighed through the trees, and the rumble of the distant river filled the air, but all the little songbirds and chipmunks had fallen silent.

Grover should have taken more notice, but the idea of calling King Douglass occupied most of his thoughts—well, that and washing up to look even a shade as handsome as Lawrence.

He strode past the small stable and glanced over to see what Betty and Romeo were up to. They crouched beside a small, messy nest both staring intently up in silence. Grover followed their gazes and horror flooded his entire body.

A hundred yards away, a bigtooth stood between the towering spruce trees, staring down at the ridingbirds. It stood taller than Grover's cabin, and yet its striped hide and perfect stillness allowed it to fade into the surrounding forest. The play of light and shadow fell across its olive plumes, lending them an almost botanical appearance. Then it charged, swinging its massive jaws wide.

Romeo bolted up to his feet, spreading his wings and shrieking at the giant, while Betty flattened herself over their pitiful nest.

"Don't you touch them, you ugly bastard!" Grover didn't think. He bounded forward, throwing all of his will against the bigtooth's momentum and hunger. To his shock the bigtooth turned. Its attention focused entirely on Grover.

He froze in his tracks. He couldn't outrun the thing at this distance, and he'd left his rifle in the cabin, like a damn fool. The small grip he held over the bigtooth's voracious mind offered him his only hope of surviving. But all that "hearing the stones and feeling the air" Lawrence had told him about felt impossible to concentrate on. And no way in hell was he going to close his eyes and simply relax. He couldn't sense any shining lights nor did the surrounding trees glow with a calming beauty.

Instead only a raw, savage hunger lashed against Grover like a brand burning inside his head. The need to charge, to bite and feed roiled through every part of the creature. There was no way to alter any of that. Grover simply fought with all his might and concentration to hold the bigtooth back. He didn't say a word, and yet his mind rang with the command, *Stop*.

The bigtooth snarled and shook its huge head. Slowly it lifted one massive leg and took a step towards Grover. It started for a second step, but Grover fought it for every inch. Sweat poured down his brow, and his entire body shook like he stood in ice water. The bigtooth hissed soft and low like an angry snake. Its foot trembled as it took a second step closer. Now the strangely sweet smell of its body drifted over him. It lowered its head, and Grover thought he could feel hot breath hit his face.

Suddenly a wall of blinding blue light flared up before Grover.

He felt it rise and envelope the bigtooth in flames. The animal's sense sizzled in agony—skin blackening, lungs searing and bones cracking open like popcorn—and Grover howled with it as it burned. An instant later, a tower of ash and charred bone stood before Grover and yet his mind still blazed with the shock of pain.

He heard Betty peeping at him like a frightened chick, and he turned to her. He glimpsed two white oblong eggs lying in her nest but his vision seemed to dim and blur—like he'd spent the whole day drinking whiskey.

His legs tangled under him and he hardly felt Lawrence catch him. Lord, Lawrence looked pale and stricken. Grover wanted to assure him that he was fine. In a minute he'd shake this all off.

But he couldn't.

❖ ❖ ❖

Grover lay somewhere quiet and dark. His head pounded like his brain was trying to hammer its way out of his skull. He tried to sit up but discovered his arms were shaking too much to support him. The faintest circle of gold floated from the darkness and touched his brow like a kiss. The pain eased.

He lay back, relaxing to the brink of sleep, though he sensed there were things that needed doing. Onions and potatoes. He'd dropped them, hadn't he? Lawrence would find them, he assured himself. They'd have supper and he'd enjoy his first taste of masala.

A wonderful scent drifted over him. But it wasn't new or exotic. Instead he drew in a deep breath of a man's body, traced with smoke and ponderosa.

Lawrence.

Grover thought he must have slept because he felt that little jolt of waking suddenly. He'd forgotten to do something—something critical. The answer came to him at once. He needed to bring King Douglass to them. They didn't have much time.

"I'm calling him for you, Lawry." Even to his own ears his voice sounded slurred and slow.

"Hush now, darling," Lawrence whispered through the dark. "You just rest. Don't worry yourself about any of that."

But Grover couldn't keep from feeling compelled to reach out. He hardly knew why only that if he didn't he would lose Lawrence again. Even as he drifted in his dreams, he felt himself stretching across the vast expanse of the open sky to soar with King Douglass. Cold winds swept over his wings, and he turned into them riding high above the airship speeding beneath him.

Odd how soft the clouds looked but how bitterly cold and rough they felt to pass through. He shook frigid water droplets from his body and dived low to catch the warm thermals rising off the wide dark river.

How brightly all the fish down there glowed. They were a stream of tiny lights floating out to the vast sea. Or perhaps they were stars swimming through the currents of an eternal night. Grover felt he could watch them flash and flicker forever.

"Grove, I don't know if you can hear me, but I can't wait any longer. I sighted Tucker's airship early this afternoon."

Grover heard Lawrence's words but their full implication eluded his drifting mind.

I saw it too, Grover thought, though he wasn't certain he got any words out.

"I don't want to leave you, darling." Lawrence's lips brushed over his own. "I never wanted to. But this time, I'm doing it for the right reason. I hope you'll know that."

He felt Lawrence draw away from him and heard the door creak. The room felt colder. Grover pulled his blankets closer around him.

Very slowly, like drops of poisoned honey, Lawrence's words coalesced in his consciousness.

Tucker's airship was here, and Lawrence had gone to close the rift the only way he could. He was going to pull the stones down on top of himself.

Alarm shot through Grover.

He bolted up from his bed. His head throbbed and his ears rang, but he didn't give a damn. He couldn't let Lawrence go alone, not this time. He had to do what he'd lacked the courage to manage eight years ago. Chase Lawrence down and stand with him. Grover stumbled across the room, snatched his rifle from beside the door and then was out.

The sun already hung low on the horizon and all around him the long shadows of spruce trees lay like prison bars. Grover sprinted for the tunnels. Just as the cavernous mouth loomed before him, Grover stumbled and belatedly realized that in his delirious state, he'd bolted from the cabin wearing neither his shirt, boots, nor his gun belt. Blood dribbled from the cuts running along his bare feet but he didn't slow.

He raced through the tunnel, tracing it by habit and terrifying a vixen and her kits in his wild charge. The roar of the river filled his ears, and he tasted salt mist as he gasped in fast breaths.

Nearly there.

But even before he reached the promontory, he heard a loud crash of stone and felt the ground of the tunnel shudder with the impact. Grover stumbled sideways and a terrible vertigo swelled through him. He reached out and steadied himself against the cave wall. *Damn it, damn it, damn it!*

He staggered ahead despite the tremors that shook the walls and floor of the cave. Golden red light poured in from the cave's mouth. Just a little farther and he'd find Lawrence, he promised himself. Grover bounded over a tortoise and came peeling out onto the promontory.

At the far end of the largest stone bridge, Lawrence stood with his hands raised up to the jagged maw overhead. To his left the frothing waters of the rift waterfall cascaded down the mountain face. A haze of rock dust swirled around him and caught the light of the setting sun. Cracked and burnt-looking boulders studded the ground, and a dark hole—like the socket of a missing tooth—gaped in the rock face at the top of the rift. Lawrence had obviously already destroyed one of the lynchpins. The strain the others placed on the surrounding rock played through the entire mountain, in faint tremors.

Brilliant blue light flared from Lawrence's extended fingers and rose up to the stones above him like a swarm of furious wasps. The mountain groaned, low and deep. Grover jumped to the weathered surface of the largest bridge. The rock beneath his battered feet strained like a dying animal.

Then, over the roar of the waterfall and the low groans of the mountain ahead, Grover heard a high-pitched hum. He looked up to his right in time to see the Tuckers' star-spangled dirigible clear the cliffs overhead and descend into the ravine. A big brassy cannon turned towards Lawrence.

"Lawry! Get down!" Grover's warning didn't carry over the thunder of the cannon fire. A smaller stone bridge to Lawrence's right shattered. Lawrence fell against a boulder as rock debris flew through the air. The boom echoed and rebounded through the ravine.

Lawrence pulled himself upright and turned to take in the airship but like a damn fool simply returned to reaching out for the massive boulders of alchemic stone embedded in the mountain wall above him.

The sun-shaped insignia of the Office of Theurgy and Magicum gleamed across the muzzle of its cannon as crewmen angled for a second volley. Grover guessed that only the poor light had saved Lawrence from their first shot. But they seemed unlikely to miss a second time.

Grover hefted his rifle. Then he caught sight of that beautiful, torn white wing soaring through the clouds.

Immediately he reached out to curl his senses around those of King Douglass. A sharp pain shot through his head, but he forced himself to push past it. He clenched his eyes closed and drew in a slow, deep breath, despite the hammering of his heart and his racing pulse.

King Douglass shone like a star against the frigid heavens. Grover exhaled, and his awareness rose like smoke on the wind. When he reached King Douglass, the contact felt oddly familiar and comfortable, as if they'd already grown secure in each other's company. Briefly, Grover wondered if he hadn't reached the thunderbird in his dreams after all.

Then he focused on turning King Douglass's attention to the airship and inviting the thunderbird to strike the fat balloon and rip a strip off the top of it. At that angle of attack, Grover knew the crew couldn't turn their guns on King Douglass; their shot would hit their own alchemic engine.

Delight at the prospect of defeating the ugly interloper in his sky coursed through King Douglass.

The thunderbird dived, slashing its sabre-sharp beak through the cloth of the balloon like a tailor shearing through muslin. Hot gasses rushed free in his wake, and at once the airship lurched. It began to swiftly drop. Men shouted and alarms sounded. The cannon was forgotten as the crew hurled anchor ropes out to the stone bridges and into the walls of the ravine.

Big mechanical claws scraped and grasped the surrounding rock walls. One line shot over the bridge where Lawrence stood and locked around the remains of a small, collapsed bridge. That, at last, stopped the gondola's descent. But the deflating balloon continued to sink under its own weight, blanketing most of the crew.

King Douglass soared over his defeated foe and sang the long notes of his victory.

That was all Grover could manage. He fell from King Douglass, releasing the thunderbird to wing back to his flaplings.

As he opened his eyes, he found himself sprawled out like a dead dog on the bridge. The airship hung suspended by dozens of creaking ropes, some one hundred feet above him and off to the right. The dull red tones of the setting sun lent it a particularly bloodied appearance. A cacophony of shouts bounced through the ravine. Someone bellowed for a fire suppressor, someone else for parachutes.

Grover managed to rise to his knees and look across the bridge to where Lawrence stood. He turned and stared back at Grover. Then he motioned Grover away frantically.

"Get out of here!" Lawrence's words hardly carried through the chaos of all the voices echoing from the airship. Grover pushed himself to his feet, and he supposed Lawrence took that for a sign he was leaving, because he turned his attention back to the white stones edging the mouth of the rift.

Again he raised his arms, and this time Grover saw the sparks of blue light whirl up from the stone at Lawrence's feet to swirl around his body and finally burst from his fingers in a flurry.

Above Lawrence and to his left, a large hunk of rock began to shake. Pebbles and dust rained down. Clumps of wild grass tumbled. If Lawrence noticed any of the debris streaming down on him, he didn't shift an inch.

Grover felt the tremors spreading below his feet. The boulder crashed down like a cannonball, and the entire stone bridge seemed to buckle. Grover fell forward. Only his sprawled arm cushioned his skull from cracking into the rocky surface of the bridge. His rifle skittered over the edge and plunged down into the river.

Lawrence had been knocked to his knees. Grover thought he saw blood dribbling down the side of Lawrence's head, but he couldn't be certain through the huge clouds of dust that billowed up. Lawrence immediately scrambled to his feet and clambered into the rubble. He laid his left hand over a large opal shard, and in an instant it blackened and crumbled like the ash dropping from a cigar.

The mountain groaned and hunks of rock all along the rift cracked and rained down as the remaining lynchpins strained against tons of rock. Lawrence sagged on his hands and knees amidst the wreckage. Grover stumbled forward.

He made it halfway across the bridge when he noticed a motion to his right—coming from the airship. Two figures zipped down the line of one of the anchor ropes. They swung directly over the bridge Grover occupied, and dropped.

Neither of them landed with any grace but they kept their feet. Grover glowered at the two blond uniformed men plunked down between him and Lawrence. Even with their backs to him, Grover recognized the Tuckers. The nearer of the two stood less than twenty feet from Lawrence as he eased his pistol from its holster.

Grover let loose a furious roar and charged them. They both glanced back but not fast enough. Grover caught the nearer one around the neck and held him in a headlock.

But the other Tucker fired his pistol.

Lawrence lurched and fell amidst the rubble. Grover felt as though his heart had been stuck through with a stiletto knife. He squeezed hard, choking the Tucker brother in his grasp. His twin spun on Grover and lifted his pistol.

"Release David at once."

"Hell, no!"

The light was poor, and Grover knew Nathaniel Tucker didn't have the balls to risk shooting himself. If he had, he would have already fired. No, the Tuckers were the sorts of bastards who shot a man in the back when he was already risking his life to save the entire country from an endless flood.

David Tucker attempted to pull free of Grover's choke-hold, and Grover plowed his fist into his kidneys. That took the fight right out of the snot. At the same time, Nathaniel grunted and paled from the blow. That, Grover found very interesting—maybe even useful.

"You can't think you'll get away with this, you son of a—" Nathaniel cut himself off short, as if it had just occurred to him that insulting Grover might not incline him to release his grip on David. "I don't know what lies Lawrence Wilder told you, but let me assure you that if you cease this beastly behavior at once, he—but not you—will be the only one held accountable. You might even earn a reward."

Grover hardly heard Nathaniel's words as he frantically scanned the dust and shattered boulders for Lawrence. To his shock he glimpsed a spark of blue light flicker up to the mouth of the rift.

He was alive!

And still intent upon pulling the rift closed. Grover had to get him out of there before the next stone came down right on top of him.

If Grover hadn't felt so weak, he would have simply hurled David into Nathaniel and hoped that one of the two toppled over the edge of the bridge. But as it was, he wasn't certain he possessed the strength to keep his stranglehold on David much longer.

"Lawry!" Grover called.

"He's dead, you dolt. I shot him," Nathaniel snapped with a self-satisfied smile. "I'm the only one who's going to give you orders now."

"If you know what's good for you, boy, you'll release me at once," David rasped.

Grover considered responding with another kidney punch, but instead he simply dragged David with him towards Lawrence.

The shit didn't resist. He went limp, offering Grover deadweight to pull across the slick stone. Nathaniel followed their movements with his pistol raised and at the ready. Something in Nathaniel's calculating expression made Grover wonder if the man wasn't trying to work out what exactly would happen to him if he missed and shot David.

His earlier reaction to the punch assured Grover that so long as he could keep his hold on David he had Nathaniel as well. They were the same man. David was the embodiment of Nathaniel's past and what happened to a man in the past carried through to him in the present moment.

Alter the past and the present would already be changed, because the here and now arose from the past.

Grover edged by Nathaniel and steadily backed towards the Lawrence. His leg brushed against a rock, and he stole a fast glance back at the chaos of ragged boulders.

"Don't even think about chancing a shot." He snapped his attention to Nathaniel. "Because if you were dead five minutes ago, then you'll sure as hell be dead now."

That seemed to startle both Nathaniel and David. Maybe they'd imagined that no one could ever work out what they truly were—or maybe they were just surprised that Grover had figured it out. Either way Grover didn't get the opportunity to exploit the instant, as a massive tremor suddenly passed through the bridge and his footing slipped.

David slithered out of his grip and darted to the cover of a rock far to the right. Nathaniel fired. Between the growing gloom, dust and shaking ground, the shot went wide. But not by far. A splinter of stone smacked Grover's shoulder. Grover lunged to the left as a second blast tore through the air. He ducked behind a cracked, charred boulder and found Lawrence leaning against it as well.

Dust powdered Lawrence's entire body to the deathly pallor of chalk. Except his right arm. The sleeve of his shirt looked burned and stained with dark liquid.

"You're bleeding—"

"Just oil," Lawrence whispered. "The fool shot me in my missing arm."

Another blast sent chips of rock flying several feet from them.

"He's to your right!" David shouted.

"What you said about him dying five minutes in the past making him dead now, you think that's true?" Lawrence asked.

"I'm pretty certain."

"Good." Lawrence closed his eyes and drew in a deep breath. "You run for it as soon as I start." Lawrence heaved himself to his feet, and all at once an immense geyser of blue fire gushed up around him. Cerulean flames cascaded over the blackened stones overhead and wound around one huge outcropping. Nathaniel Tucker took aim but Lawrence didn't flinch.

Grover threw all his concentration against Nathaniel Tucker's will. The raw drive that he'd felt in the bigtooth was nothing compared to the rage pervading Nathaniel Tucker's mind. The man roiled with hatred and grievances, but at the core of him a vast fault of thick self-loathing boiled and heaved. He'd destroyed his family home. Drowned his mother and wife. Ruined nations with his incompetence. Shamed his father so deeply the man had taken his own life at the end of Nathaniel's pistol.

He gagged on the bitter truth of these things, and at the same time Nathaniel blamed anyone and everyone else for his failings. That withered hag, Honora Astor, had been too old to perform the spell properly. Lawrence Wilder had been too green, Gaston Jacquard too lazy. *They* had been responsible for the catastrophe, not him.

And now Lawrence and this black boy spited Nathaniel further, refusing to let him transform the gaping rifts into national treasures. A wailing rage gushed through Nathaniel. He would be vindicated—proved a hero!

Grover wanted nothing more than to pull himself free from Nathaniel, but he let the swearing, sick anger pour over him. He felt as if he were diving through a sea of vomit. He focused on Nathaniel's right hand. Dragging up his own memory of broken bones, he drove that agony into Nathaniel's nerves.

Nathaniel let out a frustrated scream. The pistol fell from his grip.

At the same moment Lawrence wrenched a boulder down from the mountain. A sickeningly brief cry escaped David Tucker as the stone slammed down with crushing force. Its impact shook the ground like a hammer striking a drum. Stone debris pelted Grover, and new clouds of dust filled the air like smoke.

Lawrence's blue fire gutted. He crumpled to the ground. Grover scrambled over and between the splintered rocks and boulders. His foot slipped, and he tumbled down to his knees twice as massive shudders shook through the mountain and the bridge. Hunks of rock splintered like toothpicks as Grover leapt across a gaping seam in the bridge.

At any moment he expected to hear a shot ring out from Nathaniel's pistol or feel a bullet plow into his back. But Nathaniel remained strangely silent. Could he really be dead? Grover hoped so but didn't dare depend upon the possibility. He moved low and fast as he searched for Lawrence.

At last Grover found him. He lay on his side, blood caking his hair and dozens of shallow cuts marring his exposed hand and cheek. He coughed and struggled to get to his feet, but couldn't seem to muster the strength to rise to his knees. When he noticed Grover he shook his head.

"You have to get out of here, Grove," he whispered. "It's all going to come down."

"I ain't leaving you." Grover crawled across the buckling stone to Lawrence's side. "Besides, if I go how are you going to reach that last lynchpin?"

He slipped under Lawrence's left arm and, taking as much of his weight as he could, steadied him up to his feet. Lawrence sagged into him.

"I promised you for better of worse," Grover whispered, though he didn't know if Lawrence could even hear him over the grating, grinding roar of the mountain. Stone all around them strained and cracked as the mountain's immense weight bore down on the ragged opening of the rift.

Grover guided him across the quaking rock and wreckage to the shining opalescent stone of the third lynchpin. He tried not to look at the bloody pool that remained of David Tucker's lower half. The man's battered face angled to the side as if staring back at the tangled anchor lines of the distant airship.

Lawrence sank against the gleaming white stone. The symbol at its center flashed like a firefly dancing in a glass jar. Once this last one was destroyed, the rift ought to collapse. Grover suspected the bridge they stood on would go with it. But he'd already lived without Lawrence, and he didn't want to do that again.

"I'm staying," Grover said. "So let's get this done with."

Lawrence gazed at him for a moment then he reached out and interlaced the dusty fingers of his left hand with Grover's.

"For better or worse." He brought his ivory right hand down on the opal stone. Blue sparks spat up from his ivory arm and a huge bolt burst from his fingertips. The opal cracked black, and the symbol inside snuffed out in a wisp of acrid smoke.

A deafening crack split the air and hit Grover like a wall of wind.

Grover threw both arms around Lawrence as the force of the mountain at last crushed the few remaining lynchpins supporting the rift. Walls of stone plunged down. The ground beneath them seemed to lurch violently upward. They were thrown like rags as explosive crashes sounded around them and the air filled with plumes of dust. Grover tensed for the agony of slamming down into the rocks or the merciless water of the Rift River.

Almost incomprehensibly, he didn't fall. A cold wind wrapped around him and Lawrence. Immense updrafts seemed to cradle them. Suddenly the roar of crashing rock stilled, and he and Lawrence sank down to the remains of the stone bridge. Walls of dust rolled over them, obscuring everything in a gray haze.

Again that cold wind rose. The dust parted, and Grover found himself gaping at a clean, uniform-clad vision of Lawrence. His glower broke into a smile as he picked his way across the cracked, pitted bridge to them.

"Honora," Lawrence whispered from beside Grover. "Don't tell me that I actually strut like that."

"After this you have cause to, my dear lad," Honora replied, then she looked to Grover. "Mr. Ahigbe, Hell of a ride you gave us with that pterosaur. Well done."

"No trouble, sir—er—ma'am." In his exhausted state Grover couldn't help but stare. He felt like he'd somehow slipped back into a fever dream. He wondered how much Honora had witnessed from the stranded airship, and when she must have swung across to the stone bridge.

"Best stick with sir for the time being," Honora told him.

Then she whipped off her uniform jacket and placed it over Lawrence's shoulders. How strange it was to see Lawrence gazing at himself with such tender concern. If

Grover hadn't known anything else about her, that expression alone would have made him like her. As it was, he owed her thanks for saving both his and Lawrence's lives.

"The dust is clearing fast," Honora told them. "The crewmen should be here any moment to evacuate the two of you—"

"Weren't they firing a cannon at us?" Grover objected.

"That's going to turn out to have been a misunderstanding. It was quite dark after all." Honora favored him with a tight smile. "Rest assured, Nathaniel Tucker will apologize profusely to you both, before he submits his report concerning the absolute necessity of closing the American rift."

Considering that the man was dead—double dead, in fact—that struck Grover as highly unlikely.

Lawrence wiped blood and dust from his face with his sleeve and nodded as if Lady Astor made perfect sense.

"David's remains are back in the rubble." Lawrence gestured behind him. "You should find blood and hair enough to last you a couple months at least."

Then Grover remembered that last time Lawrence had mentioned Honora needing hair and blood. She meant to impersonate one of the Tuckers, Grover realized. If she could pull it off, he and Lawrence actually stood a chance of escaping the gallows. He sagged against a hunk of battered rock as relief washed over him.

"Very good. The two of you sit tight." Honora motioned with her hand, and the roiling dust opened before her like fancy French doors. She strode away into the gloom. Grover wondered briefly if Nathaniel's dead body lay somewhere among the rocks, crushed as well, or if he'd somehow simply blinked out of existence. Could a man leave two corpses?

"It's done," Lawrence whispered. He sounded dazed and relieved.

Grover nodded. They'd truly put the past behind them. Only their futures lay ahead.

Lawrence leaned into Grover, and Grover carefully wrapped an arm around him. Overhead clouds of dust drifted away to reveal a vast, open sky full of bright constellations.

Epilogue

The ridingbird chicks stood about four feet and sported downy coats of fuzzy speckled feathers. The four of them raced across the garden to Toby and Susan as the two children tossed out handfuls of feed. Betty and Romeo looked on from the cover of the apple trees but didn't rouse from their afternoon nap.

Watching from the porch of the Wilder House, Grover smiled as little Susan instructed Toby in throwing a lasso and catching the runningbirds' legs. Her father, Frank, had become an expert during the month he'd looked after Betty and her family while Grover had been summoned, along with Lawrence, across the sea to Washington.

Neither of the children managed to snag a single one of the chicks, but the hatchling ridingbirds delighted in leaping after and pecking at the ropes as if hunting rattlesnakes.

Grover glanced across the small table to where Lawrence stretched in his chair, with his hat tipped low to shadow his face. Grover felt half-certain that he'd nodded off. He'd hardly slept last night. Neither of them had—and not for pleasurable reasons either. Lawrence still hadn't received an official discharge from the Office of Theurgy and Magicum. The threat of being called back onto another battlefield haunted Lawrence. It'd made him anxious even when he settled down to draw in his sketchbook, and it woke him from Grover's arms at night. Three months had already rolled by, and they didn't know if Lawrence could consider himself free.

Very soon Grover needed to head back out to his cabin and prepare for winter. He'd already delayed a week. He supposed he'd wait longer if he had to. He wasn't about to leave

Lawrence. Together the two of them could get everything done that needed doing before the first heavy snow, Grover reasoned to himself, but he didn't quite believe it.

He swatted a fat blackfly away from the dish of corn biscuits that Cora Cody had brought over to them.

Leaning against the porch rails, Frank and Cora took turns calling encouragements to the children and the ridingbird chicks. George Cody's chair across from Grover's stood empty. He'd volunteered to fetch the first edition of the New United America News, which would supposedly carry the most recent articles from both sides of the Inland Sea.

"You know Toby's already asking about when he can go along with you and Lawrence to your place in the woods." Cora glanced back at Grover.

"At this rate he'll get there before we do," Lawrence murmured from the shadow of his hat, but his comment didn't carry past Grover to the other two.

"Clearly he hasn't been informed of Susan's plans for him yet." Frank laughed. "She's going to set up a bird ranch bigger than Uncle Grover's. Toby's going to be her foreman. And they're going to trade with Chief Niwot just like her Uncle Grover does."

"Really?" Cora smiled as she turned her attention back to the children. Both Cora's and Frank's expressions turned thoughtful as they studied the next generation playing so carelessly at the difficulties of a married couple working a ranch together. Grover read concern in both Cora's and Frank's expressions but also something like amazement.

"That would be something, wouldn't it?" Cora said at last.

"Yes, indeed," Frank replied. "Might well happen. The future's bound to be full of surprises."

A surprise would be fine at this point, Grover thought. It was the waiting that just about drove him around the bend. The only bright side to it was that the comforts of the Wilder House had allowed Lawrence to recover his strength. He looked good now, tanned and comfortable, even with his white shirtsleeves rolled up and his new ivory arm exposed for anyone to see. He cast Grover one of those sly, admiring glances. Grover's pulse kicked up from real low down.

He longed to have Lawrence to himself—both of them back in the familiarity of the mountains. But they had to wait.

In the meantime folks wanted to see the medals they'd received for their parts in closing the rift. And they wanted to know about the president and all the fine folks and places that filled the far-off capitol. A few souls, like Reverend Dodd, had even taken the time to tell Grover that after what he'd done for them—facing down dinosaurs and risking his life to close the rift—well, it made them ashamed of how they might have treated him and his folks in the past.

Most others weren't much changed. Sheriff Lee still wouldn't spare Grover the time of day, but then Grover wouldn't have deigned to ask him either.

Mayor Wilder had thrown a lavish welcome-home party a week ago. He'd presented Lawrence with his great-uncle's lucky compass. And a day later when he saw Grover walking along the drive, he beckoned him up onto the front steps to chat and opened the front door for him to come inside.

Much later, after they'd both probably imbibed far too much whiskey, he even pulled Grover into a strong, fatherly embrace and thanked him for looking after his son.

"I know…" Mayor Wilder had mumbled. "Always knew you two… You'd be the one to care for him."

"I will, sir," Grover had promised in a warm slur. "Always."

They hadn't said anything more about it since, though the mayor had quietly shared a few stories about Lawrence's great-uncle and his lifelong prospecting partner—the men who had discovered the seam of alchemic stone that made the Wilder fortune. The two had lived together most their lives, and they shared a grave in the family cemetery. Lawrence and Grover had since paid their respects to the two.

Grover swatted another fly away from the biscuits. Then he looked out to the drive. George Cody came pelting towards them with a newspaper gripped in his hand.

Dread filled Grover. Now that Lawrence was a national hero, his next posting for the Office of Theurgy and Magicum might well be printed up in the newspaper.

If that was the case, Grover decided silently, then he'd leave everything behind—Betty, King Douglass, his home and his friends. He'd register as a mage and follow Lawrence. He hated the thought of losing his home, but not as much as he loathed the idea of letting Lawrence go without a fight again.

Lawrence straightened and pushed up the brim of his hat. Frank and Cora turned as George bounded up the steps.

"What on earth is the matter?" Cora asked.

Out of breath, George simply slapped the front page of the paper down onto the table. A parcel, wrapped in weathered brown paper slid from between the broadsheet pages.

Grover glared down at the grainy image of Nathaniel Tucker, which took up a good section of the newspaper's front page.

"Nathaniel Tucker commits suicide," Lawrence read the headline aloud. "Famous Theurgist leaps to icy death in Potomac River. Final note reveals his role in creating the rifts and begs that the courage…" Lawrence's voice suddenly failed him and he shook his head.

"…that the courage of Lawrence Wilder, Gaston Jacquard and Grover Ahigbe never be forgotten!" George read out proudly. He beamed at both Lawrence and Grover. Then he snatched up the parcel and handed it to Lawrence.

"This came by airship for you."

The address looked faded and full of ornate flourishes. Lawrence took the package and stepped back from the table to open it. His expression struck Grover as grim. All four of them on the porch glanced after Lawrence, but none of them were so ill-mannered as to pry before Lawrence had a chance to take in the contents himself.

"I knew that Tucker was a bad egg." Cora went to her husband's side and picked up the paper. "I'd started to feel a little bad for him because his brother got killed but…" She trailed off as the details of the article absorbed her attention. A moment later she looked up with a shocked expression. "Oh goodness! That David fellow wasn't even his brother!"

"What's this?" Frank asked. He strolled over to the table.

Cora read out the entire article, revealing the contents of Nathaniel Tucker's suicide note. Grover had wondered how long Honora had intended to continue impersonating Nathaniel Tucker after she'd ensured the ratification of the Proclamation of Emancipation. He'd imagined that in her place, he would have slipped away discreetly, but he supposed that just proved how much less of a showman he was than Lady Astor.

He stood and offered Frank his seat, so that he could see the illustrations in the paper. While the further details of the article absorbed the others, Grover withdrew to Lawrence's side.

"It's from Honora," Lawrence informed him quietly as he turned the small package over in his hands.

"Oh? How is Lady Astor?"

"She's on her way to some destination that she can't disclose to me now that I'm no longer in the service," Lawrence said, smiling. "She's sent me my papers. I've been officially and honorably discharged."

Grover felt a surge of elation and only just stopped himself from throwing his arms around Lawrence in front of everyone. As it was, they leaned into each other, both grinning. Grover knew he owed his life to Lady Astor, but at this moment he felt more thankful to her for not dragging Lawrence back into service than for anything else.

The last vestige of the past that had kept them apart for eight years dissipated like morning dew in the summer sun. Now, he and Lawrence were free to make what they would of today and all their tomorrows.

"She promises to send me more masala soon," Lawrence added.

THE HOLLOW HISTORY
OF
PROFESSOR PERFECTUS

Chicago 1893

The Great Stage Magician, Professor Perfectus, rolled his black satin top hat over one white-gloved hand and into the other. His expression remained placid beneath his velvet half-mask. Out in the exhibition hall, hundreds of men and women leaned forward in their seats, following his every motion intently. He passed the hat over the supine body of the very pretty Miss May Flowers (actually called Geula Mandelbaum, but audiences expected a certain simplicity of name and function when it came to the assistants of stage magicians).

Slowly Geula rose off the table. Her beaded red dress draped from her legs. A comb fell from her hair, freeing one long, lustrous gold curl. She floated upward with the slow grace of a column of incense until she lay stretched out a full foot above Professor Perfectus's slim, gray-haired figure. He passed his top hat under Geula, brushing the loose curl of her hair as he did so.

And I—a dark girl standing in the shadows, where no one watched—I drew in a deep breath, taking all the strength I could from the currents of the air that filled the large hall. I concentrated and made a motion, as if to shoo a fly aside.

At once, three white doves escaped from Professor Perfectus's top hat, winging around his suspended assistant. Gasps, cries and applause burst from the audience and grew wilder when a mob of scarlet butterflies burst from the breast of Geula's dress. They followed the doves up into the darkness above the stage curtain and disappeared as a rain of red and white cut paper fluttered down.

Someone in the audience screamed. Concerned voices rose from amidst the applause and cheers.

I stepped forward into the flare of limelight, dressed as plainly as a governess. My hair had been pulled back into a severe bun, and a useless pair of gold spectacles perched on the bridge of my nose.

Glinting, golden things like the spectacles captured the audience's attention on a darkened stage, erasing its awareness of more subtle details.

"Good people, please do not be alarmed." I spoke slowly and calmly, suppressing the cadence of my natural accent. "Let me again assure you that none of the feats you have witnessed on this stage were the results of actual magic. The professor is not a mage or even a theurgist. What you have seen here were displays of the most ingenious slight of hand and misdirection, crafted and practiced to perfection, by a great master. My dear uncle, Professor Perfectus."

I waved my hand in the professor's direction, and he executed a deep bow and flipped his hat back atop his head. Then he dropped his white-gloved hands into the pockets of his dark coat. Sweat beaded the back of my neck and dampened the high collar of my gray dress. Encores like this one always exhausted me, but it was very nearly over.

"I cannot give away all of my uncle's secrets," I went on in a stage whisper as I drew closer to where Geula hung in the air. "But certainly a few of you must suspect that Miss Flowers is suspended by several very strong wires."

On cue, Geula reached up and wrapped her gloved hands around the black wires. She pulled herself up into a sitting position as if she were balanced in the seat of a swing. I knelt, retrieved her glittering, gold comb and handed it to her.

"Why, thank you so much, Abril. I must look a fright." She drew all eyes as she made a small show of fixing her blond hair and straightening the hem of her red dress before it exposed more than her dainty yellow shoes.

And while the two of us blocked the view, Professor Perfectus stepped backwards into his black cabinet, hidden in the dark velvet folds of the back curtain. He pulled the doors closed behind him and locked the clasp from inside. With immense relief, I let his lace-cut steel body slump lifelessly back onto the supports in the cabinet. At last, I allowed my consciousness to slip from the automaton.

I took Geula's hand and helped her hop down from the wires. Then she and I stepped apart to reveal the seemingly empty stage behind us.

A roar of happy applause went up through the crowd. Young men who had become regulars at the fair tossed flowers onto the stage while a few brave women threw handmade sachets embroidered with hearts and scented with lavender.

Strange to think how much they loved to be fooled momentarily into believing they'd witnessed genuine magic, which they'd all but outlawed across the eastern states and most of the western territories. Yet six days a week, huge crowds paid to cheer at slight of hand and misdirection. They relished the smoke hiding all the wires and mirrors because it allowed them to conjure the presence of something amazing and dangerous. Here in the dark, they longed for mysteries and magic. But out on public streets, with carriages careening past and newsboys shouting sordid tales of scandals and murders, the last thing these decent folk wanted was to discover a free mage lurking in their midst.

That hadn't always been so.

But in 1858, during the Arrow War, mages had torn open a vast and unnatural chasm, flooding out most the southern states and dividing the east and west of America with a the Inland Sea. And up in the Rocky Mountains, behind the roaring saltwater, had come ancient creatures. Theurgists and naturalists called them dinosaurs, but most folks knew them as monsters. Twelve years after that, just as the waters had calmed and cattlemen had learned to rope and drive herds of burly leptoceratops, another battle between mages had unleashed the Great Conflagration. Eastern towns all across the salt marshes and as far north as Chicago had caught light. In Peshtigo, more than a thousand people had burned to death.

Twenty-two years on, people still hadn't forgotten the terror of those merciless flames. Hell, I'd been three then, but even I still woke shaking from dreams of my parents screaming as a blazing cyclone of brilliant embers engulfed them.

So I understood what all these good, natural folks feared. I even understood why they wanted free mages like me rounded up and placed under the godly thumbs of theurgists. They felt terrified and powerless. They wanted magic if it came with assurances, federal offices and communion wafers. They wanted mages in the world—transmitting messages across the oceans and powering turbines—so long as they had us on leashes and electric collars.

But I knew the man who'd created those damn collars, and he gave me worse nightmares than my parents' deaths did.

I'd also come to understand how corrupt theurgists could be. The papers were full of news of how the US Office of Theurgy and Magicum had ordered the 7th Cavalry to suppress Lakota free mages and their Spirit Dances. That hadn't been upholding the law; it had been a massacre. I'd rather live all my life as a wanted outlaw than lend my small power to the men responsible.

Geula and I agreed on that much. She didn't share my suspicion of all theurigists as much as she dreaded the attention of the men who hunted bounties. Audience expectation wasn't the only reason she'd abandoned her real name when she'd fled Boston ten years ago.

We weren't either of us angels—though Geula could look the part with a pair of dainty white wings strapped to her dress and a brassy halo pinned to her curls—but we didn't hurt anybody. Not with our stage performances, and not when we kissed and delighted each other in the privacy of our little room backstage.

I clasped her gloved hand, feeling the warmth and strength of her grip in my own. We bowed, applause and cheers rolling over us as the new electric floor lights bathed us in a yellow glow. Geula caught a sachet and smiled beautifully. I drew in another deep breath, taking power from the tiny whirlwinds that rose between clapping hands and in gusts of hot exhalations. Doors opened and fresh breezes blew in from the lobby. My skin tingled with pleasure.

Air. I ached to feel fresh air the way a landed fish desired water.

Geula glanced sidelong at me, and I caught the worry in her eyes. I forced a smile. We bowed again, and the applause very slowly died down. There were always folk who believed that if they clapped hard and long enough Professor Perfectus would reappear, though he never did.

"You worried me for a moment there," Geula whispered. "Better now, though?"

"Much," I assured her. Performing six days a week at the New United Americas Exhibition in Chicago wore me down, but if I could hold out a year, I'd have earned enough money for Geula and I to buy our own place out west where no one knew us.

We straightened, and I followed her gaze out into the audience. The usual bunch of young men winked and ogled her. A number of older gentlemen stared at the stage with expressions of distant longing. Then I surveyed the upper crust we'd pulled into the box seats. I raised my hand, pretending to straighten my spectacles and hiding my scowl.

Three women, wearing silk, lace and dazzling strings of pearls, gazed down at me from their gilded box. I recognized them, of course. The three "Jewels of Chicago Society", papers called them. (Though the same newsmen deemed Fatima Djemille's graceful dancing "obscene", so their taste clearly didn't align with mine.)

Tall, long-faced Jane Addams and her mousy little companion, Ellen Starr, weren't either of them much past thirty but already famous for their philanthropy and Christian charity work. Beside them, the elegant, silver-haired widow Mrs. Bertha Palmer looked like a bird of paradise perched alongside two pigeons. She controlled a vast fortune of properties and was rumored to know more about financing bars and brothels than any society lady ought to. She looked like the kind of woman who laughed a great deal at everyone else.

But what truly set the three of them apart from most women in the country and made them a trinity were their statuses as Official Theurgists. With a word, any of the three of them could order me captured, jailed and collared.

My stomach clenched like a snail dropped in a snowbank.

"You see who is up in the box seats?" I asked quietly.

Geula didn't appear the least bit surprised. She simply nodded.

"I told you I found us patrons, didn't I?" Geula whispered.

It took a moment for that to sink in. She'd invited them here. How much had she told them?

"Abril, you can't keep working like this. It's wearing you down to your bones." Geula cast me one of her soft, sweet looks. "You're making yourself sick, darling. I know you want to make more money, but—"

"You don't know anything," I responded in a less-than-pleasant sort of hiss. I jerked my hand from hers.

Fortunately, the stage curtain came down before anyone in our audience could see Geula's dismayed expression or witness my dash for the back door.

❖ ❖ ❖

Geula found me across the man-made lagoons, up on the observation deck that overlooked the resplendent Hall of Natural History. I stared down at the long swath formed by thousands of people, dressed in their best hats and coats, as they poured between the huge plaster statues of proud and savage beasts. Lions, plesiosaurs, elk and elephants posed on massive pedestals, while pigeons and small brown pterosaurs flitted overhead.

Cold winds rushed up from Lake Michigan and surged over me. I drank in the force of them, calming the air around me and at the same time regaining some of my strength.

How I loved the wind—I didn't even care if it stank of fish or coal smoke. I felt as if the gusts could sustain me. Though in truth, not even the most powerful of wind mages could live on air alone. And contrary to popular opinion, none of us actually controlled the wind. We drew our power from it, just as earth mages needed the ground beneath them to cast spells and sea mages required water to maintain their power.

Theurgists, on the other hand, built spells as complex as engines and powered them with alchemic stone—the same way an engineer might shovel coal into his boiler.

(Though not so long ago theurgists had wired mages into their spells, using us like batteries and leaving us as drained husks.)

I'd learned that much history from my uncle—not the masked automaton that I'd dolled up to pass for him on stages and in hotels, but the gentle old man who'd died to keep me and his invention from falling into the hands of theurgists or the monsters who served them.

I glared into the distance.

Studded with electric lights, Mr. Ferris's Great Wheel rose so high into the twilight sky that it appeared to harvest shining stars as it slowly descended. Beyond that, veils of coal smoke spread a haze over the dark streets of Chicago, making the city seem as a far shore, vastly distant from the miles of verdant fairgrounds claimed by the New United Americas Exhibition.

"So you gonna say anything or just stare off sulking?" Geula leaned against the cast-iron railing of the overlook. She'd brought her willow lunch basket and wore a long black coat over her beaded red dress. Several ivory-capped hatpins secured her wide black hat to her hair. One stray curl hung against the graceful line of her neck.

"I'm not sulking," I replied—though my tone wasn't so convincing, not even to my own ears. "I'm thinking."

"About?"

"Things." I adored every inch of Geula—absolutely loved her laughter and easy conversation too—but for the first time, I faced how little I truly knew of her. Three months wasn't a long time together, not even if it had been a giddy, glorious three months. I'd kept back much of my own history, not wanting her to think poorly of me. For the first time I pondered how much she might not have told me.

"Things…" Geula hefted her small lunch basket and drew out a sandwich. She took a bite and chewed with a contemplative expression. "Could be better, could be worse."

She offered the sandwich to me, and I accepted it. We were making decent money at the exhibition, but not so much that we could often indulge beyond sausages and mustard on a rye roll. With only one railway bridging the Inland Sea, tickets didn't come easily or cheap. Though now I had to wonder how foolish that fantasy might be if I couldn't even trust Geula not to bring theurgists to my doorstep.

I took a couple bites and returned the sandwich to Geula. She finished it off. We both watched as a young couple strolled past us, trailing a matronly chaperone. Geula's fingers twitched, but she didn't pinch anything from them.

"I packed up your props and the professor's cabinet," Geula informed me quietly. "It's all locked up in the dressing room."

"Thank you." I felt slightly guilty about having left her with all that heavy work, but on the other hand, what had she expected me to do at the sight of three theurgists? Two days back, when she'd mentioned finding patrons, I'd imagined the usual bored, bearded old men who enjoyed throwing their money around in front of young women. I certainly hadn't pictured myself facing down the Chicago Jewels.

"What did you tell them?" I asked. "About me."

"Nothing except that I thought you were smart and quick. Obviously I didn't know the half of it, seeing how fast you rabbited off." Geula shrugged. For a few moments, she stared out at the vast crowds passing below us and filling the air with their conversations and laughter.

"Did you really think I'd turn you over for a reward?" Geula asked me.

"I..." I had feared as much, but I felt ashamed of myself now, with Geula giving me that disappointed look. We hadn't been together long, but I *did* know her. I'd seen her stand up to hecklers and bullies, and I'd stood beside her when she'd block the path of a patrolman bent on beating down a beggar. Geula stuck to her principles. She wouldn't sell out a friend, not even for a hundred-dollar mage bounty, I truly believed that.

"I didn't really think. I just ran," I admitted.

"Those Jersey theurgists put some real fear in you, didn't they?"

This time I shrugged. It hadn't been the theurgists themselves who'd ingrained this terror into me; they hadn't needed to bother. The mere threat of them had been enough to keep my family constantly moving—abandoning homes and jobs in the dead of night, changing our names and always keeping our bags packed. I'd been brought up afraid.

And when my uncle had finally found something like a stable home for his wife and me, it had been in the isolated grounds of Menlo Park, in New Jersey. There, Mr. Edison had provided housing and employment, all the while hammering in all the horror we would suffer if we forced him to report us to the Office of Theurgy and Magicum.

"They will lock you in a prison laboratory. Feed you gruel and then dissect you like a rat," he'd often informed me with a smile. "That would be a shame."

The shocks and burns I'd endured while he had tested his electric collars had been accompanied by reminders that official theurgists could and would do far worse to me, my uncle and my dear crippled auntie.

"I guess I should have given you more warning about the three of them coming to the show." Geula's words brought me back from my troubled memories. "I worried that knowing sooner would make performing all the harder for you."

Likely I wouldn't have set foot on stage at all. I didn't feel like admitting as much.

"So what were the Jewels after you for anyway?" I asked.

"Well, it was Mrs. Palmer who I'd worked for before," Geula replied, but then she cut herself off as a group of men in musty fur coats strolled past us, loudly proclaiming their wonder and excitement over the Machine Maid in the Technology Hall. Apparently the new automaton might well "unburden men from the hysterics imposed by the fairer sex".

Geula scowled at the men and I just smirked.

They weren't such catches that any of the fairer sex was likely to impose anything on them but a steep entry fee.

"Four years back"—Geula returned to her story, leaning close to me—"Mrs. Palmer's favorite cook went missing. I tracked the woman down and managed to barter her back from Roger Plant—"

"I don't know who that is," I admitted. Most of the five months I'd been in Chicago, I'd worked here at the exhibition. I'd rarely even wandered far from the theater complexes. The one exhibit I'd convinced myself to pay the ticket price to enter had been the Wonders of the Western Territories. There they'd had towers of fruit from California, heaps of Nevada borax, and live specimens of beautiful, feathered dinosaurs from Colorado farms. (Their plumes adorned a great many expensive hats worn by society ladies, I'd learned.) What I knew of the city beyond the exhibition grounds came largely from the papers and gossip. I'd heard nothing of a Roger Plant.

"Nice for you, then." Geula made a face like she was recollecting having a tooth pulled. "He runs a place called Under the Willow in the Levee. His beer isn't worth the nickel he charges, but he pulls certain men in with the girls he keeps in his backrooms. Not all of them are there willingly. It took a little doing with my pistol, but I managed to convince him that the cook wasn't worth the trouble he'd bring down on his own head if he kept her."

I stared at Geula. I'd known she'd traveled in tough company and had been more than an actress before I'd met her in the theater, but I hadn't quite imagined this.

"So they want you to find someone again?" I asked.

"They're offering seven hundred dollars," Geula said quietly. I stared at her. That was more than I could've hoped to earn in two, maybe even three, years. I didn't doubt the Jewels could afford as much, but I did wonder who they could value so highly…or who they feared crossing so badly.

All around us, small electric lights lit up, like ornate constellations thrown across the exhibition buildings. Four of them on the far wall formed a shining crown behind Geula's head.

"This time Miss Addams has a girl missing from her charity house." Geula's expression went a little distant and hard. "Liz Gorky is the girl's name. She's nineteen, dark-haired and doe-eyed. She took work at a hotel called World's Fair but hasn't returned for a week now."

"Seven days isn't so long, particularly not for a grown woman who's found work. Maybe she's had enough of living under the thumb of a bunch a nosey temperance women."

"I thought that too. But it turns out she left her infant daughter in Miss Starr's care," Geula went on. "And according to both Miss Addams and Miss Starr, Liz doted on her daughter and fretted over leaving her for even one afternoon. Neither of them believe she simply abandoned her child."

I didn't see what Geula or I could really do about the situation, but at the same time, I wasn't entirely unmoved. I'd lost my parents quite young and still wondered what they might have thought of me if they had the opportunity to know me. I couldn't keep from feeling sympathy for the child.

"Have they gone to the police?" Plenty of missing folk turned up in their morgues. If she wasn't there, then the Jewels likely had the pull to get a citywide search started. That was more than Geula or I could do for them.

"Miss Starr went to them right away, but they weren't much help. They questioned Liz Gorky's employer, a man named Herman Mudgett. He insisted that Liz had met a salesman and run off with him, which was good enough for the crushers, apparently. But then three days ago Miss Addams saw Liz Gorky here—"

"So, she ran off but not very far?" I asked.

"She wasn't attending the exhibition," Geula whispered. "She was an exhibit."

"What?"

"I'm going to see her for myself." Geula started to turn away but glanced back at me over her shoulder. "You coming?"

❖ ❖ ❖

Inside the lofty Technology Hall, a promenade wider than most city streets looped through hundreds of exhibits. The air hummed with thrilled voices, engine sounds and the bright calls of the various men presenting the inventions on display. Here and there mechanical devices stood cordoned off behind curtains and velvet ropes; some were staged like studies, kitchens or even gardens (complete with flowerbeds and trellises of ivy). Other innovations, like Mr. Moreau's silver alchemic train engine, served as structures in and of themselves.

Throngs of men and women dressed in their best clothes—hats, bonnets, gloves and a treasury of jewelry, watch fobs, buckles and cufflinks—crowded around magnificent displays of gleaming brass and whirring clockwork. Children, dolled up in suits and gowns, capered between wonders, exclaiming over steam-powered miniature trains and gaping as toy-sized alchemic airships whizzed over-head.

Towering above everything else, two huge silver columns of electric coils rose up from a stepped platform like gleaming monuments. I paused as a bolt of violet light arced up from the polished silver orb topping one of the columns. All around me, the air suddenly raced with charges. Tongues of lightning crackled through each breath I drew and seemed to set my blood bubbling like champagne. The hairs across my body stood on end like they always did when I felt a storm coming.

Geula cast me a sidelong glance and followed my stare up to the violet bolt as it reached the second tower. "I read something about Mr. Tesla's coils making coal and alchemic stone obsolete," she commented. "But I don't recall exactly how."

"Me either, but I feel like I might start spitting lightning and thunder if I come any closer to them."

We skirted around the two columns, passing a lovely-smelling exhibit, where attendants in white aprons worked at ornate machines that stamped out exquisite bars of chocolate. Geula and I both accepted the samples offered. (If we hadn't been on something of a mission, I would have circled around for a second bar.)

At last we came to the various displays of clockwork automatons and alchemic prosthetics. The wandering narrow alleys created by the numerous exhibit stalls stood largely empty compared to the crowded isles surrounding the displays of engines, guns, sewing machines and chocolates. Most of the other sightseers wandering the narrow avenue appeared to be war veterans and medical men; several even carried their surgical bags with them.

I knew that many people found the sight of artificial limbs disturbing, even those crafted from oak and hickory and inlaid with copper and gold spells, like these resting on satin pillows in glass cases all around us. But I gazed at the displays with a feeling of nostalgia and comfort. The sight of ivory fingers carved with lacey spell patterns brought memories of my aunt and uncle back to me in a rush. The subtle scent of machine oil and rose perfume seemed to float around me as I recollected carrying my uncle's creations from his cluttered workshop to my aunt's parlor. She always took a little time to fit on a new leg. I waited for the moment when she reached out and took my hand and slowly danced around the room with me.

My uncle always etched a heart into each of his designs for her.

Now I found myself looking through these disembodied limbs for that telltale trace. I stopped myself just as I extended a finger towards a delicate, outstretched hand. Of course the heart wasn't there. Both my uncle and aunt were dead. The only remains of them rested in a black cabinet back in my backstage dressing room. The one thing I was likely to do if I touched one of these finely tuned prosthetics was to jolt a spell to life and give myself away as a mage. I carefully tucked my hands into the pockets of my coat.

Beside me, Geula craned her neck to take in the banners and signs hanging in the distance.

"It's the Mechanical Maid we're after," Geula informed me. She drew a small square of paper from her pocket and studied it. A pale, round-faced young woman with her hair in ringlets and startlingly large, dark eyes stared up from the photograph.

"Is that Liz?" It struck me as odd that a girl so poor that she was living in a charity house could afford to have her photograph taken, much less look so imperious when she did.

Geula frowned at the image but nodded. An instant later, she slipped the picture back into her coat. We walked deeper into the exhibits, encountering more and more complete automatons amongst the prosthetic limbs, false teeth and glass eyes.

Clockwork birds sang from atop tiny metal perches, and delicately glazed butterflies fluttered tin wings. At the entry of one large stall, two automatons balanced atop pedestals like sentries. One stood about two feet tall and a child's pinafore covered the joints of its abdomen and groin; in place of the normal porcelain mask, its clockwork inner workings lay exposed around the two wide glass eyes. The automaton standing opposite it resembled an organ grinder's monkey, complete with grimacing white canine teeth. A key, carved from pearly alchemic stone, hung from a string around its neck, awaiting a human hand to slide it into the hole over the creature's machine heart and bring it to life.

"Can I assist one of you, miss?" A neat man, sporting a mustache so waxed that it looked like a pastille of black licorice, stepped out from between the two automatons. He looked to Geula, though I'd been the one lingering to study the exposed gearworks. (It didn't possess half the lustrous alchemic stone that powered the spells etched in Professor Perfectus's armature.) Between my dark complexion and quiet manner, it was common for people to mistake me for Geula's lady's maid. They were often shocked almost speechless if they discovered that I employed her as an assistant.

"No. We're simply looking," Geula informed the fellow. He frowned and stepped forward to partly block our way.

"Many of the devices farther along this aisle aren't all that suitable for the delicate sensibilities of women." He spoke in the hushed tone of an undertaker cautioning against opening a casket. "But across the hall there's an entertaining demonstration of a mechanical loom that produces the prettiest dress fabrics. And back the way you came is a charming music box shaped like a white kitten. I'd imagine that would be more suitable, wouldn't you?"

"I certainly have no idea of what you might imagine, sir. Suitable or otherwise," Geula replied, and she stepped past him. I laughed and followed her.

It soon became obvious why he'd been so anxious to keep us from strolling any farther along this avenue. The designs of the automatons we passed steadily turned from entertainment or medical purposes to warfare. Blades and clubs replaced limbs, while the dark barrels of heavy guns loomed up at head-level. Few of these automatons resembled human beings, much less songbirds or butterflies. Most looked more like gigantic crabs, scorpions and spiders but assembled entirely from armories.

And I did find it disturbing to see several of the things painted not only in military colors but with police seals emblazoned across them and badges soldered to their housings.

"As if the crushers aren't nasty enough already with their billy clubs and pistols," Geula muttered.

I considered the automaton, remembering the comments my uncle had so often made about such creations when they came up at the labs in Menlo Park.

"No city could afford to actually maintain a force of those things. Maybe they'd order one, but it would cost too much to risk on actual raids. I bet it's really meant to stand guard and simply appear threatening," I assured her. "All those joints are incredibly expensive to build and repair.

And the amount of alchemic stone needed to power a platoon of them would cost far more than it would to hire an army of men."

"But there are some things—truly evil things—living folks flat out won't do," Geula said. "Whereas an automaton couldn't care, could it? Whoever's registered on its collar as the owner could make it do anything."

"True, but that doesn't mean it would succeed," I replied. "Between the gold wires and the alchemic stone used for their cores, I suspect that even if an army of these spiders were let loose they wouldn't last too long. See that seam between the inner workings and the top where the alchemic stone is housed? It wouldn't take a minute to sever the couplings there. Once they're shut down, then, easy as you please, anyone can rip them up and even resell their parts."

Geula pulled her gaze from a looming automaton with a head like a spider's and half a dozen sabre-tipped legs. She looked to me. I wasn't sure what she read from my expression, but it brought a grin to her face.

"You really are a genius, aren't you?" Geula whispered to me. "And I bet you could stop this monster dead with your bare hands."

Briefly, I considered the hulking, insect-like machine. All the ambient power in the air seemed to crackle around me. Right now, with a touch of my hand, I could burn through the automaton's wires and cogs. Another time or somewhere else, it might be a different matter. But I loved it when Geula looked at me like this, and I wanted her to think the best of me being a mage. So, I simply smiled and nodded.

As we turned around a bend, we suddenly bumped up against a dense crowd of men. The vast majority appeared cued up to shoulder their way into the blue-velvet tent displaying a red banner that proclaimed the many advantages of the New Mechanical Maid.

Devoted! Obedient & Adoring!
Woman, as She was Always Intended!
Built to Serve Every Need!

A voluptuous line drawing of a parlor maid with little wheels attached to her heels and a doll-like face hung beneath the banner.

"Two cents says this is nothing but a couple working girls rubbed down with silver powder and wearing copper-wire pasties on their tits," Geula whispered against my ear. "Bet they're selling the world's oldest trade as new technology."

"Maybe…" Something in the air disturbed me, and it wasn't just the dust of too much face powder. A definite and terribly familiar vibration pulsed from behind the curtains. I couldn't get a clear view of the big fellows at the front through the crush of men surrounding us, but their bulky figures made me extremely uneasy.

"It might be more simple than expected to get Liz out of this," Geula went on as we crept forward with the line of men. "Whoever's putting up this front won't want to have it exposed here by a scene."

"I don't know. I think there might be more going on—"

All at once, the crowd of men surrounding us rushed and jostled forward, pushing Geula and I ahead into the dim interior of the tent. The warm air inside felt torpid and smelled of sweat and stale cigar smoke. The mob flooded around a raised brass-colored platform and carried Geula and I near enough that I could make out the lines of the dark curtains behind the platform. Two rows of electric lights lit up its floor. It was a portable stage, complete with a hidden space in back and a generator humming below the platform.

A stocky man in his late forties, wearing a dapper brown tweed suit, parted the curtains and stepped into the light. A thunderclap of applause went up from the men all around me, and I caught my breath in horror. My pulse seemed to race so fast that it sent tremors through my hands.

Next to me, Geula appeared perplexed as she took the man in.

"Is that—"

I forced his name out. "Edison."

Looking back, I realized with growing panic that there would be no way through the throng of men behind us. The only way to escape would be to wait until the end of the demonstration and file out past the platform and through the back flap of the tent, where two of Edison's big toughs stood guard. I recognized the stocky red-bearded man as the brute Edison had often sent after me when I'd refused to present myself at the laboratory.

After nearly nine years of hiding, I'd strolled directly back into Edison's grip.

At that thought, I felt the blood drain from my face and a sick vertigo washed over me.

He's in the light and I'm in the dark, I told myself. *He won't see me. He's too arrogant to care who's in the crowd. He won't notice me from the rest.*

I did my level best to believe that I could be right. I could get out of this place. Then, to my surprise and absolute relief, Geula caught my hand in hers and squeezed my fingers. I gripped her hand in return—just as I did on stage—sharing the assurance that we were there for one another.

"Are you all right?" she whispered.

"I…" But I didn't dare say anything surrounded by so many other people.

Geula glanced between me and the platform, and that

quick look of knowing came over her. I hadn't told her any-thing about the years I'd spent as a prisoner at Menlo Park, but she seemed to understand it was Edison who terrified me. At the very least, I supposed she understood what danger a man like Edison, who worked directly for Federal Theurgists, posed to a free mage like me.

"As soon as we can, we'll slip out of here, like shadows. I promise," Geula assured me. "As long as we stay calm and don't draw any attention, we'll be fine."

I nodded and squeezed her hand again.

Up on the platform, Mr. Edison basked in admiration and applause, spreading his arms wide as if his mere exis-tence was a marvel worthy of this entire exhibition. His hair had turned grayer than I remembered, and his paunch had become too prominent for mere tailors to disguise, but his bland face bore hardly a single worry line.

After a few more moments, he motioned for silence. The crowd quieted.

"Good evening, gentlemen," Edison called out warmly. "It's a pleasure to see so many of you gathered here and looking so excited! As you should be, let me assure you! I am not overstating the matter when I swear that this, my latest innovation, by far surpasses any before it. Yes, pre-viously I collared magic and brought light as bright as the stars into your homes. But now, I have improved upon God Almighty's loveliest and most flawed creation. Woman!"

He turned to the curtain behind him and pulled the fabric aside to expose an automaton that almost perfectly duplicated the appearance of a young dark-haired woman. She wore a strangely dazed smile, and the light shining up from below cast unusual shadows across her face. Even so, it was obvious the woman on the platform was the same one in the photograph Geula had shown me. Liz Gorky.

At a motion of Edison's hand, she stepped forward and twirled around. The thin white shift she wore turned nearly transparent as she spun through the blazing electric lights.

Metallic ribs and an automaton's shell—an armature—encased most of her body like a second skin. Only her head, breasts and groin remained exposed, naked flesh. The tight bun holding up her long hair provided a clear view of the narrow silver collar locked tight around her throat like a choker.

Appreciative gasps and a number of hoots sounded from the men surrounding us, though a few of them appeared aghast. One portly middle-aged gentleman standing to my right looked stricken. Even in the gloom of the tent, I picked out the furious red flush rising in his pale face. His horror only increased when he glanced sidelong and caught sight of me and Geula.

"You may wish to avert your eyes, ladies," he mumbled, and to my surprise, he bowed his head to stare at his polished shoes. Clearly he'd expected something wholly more mechanical.

"Yes, lest we discover what's under our own clothes," Geula whispered to me. Then she returned her attention to the stage. "If that's makeup, it's the best I've ever seen. The joints of her fingers really do look like an automaton's. And not merely any automaton's hand, either..."

I edged a step forward to study Edison's Mechanical Maid.

Geula was correct; it wasn't any automaton's armature holding Liz Gorky up on that stage. The long, graceful fingers were my uncle's design, though the wrists and ankles hadn't been crafted with the same exquisite care and looked stiff, almost chunky. Nor had the armature been fitted perfectly to the woman's body. The silver planes caging her thighs dug into her full buttocks, leaving red welts.

I didn't dare push my way closer to the platform for a better view, but I guessed that Edison had cobbled together two or more of my uncle's early blueprints. Though the inclusion of Edison's own collar and the dazed look on the woman's face assured me this creation was far from what my uncle had intended.

The automaton's armature wasn't serving to give a disabled woman back her freedom of motion, or to empower her with even greater strength and speed that she could have hoped for from a body of flesh and blood. Edison had gutted all my uncle's ideals and crafted the remnants into a shining steel prison.

Up on the platform, Edison grinned and leaned theatrically towards the Mechanical Maid.

"Why don't you give the fine fellows of our audience a bow?" As Edison spoke, I felt a crackle in the air around the Mechanical Maid's throat. I remembered the same feeling from when Edison had tested his collars on me. The Mechanical Maid twitched once, her expression remaining wide-eyed and smiling, and then she bowed low and rose back upright.

Applause and a few murmurs arose from the crowd. The portly man looked up from his shoes and scowled to see that the demonstration had not ended.

"A few skeptics among you might think that I've hired an actress to present to you on stage, but I assure you that this is the genuine result of my patented Mechanical Maid Automatonic Armature! At one time, this woman was a loose creature who ran wild, bringing no end of shame to her good husband. You needn't take my word. Listen to what her husband, Dr. Mudgett, has to say."

A slender man sporting a thick mustache and oily dark hair stepped from behind the curtain to join Edison. Hadn't Mudgett been the name of the proprietor of the hotel that

Liz Gorky had disappeared from? Geula and I exchanged a glance, but neither of us said a word. Not in this crowd.

"Mr. Edison has indeed created a miracle here," Dr. Mudgett stated. "Before he consented to treat my wife with his amazing automatonic armature, I'm ashamed to say that Liz was a disrespectful creature, prone to hysteria and wanton disobedience. She could neither keep a fit house nor control herself. She spoke back to me endlessly, spent my money furiously, and wept when she could not have her every wish. I know in these modern times she wasn't unlike many of your wives, daughters, mothers or sisters."

Mudgett took a moment to look out at the men gathered around him with a sincere and serious expression. And a number of them called out their agreement and grievances. Few women knew their places, these days. They took work, rode bicycles, demanded votes, and all at a man's expense. Apparently, even the colored women were getting above themselves.

Geula rolled her eyes, and I fought the urge to send a shock through the crowd. Though there wasn't much that would have given me away more quickly.

Mudgett nodded.

"Now, we mustn't hate them for their frailty and failings. As a medical man, I can tell you that such women do themselves as much harm as they do their families." He spoke soothingly, almost as if he didn't realize that he'd been the one to stir up the audience's ire. "I have seen any number of women suffering from nervous disorders, neurasthenia and even sterility, all because they have foolishly attempted to live as men, instead of joyfully living in obedience to men."

"Women like that aren't natural!" a spotty young man across the room shouted.

"No. Nor are they Christian, despite what they may call themselves and their organizations," Mudgett agreed, while

Edison looked on like a well-pleased ringmaster. "Sadly, until now the only way to deal with women like my own dear wife was either to confine them in madhouses or school them through brute force. But no longer! Mr. Edison has solved the problem without causing the slightest suffering or hardship for the weaker sex. Isn't that true, darling?"

Liz Gorky nodded.

"Gentlemen, thanks to Mr. Edison, I could not wish for a more pliable or dutiful spouse." The doctor smiled and reached out and pulled Liz Gorky close to him. Her expression didn't change in the slightest as she leaned into his arms.

"Doesn't the good book command that a wife should be her husband's in everything?" Mudgett asked her. I felt the air around her collar sizzle and knew from experience that fire seared through her mind, punishing her impulse to resist. But she betrayed no sign of the pain.

Liz—or the Mechanical Maid imprisoning her—nodded again and wrapped her arm around Mudgett, who grinned.

"Now that my Lizzie knows the pleasure of rightful submission and deference, we're both happy. And it's all thanks to Mr. Edison's Mechanical Maid Automatonic Armature!"

This time, the applause sounded like thunder. Even the man next to me gave a hearty cheer. I felt so repulsed that I had to fight down my bile.

"Well, that's mighty kind of you. And thank you, Doctor, for trusting me with the transformation of your wife," Edison said once the clapping quieted. "And thank you for allowing these gentlemen to share her story."

Again, the tent filled with applause. Neither Geula nor I even pretended to clap along.

Dr. Mudgett tipped his hat to the crowd and escorted Liz back behind the curtain.

Edison remained up on the platform, beaming through the gloom at the crowd.

"It has been my pleasure to see all the good done by all my innovations, but none more than this one," Edison announced. "Now, if any of you gentlemen feel that my Mechanical Maid Automatonic Armature could help you to shepherd a woman in your care back to her proper place, I would advise you to leave your cards with my associates. Mr. Kern or Mr. Hays are there at the back of the tent. We are taking advance orders. I look forward to working with many of you to improve your lives."

A shaft of light speared into the tent as the flaps in the back drew open. Hays's red beard appeared almost unnaturally bright in the sudden glow. Across from him, Kern straightened his bowler, which looked absurdly small in comparison to his hulking body and giant melon of a head. They'd both worked for Edison at Menlo; as well as I remembered them, I prayed that I hadn't made an equal impression upon either of them. The fact that I'd burned down one of the laboratories made that seem unlikely, but I bowed my head and forced myself to step forward as the crowd filed out of the tent.

Twice I found myself edging forward, and both times Geula touched my hand.

"Running will only draw their attention and everyone else's," she said softly.

I dropped my head again. Shoving my hands into my coat pockets, I shuffled behind Geula. The men ahead of us slowed our exit to a snail's pace, as many stopped to take or leave cards with Edison's burly associates. We edged forward, stopped, edged forward again.

Then Geula and I stepped through the tent flaps. The air outside the tent felt fresh and clean. I pulled in a deep breath and started ahead towards a display of towering automatons built to conjure up the thrill and terror of the great dinosaurs of the west. A toothy tyrannosaur gaped down, while a huge white pterosaur hung on a chain from the ceiling. Nearer to me stood several massive horned creatures, the plates on their sides lay open, exposing the cogs and springs that would lend the thing the illusion of life with a mere spark of power.

"There's more going on here than just one girl being carried off by a pimp," Geula muttered. She turned her gaze to me. "And what was the matter with you in there? Was it something to do with—"

"You! Stop, right there!" Hays shouted from behind us. I knew his voice better than I did his flushed face or red beard. I tensed but managed not to turn back. Next to me, Geula scowled but then quickened her step slightly. Men around us turned, confused as to who Hays addressed.

"Thief!" Hays roared.

We marched deeper into the displays.

"Come back here, you dirty little thief!"

Several startled shouts warned me that Hays followed us, shoving his way into the crowd. I wanted to run but knew that would bring the security men down on me all the sooner. No one was easier to pick out from a milling herd than a single woman sprinting away.

"Ashni Naugai! I know that's you!"

Hearing my real name for the first time in nearly a decade, I couldn't keep from looking back. Hardly fifteen feet from me, with only twenty or so men blocking his way, Hays leered at me. He shoved two dapper older men aside.

Far across the vast hall, purple bolts arced up and the air surged with a wild charge. I drew it in and then reached out and lightly brushed my hand over the massive horned dinosaur. The automaton sprang to life, rearing up and tossing its big head like a bull let loose in a china shop. Grown men screamed and shouted in alarm. When the dinosaur charged a few steps towards Edison's tent, people all around ran. It didn't matter that the automaton was already winding down. In the panic, Geula and I were merely two tiny figures among a mob that fled from the displays and out of the hall.

"Ashni Naugai?" Geula demanded of me as we made our way up the stairs leading into the Women's Hall. Plaster goddesses, muses and amazons contemplated us from pediments lining either side of the stone steps.

"Yes, Miss *May Flowers*?" I responded. That only made Geula glower at me all the more.

"I told you that wasn't my real name." Geula stopped to look around. Deep shadows spread between the electric lamps that lined the wide walkways of the exhibition. Twenty yards from us, repairmen in green uniforms mounted ladders to change the lamp bulbs that had already burned out. Around them, small groups of people wandered together, taking in the wonder of a world illuminated against the night.

I scanned the shadowy figures as they moved in and out of pools of electric light. Neither Hays nor any of Edison's other men appeared to have followed us this far. Geula and I had certainly led them on a long enough chase, crossing back and forth across the lagoons and even ducking into the terminal building as if we meant to catch a train out to Chicago or beyond. As much as I'd wanted to race directly back to the theater, I was glad we hadn't taken the chance of leading Edison straight to my uncle's automaton.

"The first week we were…together," Geula said quietly. "I told you my name."

"And I told you I was a mage, but that didn't stop you from getting us involved with theurgists," I whispered back. The moment I spoke, I knew that wasn't the real reason for my anger and agitation. It was Edison, not Geula, who'd rattled me, and it hadn't been her fault I'd gone to his tent. I'd walked right in of my own volition.

A cold wind rolled off the lake. Geula shuddered and pulled her coat closer around her. I spread my fingers, drinking the strength from the flurry and shielding Geula from its icy bite.

"I didn't let them know anything about you, I swear." Geula frowned. "How could I, when it turns out I don't actually know anything myself?"

"You know enough to get me collared." But I couldn't summon any real anger at her.

"Yeah." She snorted. "But you didn't bother to tell me enough so that I didn't drag you straight into some trouble you're obviously running from."

I hadn't imagined the matter from that perspective. She was right, of course. How could we protect each other's secrets if we hid them from one another?

"I didn't think it would matter, not once we'd moved west together." I glanced up at the serene goddess posturing a few feet from me. A bat darted past, chasing moths that had been drawn out by all these brilliant lights.

"So?" Geula prompted me.

"Tell me about Boston first." It wasn't that I didn't trust her, but I'd never shared my history, and I didn't really know how to get the words out—or if I could.

"All right." Geula shrugged. "Judge Lowell discovered my younger brother in bed with his wife. A day later, she was murdered and my brother was charged. The judge had my brother hanged. I shot the judge."

I stared at her for a stunned moment. She made it all sound so…straightforward, as if she were describing the inevitable outcome of a mathematic equation. Perhaps, for her, she was.

"So, what about you?" Geula asked.

"It's not simple…"

"Not much is." Geula stepped up next to me and put her arm around my shoulder. "Just start at the beginning."

"I suppose it starts with my parents and uncle." I relaxed against Geula. "They came to Chicago after the floods. There were a lot of jobs then for wind mages repairing and replacing telegraph lines. They were happy, I think. My uncle met my aunt here and trained under her father as an automaton builder. Then the fire came through." I had to pause a moment to steady myself against the guilt that welled up behind that one sentence. My parents had burned to death, and my aunt had risked her life to rescue me from the inferno of their house. She'd lost her left leg and most of her right hand protecting me. "We lost my mom and dad. Abril, my auntie, she was very badly burned. After that, the Mage Law passed, and my uncle took my aunt and me into hiding. We left Chicago and moved from place to place until my uncle finally found work at Menlo Park—"

"In Mr. Edison's laboratories?" Geula asked like she was guessing the answer to a riddle.

"Yes. At first it seemed like an answer to all our prayers. Uncle Neelmani set to work improving the designs for automatons, I assisted him and cleaned up the machine labs, and Auntie Abril read to Mr. Edison's wife, Mary. We lived on the grounds and were well paid." I could still remember how delighted we'd all been. Uncle Neelmani had insisted on toasting Mr. Edison at every meal. He'd been certain that with Edison's resources he'd at last be able to build an automatonic armature that would allow Auntie Abril to dance and draw as she had loved to do before the fire.

How naïve he'd been—how foolishly kind and utterly devoted. I missed him so much that it hurt to remember him and know he was gone forever. I frowned up at the dark sky overhead until my urge to cry passed.

Geula quickly pressed a kiss to my cheek. Her lips felt hot against my skin, and a hint of chocolate lingered on her breath. She knew exactly how to reassure me without saying a word.

"Nothing like goodness inspired Mr. Edison to take us in," I went on. "He wanted me so that he'd have an unregistered mage to test his mage-collars on without having to report his failings—"

"The scar on your neck?" Geula asked in horror. "Edison did that to you?"

I nodded.

"He wanted worse for his wife," I told her. "The reason he allowed my uncle to work on an armature wasn't to develop a device to improve the lives of the injured and crippled. He wanted my uncle to build a shell that would let him lock his wife up and keep her from indulging in laudanum."

"An addict, was she?" Geula asked.

"And a mean one at that. She'd call my auntie every filthy name she could think of and hurl plates at her if she was denied her doses."

At the time, I'd despised her for treating my aunt so badly. I'd sometimes wished Edison could have locked her up. But remembering the dull deadness of Liz Gorky's gaze, I realized now what a terribly cruel act it was to so completely deny any person control of themselves—whether or not they made poor choices. Those decisions were theirs to make and defined who they were.

"So what happened?" Geula asked.

I didn't want to go on. In some childish way, it felt like I was letting them die all over again by saying more. But I wanted to be honest with Geula. I did owe her that.

"Auntie Abril fell ill. Her lungs had never recovered from the fire, and she was very susceptible to ague. She passed away on the thirtieth of September, only hours before Uncle Neelmani convinced Edison to allow him to use the armature he'd perfected to help support her breathing—"

"It could do that?" Geula asked.

"Uncle Neelmani thought so, but he couldn't get to us in time to try it. Aunt Abril died two hours before he arrived with the armature and its cabinet." I stopped for a moment, fighting back the memories of my auntie lying in her bed like a sunken, waxy doll. I didn't want to think of her that way; it wasn't who she'd been. I wanted to remember her dancing and laughing at both her missteps and mine. But the cold image of her corpse hung in my mind.

"Without her in the house to hide the laudanum away, Mary Edison had free access. She died twelve days later of overindulgence," I said. "Mr. Edison took it very badly. He blamed our family, and in a rage, he had his assistant Hays collar me so that he could test how long a mage could survive if the collar malfunctioned and didn't stop burning. I was only saved because a newspaperman dropped by the laboratory unexpectedly to interview Edison. My uncle found me a few hours later and realized that we had to escape immediately. He packed up his armature, and we managed to get to the train station before Edison and his men closed in. I was already aboard with all our luggage... and I guess my uncle realized that if he fled he could draw Edison and his men away from me and his invention..." My voice failed me then.

Geula didn't ask me to go on. I drew in a deep breath and concentrated on the rushing, pleasant feeling of excitement in the air. Perfumes of machine oil and coal fires twisted around night-blooming jasmine. Faint vibrations rolled up from a music hall, and somewhere on a balcony above us, a woman hummed to herself and applied a spritz of lavender perfume.

I exhaled slowly, feeling that I was placing this vibrant living world out between me and the painful memories that lay dead in the past.

"I think he must have circled back to ensure that the fire I started destroyed all of his blueprints," I said at last. "It was a month later that I read about his death and how much of Edison's automaton laboratory had burned down. I was on my own from then on."

"How old were you?" Geula asked.

"Sixteen," I replied. "Old enough to know that a woman couldn't travel on alone without trouble. But if I accompanied a frail old relative in a wheeled chair, folks were far more likely to let us alone. So I stuffed a mannequin into my uncle's automaton armature and dressed it up with a wig. I explained away his mask as part of his eccentric flair, him being a stage magician."

"And abracadabra! Here you are with Professor Perfectus, yeah?" Geula smiled wryly.

"Well, nine years on," I pointed out. "But yes. That's my story."

"So you aren't Mexican, at all?" Geula appeared slightly chagrined. "And to think I've been trying to learn Spanish all this last month."

I laughed at that. (I'd been trying to pick the language up myself.)

"My parents and uncle came over from England, but my grandfather was an Indian sailor and a wind mage." After everything else, this seemed like such a small confession. "I used my aunt's name because I had some of her papers mixed in with my uncle's luggage. Her birthdate wasn't too hard to alter. And I knew the Edison had never known her maiden name."

"Clever," Geula said, but her expression turned troubled. "The armature that they trapped Liz Gorky inside? That was your uncle's design?"

"Based on it," I admitted, though the idea of how terribly my uncle's intentions had been misused repulsed me. "But it's nothing like his actual work. If you put on the Professor Perfectus armature, it couldn't restrain you like that thing Edison created. My uncle built spells into it to ensure that it responded to the desire of the wearer. It would fit and move like a second skin, not trap you in a cage."

"A second skin of steel," Geula added.

"My uncle can't be blamed for what Edison did with his design."

"No." Geula sighed and craned her head up at the statue looming over us. "How hard do you think it will be to break Liz out of that thing?"

For an instant, the question surprised me. But of course Geula hadn't immediately discarded rescuing Liz Gorky and turned her mind to putting as much distance between herself and Edison as possible. She wasn't like me—she fought instead of running away.

"I don't know. Professor Perfectus releases with a touch. But I'd bet that Edison is using a lock like the one that closes his mage-collars." I scratched absently at the high collar of my dress. "Those have to be released by the registered owner."

Geula's scowled.

"No way around that?" she asked.

"I…" I didn't want to be dragged back into Edison's proximity. I wanted to pack up and leave with Geula tonight. And yet the thought of Liz Gorky gnawed at me. "I managed to open a few by draining their power so that the registration spell failed. It isn't easy, but if there was enough time, I might be able to do it."

Geula smiled at me and then nodded thoughtfully.

"Hopefully, you won't have to." Geula clasped my hand in hers and started up the steps. "We're not alone in this, remember?"

This time, as much as I wanted to, I didn't run. We strolled up the stairs side by side.

❖ ❖ ❖

An hour later, upon the second story of the Women's Hall, seated under a glass dome and surrounded by the perfume of hundreds of costly greenhouse orchids, I wondered if perhaps I'd made the wrong choice. Or maybe Geula had. We certainly didn't seem to be making much headway on Liz Gorky's account.

The Jewels were gracious hostesses, and the table Geula and I sat at all but overflowed with delicacies and indulgences. Peaches, figs and bright gold oranges (all from California) were piled high on silver trays. Gilded chocolates, in the shapes of songbirds, studded an exotic coconut cake, and we'd already eaten our fill of lobster, potato gratin and sweet peas. Flutes of bubbling champagne percolated in front of us.

Across the table from Geula and I, Bertha Palmer sipped her champagne and watched the two of us with the hard, keen look of a landlady intent upon evicting undesirable tenants as discreetly as possible. To her right, meek Miss Starr poked at her serving of cake with a gold fork but didn't actually take a bite. During the entire time that Geula had described what we'd witnessed in the Mechanical Maid display, she'd not spoken a word, nor had she appeared much surprised. To Mrs. Palmer's left, Jane Addams hunched in her chair, looking too long and angular for its dainty proportions. She'd refused both cake and champagne in favor of a strong black coffee. She worried the column of pearls wound around her throat, and then seemed to catch herself and curl her large hands around her coffee cup.

Of all three Jewels, Miss Addams alone had reacted with dismay to the revelation that Mudgett had claimed Liz Gorky as his wife. Outrage had shown clearly in her face and she'd looked to Miss Starr immediately. Then, as now, Miss Starr kept her demure head down, revealing nothing and offering nothing.

"Now, I know that all you asked me to do was track down Liz Gorky…" Geula took a bite of cake and went on. "But there have to have been other women Edison and Mudgett have done this to. The exhibition has been going for months, and Liz Gorky could only have been part of their Mechanical Maid display for a week at most. So who did they have on display before this, and what's become of her?"

Mrs. Palmer turned her champagne glass in her hand. The other two were silent as well.

"If Mudgett is running a hotel, he likely has access to a number of women." I spoke up for Geula's sake. "Not merely his staff but guests too. The exhibition has been drawing thousands and thousands of people from both halves of the country. Some are bound to go missing…"

"Damn it," Miss Addams muttered. She cast a brief glower in Mrs. Palmer's direction. "Didn't I say there was more to this?"

"Let us not jump to foolhardy conclusions. It isn't impossible that Liz did marry Dr. Mudgett previous to her coming to you at Hull House." Mrs. Palmer spoke very deliberately and coolly. "He could be the father of her child, for all we know."

At this, Miss Starr's head came up fast. For the first time all evening, I saw clearly how furious she was. A flush colored her cheeks, and though she glowered, her dark eyes seemed to glint with unshed tears. The moment she met my gaze, she bowed her head again and crushed a piece of her cake between the gold tines of her fork.

Miss Adam's hand jumped to the pearls and gripped them as if attempting to rip them from her neck.

I remembered the photograph of Liz Gorky that Geula had shown me. This close to Miss Starr, I recognized more than a passing resemblance—the same dark eyes and angular jaw. Miss Starr's bowed head and downcast gaze hid the very features that made Liz Gorky striking. Liz Gorky was too old to be her daughter, but could have been a younger sister, a cousin or even a niece.

"Liz was not married," Miss Addams said firmly. "She told us that her family disowned her for engaging in relations while still unwed."

"So she says, but there is only her word for any of that." Mrs. Palmer favored each of us in turn with a hard, direct glance. "If we were to act directly—publically—against a man of Mr. Edison's reputation and reach, we would certainly need more cause than the word of an admitted adulteress."

I didn't recall anyone saying anything about Liz Gorky being involved with a married man, but neither Miss Addams nor Miss Starr objected. And if that was the case, it made even more sense that Mrs. Palmer feared legal charges against Edison on Liz's behalf wouldn't hold up.

At the same time, Geula's point about Mudgett and Edison going through other women troubled me deeply. Even if Edison's cobbled-together copy of my uncle's armature did function perfectly—and I very much doubted that it did—how long could a person survive having her will so completely suppressed and violated? How much time did Liz Gorky have before she went utterly mad or died? She'd hardly been missing a week, but already she'd struck me as a dull, dying thing. How many more would there be after her?

"We must do something," Miss Starr murmured.

"Is there any way of finding out where they're keeping Liz Gorky?" Geula asked. "We might be able to steal her away from them if we knew that much."

Unwillingly, I thought of the cabinet where I stored Professor Perfectus.

"We could have them followed, but it will take time and would involve bringing even more people into the matter." Mrs. Palmer glanced to me. "Since it seems that the two of you were noticed by Mr. Edison's associate. He thought he recognized you in particular, didn't he, Miss Nieves?"

Geula and I exchanged a quick glance. Neither of us had mentioned that.

"No," I replied. "He mistook me for another woman, but after witnessing that Mechanical Maid, I wasn't inclined to remain in his company long enough for him to realize his error."

"I see." Mrs. Palmer's level gaze reminded me of the unwavering stare of a snake. "Well, it would seem that after that incident, Mr. Edison took it into his head that this other woman was here at the exhibition. He appears to be quite interested in an automaton in her possession. If we could somehow locate that, then we might have a chance at trading it for Liz's release."

"He actually said that?" Geula asked.

"He has his agents searching the exhibition grounds," Mrs. Palmer replied.

I had to suppress the desire to leap up and rush back to the theater. I had no doubt Hays would recognize the cabinet if he found his way into the theater's dressing rooms.

"Of course, I've made certain that, for propriety's sake, Edison's men were not allowed to intrude into the private rooms or dressing rooms of any women. I informed him that I would oversee any such search beginning tomorrow morning."

"Oh for Heaven's sake," Miss Addams cried out, and she looked to me. "If you have the damn thing, then say as much. We'll pay whatever you ask. Just let us get Lizzie back."

"Yes!" Miss Starr cast me a pleading look. "Whatever you want, it's yours."

I didn't miss Mrs. Palmer's annoyed expression or Geula's pleased smile as she looked between Miss Addams and Miss Starr. I said nothing, but Geula leaned forward on her elbows like a card sharp preparing to reveal a winning hand.

"Two thousand dollars and two tickets for California," Geula said.

Mrs. Palmer made a face like she'd bitten her tongue, but Miss Starr and Miss Addams agreed to the price. I glowered at Geula. She couldn't actually believe I would ever hand my uncle's armature over to a man like Edison. He'd made a monstrosity of the imitations he'd built. I didn't want to find out what horror he'd create if he got hold of all the subtle innovation and spells that made up the real armature.

"You do realize that this won't stop Edison and Mudgett from replacing Liz with another woman," I said. "Or doesn't that matter?"

Miss Starr shot me a look of raw fury.

"I don't know how things are done where you come from, Miss Nieves, but here in America, we look after our own!" She jabbed her gold fork at me. "Lizzie is one of us, and we are going to do whatever it takes to get her back safe and sound to her daughter!"

Instinctively, I drew in a deep breath and felt the air around me grow cool as I drained the power from it. Geula must have felt the change because she straightened and cast me a worried look. As much as I wanted to slap a stinging charge across Miss Starr's face, I resisted. And not merely because I'd be a fool to reveal myself in front of three theurgists, but because it occurred to me that Geula wasn't being quite straight with them. She might promise a simple exchange of the armature for Liz Gorky, but there had to more in her mind than that. She'd been as appalled as I had at Edison's Mechanical Maid.

"Where I come from," I began, "all people are created equal and every life has value regardless of how poor or un-privileged their family and friends are. So obviously, Miss Starr, my America is a different one from yours."

To my surprise, Miss Starr's entire face seemed to quiver. She gave a sob and then leapt from her chair and rushed off to the balcony.

"Ellen!" Miss Addams called after her. She began to rise from her seat with an awkwardness that I remembered my aunt suffering when her prosthesis didn't sit quite right.

"No, Jane." Mrs. Palmer stood swiftly and easily. "She's overtired, that's all. Let me talk to her. In the meantime, I'd very much appreciate if you'd finish the rest of this up." Mrs. Palmer indicated Geula and I with an offhanded gesture, and then she strode after Miss Starr (who I could hear sobbing out in the dark).

Miss Addams sighed heavily and took a slug of her coffee like it was whiskey.

"You bring Liz here, and I'll have your money and rail-way passes waiting for you. Are we agreed?" She looked to Geula briefly but turned her full attention to me. "I'll send word to Edison that we're willing to make the exchange. It can't happen here, but would the theater serve?"

"No." The still air inside the auditoriums would stifle me. Edison wasn't likely to agree to meet out in the open air, not knowing me as he did. But the vast space of the Technology Hall would seem familiar to him—like territory he owned. At the same time, it offered me air charged with currents and the cover of countless displays for Geula. Edison and his men couldn't control them all. "I'd rather we make the exchange in the Technology Hall."

"Tonight?" Miss Addams asked.

I nodded. Best not to give Edison much time to muster more of his resources. He was a smart man but not particularly quick, so striking immediately would serve us doubly well.

"What time do you think?" I asked Geula.

"Two hours from now," she replied, after considering for a moment. Then she looked to Miss Addams. "But give us a good hour before you contact Edison. I'd like to already be in the building and prepared before he even catches wind of what's going on."

Miss Addams nodded and took a more refined sip of her coffee. She frowned and added a sugar cube. As she stirred her coffee with a gold spoon, she said, "Despite what Ellen said and what Mrs. Palmer might have indicated, we do want Edison stopped."

"I guessed as much." Geula nodded.

"But you don't want it traced back to any of you, correct?" I asked.

Miss Addams paused and studied me. I didn't bother bowing my head or lowering my gaze.

"We have to protect the movement, above all else," Miss Addams replied. "Women's national suffrage depends upon men viewing us as virtuous, kind and nonthreatening. Rightly or not, Mrs. Palmer, Ellen and I have come to symbolize those traits within the suffrage movement. We can't be publically linked to…to whatever it is that may become of Mr. Edison or his Mechanical Maid project. You understand that, don't you?"

I did. We couldn't have men suddenly realizing how little difference there really was between a demure society miss and a calculating murderess. I just didn't like which side of the divide that relegated women like Geula and I to.

"Yes, I understand."

Miss Addams sipped her coffee and seemed pleased with the effect of the sugar cube. Rather dismissively, she added, "It would seem that you have two hours to prepare. I wish you the best of luck."

"We don't need luck," Geula replied. "But make sure you have the money and railway tickets. Because we *will* be coming for them tonight." Then Geula raised her glass, and I took up mine as well. We tapped the crystal together and drained our small portions of champagne.

In the abandoned quiet of the Technology Hall, I picked out the hum of the distant coal-powered generators. During open hours, they provided electricity to many of the displays, but now with the exhibitors and crowds gone, they simply lit the long rows of spotlights flickering overhead. Shadows fluttered and danced across the drop cloths and curtains that covered most of the displays.

Mr. Tesla's towers stood silent, and a sleek silver train engine crouched on its track as if the short length of velvet rope in front of it had frozen it in place. Bats winged between the steel rafters far above us while a nervous chatter of clockwork cogs clicked and tapped away from behind countless displays.

I drummed my fingers against the cabinet that normally housed Professor Perfectus. It resounded with a hollow knock, and I stopped. Only a mannequin hung on the supports inside. But I felt certain that the sight of the glossy cabinet would draw Edison's attention. With luck, it would delay him from studying our surroundings too closely.

I resisted the urge to glance back to the looming statue of Hephaestus and reassure myself that Geula hid in the shadow of the lame god's hammer. I didn't need to look to feel certain that she held her pistol close to her chest, ensuring that the overhead lights didn't glint off its long barrel. She wasn't the one likely to grow nervous or make a mistake.

I took in another slow deep breath. The space overhead whirled with the tiny cyclones of my warm rising breath. I'm not inclined to pray, but briefly I thought of my uncle assuring me that wind mages like me were special to Aditi, goddess of the sky.

She who unbinds and grants freedom, she who protects all who are unique—she is surely your guardian, my dear. Never fear.

I'd always wondered at him describing me as unique. Now it occurred to me that maybe he'd known about me and accepted me, even before I had. It was a strange time for such a thought, and yet the idea calmed me.

I studied the oversized double doors at the front of the hall. The flickering bulbs made them appear to shift. A mere trick of the light. When the doors did open, I'd feel fresh air pouring in between them. That was one of the reasons Geula and I had picked this spot. It also offered us a quick escape if things went badly.

As my thoughts drifted, the lights overhead flared. I concentrated, focusing on pulling the energy from them, and they dimmed again. I wanted Edison in the dark in every sense.

Suddenly, clockwork timepieces throughout the hall rang, gonged and shrieked. I started and the lights flashed out of my control. Then I realized all the uproar simply heralded the arrival of midnight. I clamped down on the electric lights, drinking in as much of the power flowing to them as I could manage. Tiny tongues of light sparked in my hair, and my skin felt as if it was humming.

As the last mechanical clock chimed its twelfth note, both doors in front of me swung open. Edison, dressed in a formal black swallowtail coat, strode in with Liz Gorky gripping his arm. Her hair hung in ringlets, and the white gown she wore disguised most of the armature holding her, except the silver collar around her throat and steely plates that encased her arms. She stared off past my head. Edison glowered at me directly.

Cold gusts whipped through the air, and lamplights from the walks outside shone like distant constellations. Then Mr. Kern and Mr. Hays stepped in behind Edison, and the doors fell closed after them. I wondered if he hadn't been able to call Mudgett to him on short notice, or if he hadn't wanted to inform the other man that he might barter away his "wife".

"Miss Naugai," Edison called out. He smiled at me like a monkey baring its teeth. "I received your message, and I'm here in all good faith."

I didn't have to see clearly through the flickering light to recognize that Mr. Hays carried a pistol. Mr. Kern appeared to feel that a blackjack would be enough to deal with me. It had been when I was twelve, so why not now as well? Though from their almost bored expressions, I guessed they weren't either of them expecting much by way of a fight.

"Take the collar off Liz Gorky, and you can have what you're after." I laid my hand on the cabinet.

All of them but Liz looked intently at the cabinet. For just an instant, I imagined Edison might comply—it would have been so easy if he did. But Geula had been right. A man who double-dealt, stole and lied as much as Edison wouldn't be easily fooled. At least I had their attention focused on the cabinet.

That bought Geula a moment more to take her aim.

"I tell you what," Edison said. "I'll send Miss Liz here over to fetch that cabinet, and once she'd done, she's all yours."

The air around Liz Gorky's collar crackled wildly. She shoved her hands into the folds of her dress.

We hadn't planned on it being Liz that Edison sent across the distance to retrieve the cabinet, but I could hardly object. I had to hope Geula could still manage a clean shot. If not, we'd have to improvise.

"All right, send her over," I called.

Liz Gorky lurched forward, still clutching her dress. Earlier, she'd twirled quite gracefully, but then her collar hadn't been searing the air with electricity as it overpowered her will. As much as she must have hated putting her arms around Mudgett this afternoon, there was something in this walk towards me that she loathed much more. She fought against each step with all her will. She'd nearly reached the halfway point that Geula and I had agreed upon, when I noticed a dark shape buried in the folds of her dress.

I wanted to call out, but for Geula's sake I couldn't. Everything depended upon me releasing the brilliant flare of lights to blind Edison and his men and keep them from seeing Geula when she broke from her cover.

Liz stepped over the marker and started to raise her hand. At the same moment, I released all the power I'd held. The overhead lights flared, and white arcs of light gushed up from my hands to flash across the stage mirrors that we had so carefully positioned earlier.

I clenched my eyes closed against the blazing brilliance. Loud explosions of pistol shots burst through the hall. Bulbs overhead burst. A man shouted, and I heard someone fall heavily. Then something hit me hard in the shoulder, and I stumbled back a step and opened my eyes.

A few lights continued to flicker through the hall. Deep shadows enfolded the far walls.

Both Hays and Kern lay deathly still on the floor behind Edison. Out of the corner of my eye, to my left, I glimpsed Geula gripping her pistol and aiming for Edison.

"Liz shoots and I will kill you, old man," Geula snapped.

Liz stood in front of me, also holding a pistol and aiming it directly at my head.

"Well, well, well." Edison displayed another ugly grimace of his white teeth. "It would seem you've grown up into quite the conniving little heathen, Miss Naugai. And your pretty friend must be Annie Oakley."

Liz Gorky trembled, but her aim remained steady. The barrel of the gun pointing at my face seemed huge. I couldn't bring myself to look away from it, even to see what her first shot had done to me. My left shoulder ached, and the blood pouring down the inside of my dress sleeve felt scalding hot.

"Now, you, Annie," Edison addressed Geula. "I imagine that a white Christian woman like yourself would be most interested in aiding another white woman. You're the one who wants Miss Liz back with her daughter, aren't you?"

Geula gave him no reply, but I caught her gaze flick to me for an instant. Was she weighing the likelihood that she could shoot Edison before he had Liz blow my brains out?

"What are you suggesting?" Geula asked, and I realized that she had to be stalling—gaining me time to act.

I looked at Liz—at the collar tight around her throat. I didn't even register Edison's response to Geula. Instead, I focused on that seething band of silver.

Sweat soaked the back of my neck. My heart pounded so fast and hard, it seemed to make my vision jump and flicker like the dying overhead lights. I'd spent all of my strength in a brilliant flash, but I still turned my will against the silver collar wrapped around Liz's throat. It seared my senses as I pulled at the heat and power rolling off it in waves. Liz's hand dropped slightly. I took in another gasp of the electric air, swirling up from the collar; it tasted like smoke in my lungs. Liz's arm lowered a little more.

I thought I saw something like pleading in her face.

Both Edison and Geula must have noticed the shift in Liz at the same instant.

"Shoot her!" Edison shouted in a panic. I threw all my strength against the lock of the collar. And in that moment, Geula leapt for me. She wrapped me in a shielding embrace. I felt it as the bullet slammed into her back. She stumbled, and we fell together.

"Shoot her, God damn it!" Edison screamed.

Liz spun around, and I saw her collar lying on the ground at her feet.

She fired the pistol. Edison fell groaning and bleeding to the floor. I thought Liz shot him again at much closer range—he went silent after that. But I wasn't paying attention; all I cared about was Geula, lying so still against me. Tears filled my eyes, and I clutched her.

My hand brushed over the ragged hole torn through her coat and dress. My finger caught on the hard surface of the bullet. It fell from the steel armature under her clothes and dropped into my shaking palm.

"Next time we go with your plan and just run off together, I promise." Geula gave a cough and grinned at me.

I wrapped my arms around her and kissed her.

The carriage floor trembled with the steady vibration of wheels rolling over rails. My fingers slipped, but then I caught and unfastened the last button of Geula's dress. The heavy fabric slid to the floor, revealing her lovely bare skin and the lattice of armature that clung to her like an immense silver mehndi. She shifted, and the armature bent with her. It felt almost silken under my fingers as I stroked Geula's back.

She hadn't taken it off since it had stopped Liz Gorky's bullet from killing her, and we'd both grown used to the sight and feel of it.

The sleeping car swayed as our train curved along the track.

Geula kicked her dress up onto the empty bed on the far wall and settled down beside me on my bed.

"According to the conductor, these mountain passes grow very cold, so we may have to get inventive about keeping ourselves warm all through the night," Geula said.

"Don't worry, I happen to come from a long line of inventors."

Geula rolled her eyes at the joke but also grinned happily. We'd both had wine while in the dining car and were feeling warm and carefree. Geula kissed my bare shoulder. Then she paused a moment, frowning at the red, dimpled scar.

Miss Starr had been so delighted when we'd brought Liz Gorky back to her that she'd treated my injury. But the skin still felt tender and ached when I extended my arm too far. Given time, the scar would stretch and toughen up. Already it bothered me far less than it had a week ago.

"Does it hurt?" Geula asked.

"Not a bit," I assured her. I picked up the newspaper that the conductor had purchased for me at our last stop in Colorado. Very briefly, I took in Dr. Mudgett's baleful stare gazing up from the front page. He'd been condemned to hang two days ago—after the Chicago police had discovered the bodies of four murdered women in the basement of his hotel. It seemed that he'd been making a sideline selling their skeletons to medical students. A maid at his hotel, Elizabeth Gorky, had informed the police.

I felt relieved to know that Mudgett had seen justice, but also happy that it now had nothing to do with Geula or me. I tossed the papers off the bed and drew back the duvet. Geula slid in next to me.

We kept each other quite warm all the rest of the night.

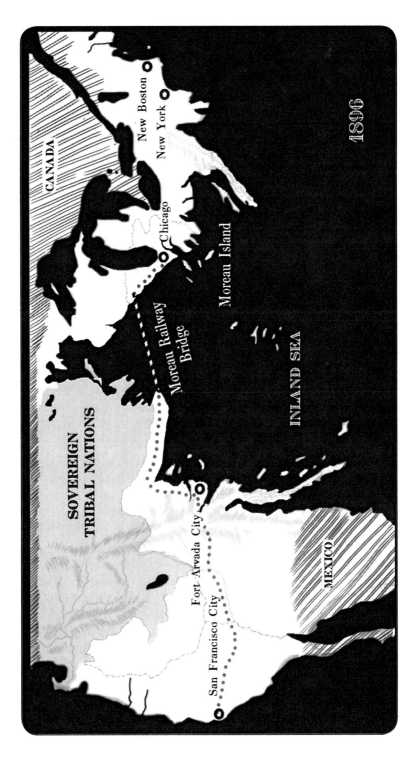

GET LUCKY

Prologue

Riverain County, Illinois 1896

Dalfon Elias drew his horse to a halt at the top of the wooded hill, considering the overgrown road ahead of him. As he dismounted, a little green pterosaur that had been occupied drinking from a muddy rut took flight into a flowering dogwood. Otherwise the road appeared largely abandoned, and the surrounding lush forest stood quiet in the early-morning sun. Dalfon crouched. The tracks that he followed weren't difficult to pick out; the two nails missing from the horse's hind shoe left a particularly distinct impression.

If Jo "Killer" Curtis had been smart he would've allowed the farrier to finish shoeing the animal before he shot the man and stole the mount. But like so many other outlaws that Dalfon had hunted and gunned down, Curtis was quick to draw but slow to think. Double-crossing the members of his own gang and raping a marshal's daughter hadn't won him any friends—certainly no one willing to risk their own skin to shelter him from angry gunmen and marshals toting rifles loaded with alchemic ammunition.

Curtis's decision to leave West America and flee cross the vast Inland Sea to the old states of East America could've been the only bright idea his rotten little brain ever produced. Curtis might just have disappeared into obscurity if only he'd managed the basic decency to pay his way instead of knifing the porter who'd requested to see his train ticket.

Committing murder on a Trans Americas Railcar had been an astoundingly stupid act. It had spooked regular passengers and ignited an outcry in the press over public safety on the rail lines. Worse it had roused the ire of railroad baron Louis Moreau.

Old man Moreau could afford to hire earth mages to open up mountains for him, and whole armies of gunmen to clear away any belligerent sauropods. The bounty his Trans Americas Railroad offered to have Curtis delivered—preferably dead—had been generous enough to decide Dalfon against retiring from the bloody work of hunting men. (In truth Dalfon had never felt so committed to peaceful employment that he'd sold his revolvers or ceased plying certain telegraph operators with coins and company to ensure that he knew exactly when a good bounty arose. But he'd thought about it…in passing.)

"Looks like the bridge washed out." Dalfon spoke softly to himself just to hear a human voice. It had been a long time hunting Curtis across a swampy wilderness. But he was close now. He knew it.

The pterosaur perched among the white dogwood flowers produced that little string of grunts that always made Dalfon think the creatures were chuckling over private jokes. Two more of the little beasts flapped into the branches. Dalfon's mare helped herself to a mouthful of wild grass, while Dalfon considered the remnants of a wooden bridge and the wide, dark river flowing between him and Curtis's hometown of Edgewater.

He didn't believe Curtis possessed the means or forethought to demolish a bridge, so more than likely this was a matter of bad luck rather than tactical maneuvering. (Triceratopses sometimes collapsed bridges under their immense girths.)

Still, Dalfon took a few moments to survey the town below for any sign of a possible ambush.

Nearly the entire population seemed to be out, dressed in their Sunday best despite the muddy streets. Streams of revelers strolled from the big, whitewashed church towards the town square. Out on the open green, veritable rainbows of bright ribbons fluttered alongside East American flags, and a number of women appeared to be in a desperate race to bury several big tables beneath a mountain of pies and cakes. Groups of men gathered around pens of livestock and paused beside gleaming displays of clockwork automatons. Between the clusters of bustling adults, children chased each other and paused now and again to gawk at the fat troops of roan leptoceratopses romping in wooden enclosures.

Four young men hauled a yellow banner into the air. *Give Thanks for Flood's End*, it proclaimed in brilliant blue letters. Despite himself Dalfon felt a whisper of nostalgia curl around him. In California, they celebrated Flood's End earlier in the year, but there, just like here, the day of thanksgiving brought out large crowds and reminded folks of how precious the common joys of their daily lives were.

The great flood that began back in '58 could have destroyed everything. For six years saltwater inundated lands around the world—states and then entire countries disappeared like Atlantis. Monstrous beasts emerged from the rifts where the water poured out. Tyrannosaurus devoured people, mosasaurs capsized supply ships and gigantic pterosaurs ripped airships from the skies. It had probably seemed like the apocalypse to most the people living back then. But the floods had been stopped, thanks to the courage of a Black trapper and a one-armed mage. (Dalfon had been honored to meet the old-timers a year prior while recovering from a dustup with the Younger gang in that "Paris of the Rockies", Fort Arvada). The dinosaurs remained, but folks now knew how to fight and domesticate them.

People across the divided Americas, and most of the wider world, still commemorated the end of the flood. In San Francisco the day was always celebrated with parades, fireworks and street carnivals. Dalfon's parents embraced the holiday with a rare, unrestrained revelry they didn't even display during Purim—probably because they were old enough to know firsthand what the world had been like before the long inundation and just how near they'd all come to death.

Dalfon felt a dull hunger gnaw at his empty stomach as he recollected the feasts he'd left behind when he'd abandoned his pious family—all those penny pies, corn cakes, fragrant, sweet oranges and cups of spiced cider. He'd taken all that abundance for granted, he supposed. But he'd also known, even at fifteen, that he wasn't ever going to become a rabbi like his father or wed any of the pretty girls his mother always pointed out to him. When he'd met a rugged older ranger, he'd joined the man and his band to ride the wilds of the Rocky Mountains. He didn't regret the decision, but he did sometimes miss the decency and comfort of the life he'd left behind.

"You hunching there in the middle of the road for a reason, mister?" A man's voice sounded from behind Dalfon, and at once he sprang up and spun to face the youth striding up behind him. The pterosaurs startled from their perches, but Dalfon's mare continued grazing.

"Some lookout you turn out to be," Dalfon muttered to her. Then he turned his attention and most winning smile on the ragged young man before him.

The fellow wasn't unattractive—in fact there was something charming about his dark unkempt hair and amused expression—but being soaked to the bone and spattered with mud from his patched shirt all the way down to his bare feet wouldn't have brought out the best in any man. His slim build and complexion made Dalfon think that at least one of his ancestors hailed from across the Sea of Sanji, but his dialect sounded a little French.

As far as Dalfon could see, the young man wasn't armed beyond the hunting knife that hung from his belt. But the fact that he carried a dead juvenile crocodile slung over his wiry shoulders certainly testified to a lethal capacity. The reptile's pale tongue lolled from its grimacing mouth, and it seemed to pin Dalfon with one warning yellow eye.

"Hail fellow and well met!" Dalfon tipped back his hat to the young man. "The name's Dalfon Elias."

"Luc Spivey. But everybody calls me Lucky."

"Ah. Well, Lucky, you've caught me in the midst of pondering the bridge," Dalfon informed him.

"You mean that what ain't there? Seems like either a whole lot to consider or nothing at all." Lucky smiled as he teased Dalfon, and the expression seemed to light him up.

"As the bard wrote 'what need the bridge much broader than the flood? The fairest grant is necessity,'" Dalfon stated, but he could see that Lucky didn't follow him. "Anything that would get me across the river would do, was what I was thinking."

"Oh. Heading into Edgewater?" Lucky's expression turned slightly assessing, and Dalfon could almost feel him trying to work out what possible connection Dalfon could possess to the literal backwater of Edgewater.

Dalfon considered spinning one of his yarns about a long-lost brother or newly discovered cousin, but today he didn't feel like lying. And there was something canny in the way Lucky studied him that warned Dalfon the young man wasn't a fool.

"It's been a while since I've taken in a Flood's End celebration," Dalfon admitted. "I've enjoyed plenty of bang-up parties—one that nearly burned an entire town down—but it's been a long, long time since I last strolled across a green, sipping tea and sampling pie and just feeling…decent. I think it'd be nice to go."

"It does look like it could be a good time." Lucky's dark gaze turned from Dalfon, and he stared down at the town as if studying the bright poster for a play he longed to see but couldn't afford the ticket to attend. Considering the young man's appearance, Dalfon supposed the good folks of Edgwater didn't treat him with much respect.

Civilized, genteel people—Dalfon's parents included—would likely take a wide route to avoid acknowledging much less speaking to a man who looked like Lucky. But Dalfon had traveled far and encountered all kinds, from slick, handsome devils to dirty, old saints. He'd been himself accused of being diabolical more than once. And with twenty dead men to his name, he didn't argue. But something about this young man struck him as more genuine than Dalfon had ever been. Simple, in the better meaning of the word.

"They charge a nickel to get in if you don't live in the city." Lucky shifted the weight of the crocodile slung across his shoulders. "But it don't cost anything to watch from up here when they'll set off the fireworks tonight."

"A nickel?" That wasn't cheap. A dime could buy a man a pound of sugar and a quarter would set him up with more dried beans than he'd want to eat.

Lucky nodded like a world-weary old prospector. His eyes remained focused on the festivities taking place across the water. Dalfon would have had to be blind not to see the longing there. Again he recalled the pampered luxury of his own boyhood when he'd sampled sweets and jumped on carousel rides just as he pleased every Flood's End. Since those days he'd figured out how easy his life had been and how much luxury he'd enjoyed, but until this moment it hadn't occurred to him that it was one thing to feel grateful; that was a sort of childish state, being provided for and only having to say "thank you". It was different to think of providing something to another soul—finding a way to pass on a little happiness, a little joy. Not that he had time for such things. There was Curtis to hunt down. But it might feel good, one day, to allow someone else to experience the pleasures he'd enjoyed.

A band began playing on the green. Big brassy notes trumpeted through the air. Dalfon frowned at the river.

"I don't suppose you know where there's another bridge?" Dalfon asked.

"Four miles or so south, on Swaim property," Lucky replied, but he shook his head. "If the Swaims see you, it could mean a whole mess of trouble. Or you might try the shallow spot about four miles east, but you'll get plenty wet. You'd be best off rafting across."

"If I had a raft, you mean? Maybe hidden in my coat pocket or slipped down my boot?"

"They do look like awful big boots." Lucky smiled. "Maybe you could hire a fellow to take you across."

Dalfon laughed at the obvious lead-up. Lucky's smile widened into a grin, assuring Dalfon that he did indeed possess a raft that could ferry Dalfon across the river. Depending on the route Curtis took, Dalfon might well arrive in Edgewater ahead of the killer.

"All right, how much will it cost me to hire you to convey my-poor-self and my steed across?" Dalfon asked.

"Poor-self! You ain't all that poor. Not with a jacket that nice and those slick-looking boots." Despite his words Lucky appeared suddenly uncertain. "I ain't trying to take advantage, I mean if you're bad off... Judge Swaim and his family are surely all over there at the Flood's End celebrations, so it would most likely be fine to cross their bridge now. I can show you the way."

"What about this." Dalfon found himself speaking before he considered the implications or possible complications that might arise. "I'll pay you two dollars. But not only do you have to ferry me across the river, you'll also show me around the town and give me a tour of the Flood's End celebration."

For a moment Lucky just stared at him like he knew the proposition was too good to be true but couldn't quite figure out the con.

"I could use a little human conversation after only having my horse to chat with for a fortnight," Dalfon added. "I'll want a bath and a meal first, of course. Then we'll see where the day takes us. Conversing with me wouldn't be too much of a hardship, would it?"

"No. I don't reckon it'd be any trouble at all." The mix of hope and shy admiration in Lucky's expression sent a rush of warmth through Dalfon's chest, filling him with the flattering sense of being mistaken for some sort of hero— someone better than a mere bounty hunter. That faint sense of dissatisfaction with his transient hell-raising life stirred again—just as it had been doing since he'd departed Fort Arvada. What was it that Voltaire had said?

Everyone goes astray, but the least imprudent are they who repent the soonest?

At the same time, virtue being its own reward didn't leave a man with much spending money. Certainly not enough to treat another fellow to a meal as well. So today wouldn't be the day for changing his ways.

"What do you say?" Dalfon asked.

"You got yourself a deal, Dalfon." Lucky thrust out his right hand and they shook. Lucky continued to hold Dalfon's hand for just a little too long. His fingers felt tough but also warm. That couldn't be gratitude alone that he recognized in Lucky's gaze.

They descended together towards the river where Lucky had hidden his raft away in the underbrush. Dalfon found himself telling Lucky absurd stories of his various adventures in the Rocky Mountains and delighting when he won a laugh from him.

The young man did have a certain charm, Dalfon thought. And just now the way the morning light fell on him, it lit his dark eyes like amber and exposed a brief, almost flirtatious curve to the set of his lips. Cleaned up and fed a decent meal, Lucky might prove to be quite fine. Maybe even a little distracting.

Dalfon knew it was neither wise nor practical to waste his afternoon—perhaps his evening too, if things went well —with this young man. But if there was any day to indulge himself, any day on which to relish all the joy and abundance that made a man glad to be alive, and to share that bounty with another soul, it was today.

Music rose from a far shore, and the scent of mulled cider drifted on the air. Dalfon stepped out onto the raft and led his mare after him. Overhead, a flock of pterosaurs chuckled at him and dived after fish hidden beneath the rolling waters.

My Lucky day, Dalfon thought to himself.

Well, perhaps it was.

Riverain County, Illinois 1899

Lucky studied the triceratops from the shadows of a black-gum tree. He'd come down here to fish, but folks up in Chicago would pay top price for triceratops horns and hide. And he'd smoke the meat and offer it to his sister Molly since he hadn't gifted her with anything for her dowry. Not that her husband's family expected a penny from him after he'd inherited all of Pa Spivey's debts. But he felt it might do his pride good to be able to provide a real fine spread for her baby's christening celebration next month.

His pride had been at a low ebb of late.

He slowly lifted his rifle.

The dinosaur bent its huge head to root up reeds and glasswort with the shortest of its three horns.

Lucky took careful aim on the triceratops's orange eye. His hand-me-down Sharps rifle only offered one shot. But with an animal as tough-skinned and heavy-boned as a triceratops, there was really only one shot to take. The trick was not to miss.

Lucky waited, allowing the triceratops to close the distance between them. The first night winds blew through ferns and cycads. A smell rolled off the triceratops, like old straw and goose shit; it hit Lucky in warm waves.

Standing a good ten feet tall, stretching back thirty feet and sporting horns as long as Lucky's arms, the dinosaur could probably have uprooted the trees Lucky sheltered beneath. But the triceratops moved through the reeds with surprising care, and a moment later Lucky realized why.

A dappled hatchling—hardly bigger than a piglet—trotted alongside her, snapping up the roots and tender new growth of reeds that its mother exposed.

The hatchling produced a string of little noises that sounded for all the world like the chirps of an eagle. Briefly, a turtle caught the hatchling's attention but a low note from its mother called it back. The hatchling trotted through the mud to butt its blunt little head against its mother's leg and snort as if it had won some great battle. Then it returned to feeding.

Lucky lowered his rifle.

It wasn't in him to orphan any creature, no matter how valuable of a haul he stood to gain. His trouble wasn't with killing an animal. He would have starved years ago if he hadn't been able to do that. But he couldn't bear to deprive a child of its mother. He knew that pain too well and couldn't stand to hear the inevitable plaintive cries that would fill the air. The sound resonated through him and left him feeling heartbroken for hours. It embarrassed him to be so tender, even after so many years. Probably no other man in Edgewater would have hesitated even an instant.

Then he remembered that quote Dalfon had told him once, "Everyone can master a grief but he that has it."

Thinking of his lost lover's acuity didn't help Lucky feel less melancholy but it did harden his resolve. There wasn't no use in moaning to himself over a thing he wasn't gonna do. He knew he wouldn't shoot the mother triceratops, so he'd better finish up his fishing and skedaddle before the beast noticed him and took offense.

He crouched down beside the dark water. His faint reflection peered back at him through a fringe of shaggy black hair, searching his tan face and the subtle curve of his eyes. Noting the details that set him so far apart from every other soul in Riverain County. At twenty he still looked slight as a seventeen-year-old, and he didn't hold out much hope of ever sporting the sort of thick beard that his adoptive father, Pa Spivey, had taken such pride in.

"You may be dark as a Mexican and stringy as a Chinaman, but with those big, flat feet of yours, I'd swear your pappy was a goddamn frog!" Pa Spivey had always cracked himself up with that joke, poking fun at the French accent Lucky had long since lost as well as Lucky's childhood claims that his wealthy *tante* would someday come and rescue him.

Lucky dipped his fingers into the sluggish current, breaking the reflection apart. He closed his eyes and his mind filled with the steady flow of water—here in the shallows he sensed it like a dull red pulse, as if all the rivers and sea were his own blood.

Lucky concentrated, drawing up strength from the water itself. A kind of electricity kindled in his chest—the hot, tickling sensation quickly grew disconcertingly strong. His nerves felt like violin strings being sawed at by a wild fiddler. After only a moment it seemed too much to endure. Lucky released the blazing current, and it rippled down into the body of a fat catfish below. The fish jerked once and rose to Lucky's hand, dead. Lucky took a moment to regain his composure, mopping the sweat from his brow and waiting for his pounding pulse to slow. Then he added the fish to the five others in his reed basket.

The triceratops neared the long stand of black-gum trees and snapped up a mouthful of the leaves from the sprawling branches. The smell of her caught in Lucky's throat.

Time to move on.

He swung his rifle across his back and hefted his fishing basket over his shoulder. He worked his way over the knotted roots of the black-gum trees, away from the triceratops and her hatchling. Best to take the long way around, he figured, even if it did mean trespassing onto Swaim land. It wasn't as if Judge Bernard Swaim ever ventured out to the marshes that edged his sprawling property, and neither of his two younger brothers hunted after dark. That would be too much time taken away from card tables and whiskey bottles.

Still, Lucky felt uneasy leaving behind the soft, damp footing of the marsh to slink up the dry hillocks where red maple and hickory grew. The soil turned brittle and unwelcoming against his bare feet. The faintest trace of burnt black powder drifted on the air. Since his wife Margot's death, Judge Swaim had turned particularly vicious towards trespassers. Gossip among the sharecroppers was that he and his brothers had shot a Pinkerton detective a month back and thrown his body to the crocodiles.

Lucky walked carefully, distinguishing the trunks of trees from rocky slopes more by memory than sight. If he'd been born one of those wind mages or an earth mage, he supposed he'd have been able to feel the world around him on the breezes or could have known the lay of the land at a touch. As it was, the distant, murky waters of the marshes bordering the Inland Sea did him little good at all. The sheer immensity and power of all that water became overwhelming far too quickly for Lucky to attempt much more than catching fish.

On the bright side, though, water mages like himself were so uncommon that the US Office of Theurgy and Magicum rarely dispatched theurgists to search for them. That had kept Lucky free from wearing a collar or being shipped off to some institute back east.

What they did to mages in those institutes, Lucky didn't know, but Ma Spivey had described no end of horrors after Lucky and his two sisters had tried to run off. (They'd all three been adopted by the Spiveys to work the marshy farm.) Pa Spivey had belted them black and blue, while Ma

Spivey had threatened to turn Lucky over to theurgists if any one of them disappeared again.

"They'll wire your brother up to the spell engine of a fancy airship and burn him like a fly in kerosene," she'd said. Both Molly and Effie had wept and clung to Lucky, and that had put an end to any of them attempting to escape the Spivey house.

Another time, when Lucky had failed to dowse fresh water for a new well, she'd threatened to turn him over to the local theurgist herself, commenting, "Not that a yellow heathen like you would be any use to Bernard Swaim. I reckon he'd just crack open your skull, stick in a knife and spread your brains on his toast like butter."

That image returned to Lucky in nightmares even after both his adoptive parents—Ma and Pa Spivey—had gone six feet under. That came of having too much imagination. That's what Effie always said.

Lucky scowled, thinking of his youngest sister. He'd done all he could to save Effie, he told himself, but he couldn't quite believe it.

He hated the way his thoughts returned to the past more and more. It was a world of regret and sorrow that he wanted to leave behind, and yet this year that he'd lived all alone, memories had become his only companions. Some days he felt as if ghosts walked beside him through the marshes.

A shape at the edge of his vision caught his attention. The shadows near the base of a big oak looked like a man hunching in wait. There was something excitingly familiar about the angular profile. Lucky squinted into the gloom. The wind shifted, rustling through low growing branches. The shape broke apart into a tangle of leaves, and Lucky laughed quietly at his own credulity.

Three years on and here he was, still looking for Dalfon Elias's profile in dark shadows. And the funny thing about that was that he wasn't even certain he actually remembered what Dalfon looked like so much as he remembered the feeling of him—his rough chapped lips, the heat of his naked flesh, and the musky taste of him. He'd been taller than any man Lucky had ever laid eyes on, rawboned and inclined to smile real sly, like a fairy-tale fox. Lucky supposed his memories of Dalfon were colored by his intense recollection of not knowing what to do in the dusty alley behind the saloon and then sinking to his knees, flushed with urgent desire and ninety-proof courage.

Maybe Dalfon had really been common as dirt. Just a gunslinger out to get all he could from other men. He'd only come to Edgewater to gun down Jo "Killer" Curtis. Once he'd collected the bounty, he'd lit out across the Inland Sea for his home in West America without so much as a goodbye. Never mind all those other promises he whispered to Lucky in the brief languid minutes after they'd fucked. No one had seen hide nor hair of Dalfon in three years and no one expected to either. Gunslingers didn't live long—not even sly, handsome liars like Dalfon.

No point in thinking on him for one more moment.

Lucky picked his way around a tangle of prickly holly and stopped.

Under the dogwood, another silhouette appeared. This time Lucky could almost swear he made out the silvery shape of a pistol in the man's hand. From behind came the deafening crack of a rifle. Lucky spun to see three mounted men clear a small rise. One held a lantern that illuminated all three of their faces.

The Swaim brothers: butter-blond, rich as cream and cruel as cats. They rode real, grain-fed horses, not the headless clockwork automatons that sharecroppers rented once a year to pull their plows.

"What in the hell do you think you're shooting at, Harry?" came Frank Swaim's acerbic voice. Obviously the man with the rifle up to his shoulder was flashy, young Harry Swaim. And the brother gripping the lightning-lantern looked like the eldest, Bernard—the judge and theurgist.

"I heard something in the bushes." Harry pulled at his horse's reins, wheeling the animal back towards his brothers. "If you think you could make a better shot in this gloom, go ahead!"

"I don't see the point of shooting at all," Frank replied. "If he's not dead already, he will be in an hour's time. I hit him straight on."

"Shut up." Bernard lifted his lantern and cranked the key at the base. The lightning captured within the lantern flared.

Lucky lunged into the cover of the dogwood as shafts of blinding light swept through the woods. A pheasant took flight. Harry fired again. The shot boomed like thunder. The pheasant plummeted to the leaf-strewn ground in pieces.

Lucky stared at the bloody hunk of wing lying only feet from him; his ears rang. Those weren't common hunting cartridges in Harry's rifle. More likely contraband spell-ammunition that rangers were rumored to use when they came up against big dinosaurs in the Rocky Mountains.

"Damn it, Harry! You're going to deafen me," Frank shouted.

"That's what you get for letting him overpower you and escape," Harry bellowed.

The lightning-lantern dimmed to a pale glow.

"I'm telling you, there is no point in finding him when I've already cast a crushing curse," Frank snapped. "He was dead the moment it hit him."

"He's covered a lot of ground for a corpse!" Harry yelled back.

"Both of you shut up." Bernard nudged his horse ahead a few steps. He glowered at the holly bramble where Lucky had crouched moments earlier. As he lifted his lamp, its glow fell across the bodies of two big catfish.

They must have fallen from Lucky's basket when he bolted. No way on earth anyone was going to think they got there on their own. Bernard drew his pistol and again nudged his horse towards Lucky. For an instant Lucky considered calling out, assuring the Swaims he wasn't the man they were hunting. But the Swaims weren't the sort of men who'd let him toddle on home with the knowledge they were using contraband ammunition and curses to murder a fellow. Lucky tensed to flee back towards the marsh.

Suddenly a shot rang out from behind Lucky. Bernard's lamp shattered, releasing a hiss of blue light and plunging the woods back into darkness. Bernard fired blind. Lucky felt branches near his head splinter.

Someone caught the back of Lucky's collar and jerked him ahead.

"Run," a man's low voice whispered against Lucky's ear.

Lucky didn't resist the pull of the hand at his back. He raced blindly towards the thick brush surrounding the marsh. Maple branches slapped his face and brambles caught at his coat and trousers. The man beside him gasped as they sprinted, but he kept apace. Then Lucky's foot caught on a root. He toppled only to have the man beside him catch him and yank him upright. He all but dragged Lucky through the tangle of brambles.

How the blazes this other fellow hadn't tripped even once, Lucky had no idea.

Another explosive boom rocked through the air, and one of the Swaims' horses let out a horrifying scream.

Frank shouted a string of obscenities, and Harry returned them. The shrill tones of their voices carried through the dense underbrush.

The brothers sounded a good distance back and a ways off to the north. Bernard's utter silence throughout the argument filled Lucky with dread. Chances were, he hadn't lit off in the same direction as his brothers. He could be right behind Lucky and this other fellow, even now.

Then, to Lucky's relief, his feet hit cool, wet soil. Mud squelched around his toes and spattered his ankles. A thrill of water rushed up from the soles of his feet. The man beside him whispered an oath and started to pull Lucky back up towards higher, dry ground.

"No," Lucky whispered. "They don't know the marsh like I do."

He felt the other man's hesitance but didn't let it slow him. Lucky wasn't going to linger with Bernard Swaim on his trail. He rushed ahead into the stands of tall reeds and bald cypress. He heard leaves rustling behind him and realized the other man followed. Once he'd worked deep into the cover of overhanging branches, Lucky paused.

Shafts of moonlight fell between tree branches and offered Lucky glimpses of the man behind him. This fellow looked broad in the shoulders. His pale hair hung in loose locks over his bowed head and obscured his face.

The man raised his head, and Lucky almost jumped at the sight of two large, perfectly round and milky-white eyes staring back at him. The man cocked his head, and the angle of the moonlight illuminated the strap of the man's goggles. Was he wearing moon lenses? Those cost a fortune, didn't they? But that explained how he'd navigated so well through the dense underbrush.

The man stepped back into the shadows, and a moment later touched Lucky's shoulder, assuring him of his presence in the darkness. Lucky leaned in to where he imagined the other man's head might be. He caught the strong scent of perspiration and iron. This close Lucky could smell the curse burning through the primordial scent of the man's blood and his heart sank.

Unless a theurgist broke it immediately, there was no respite from a curse. It touched living flesh and manifested instantly. That was why throwing a curse—even a half-assed one scratched onto a copper spoon—would get a soul hanged by the neck until dead. Amen. Only theurgists, with all their badges and licenses, were authorized to create, handle or transport curses.

Lucky reached out and touched the man's back. The leather of his coat felt hot and damp. Fever raged in him, and Lucky could feel shudders passing through his frame. He probably didn't have long left, certainly not enough time to get to help. Frank Swaim got it right; this tall stranger was already dead for all intents and purposes.

Lucky thought he should go, but the memory of Effie burning up in the throes of scarlet fever filled his mind. He didn't want to stand here and helplessly witness another person's death. This man had saved his life, and he deserved better than to be abandoned to the mercy of leeches and giant crocodiles like One-Eyed Pete.

Not too far behind them several branches snapped, and one of the Swaim brothers—Harry—swore at the bushes.

Lucky couldn't believe it. Despite the dark, the cotton-mouths and the crocodiles, the Swaims had followed them into the marsh. Behind them another string of profanities rose up along with the distinct scent of a furious skunk. A gunshot echoed through the marsh.

"God, Harry," Frank snapped. "You got the damn thing's brains all over my pant leg."

They truly wanted this man. Lucky wasn't certain he could stop them or if he ought to even risk the attempt.

"Go," the other man whispered.

Lucky didn't know why, but having the fellow suggest being abandoned made Lucky all the more set against deserting him.

"I know a place they won't go," Lucky whispered. "You think you can keep walking a ways more?"

Lucky heard the other man take in a strained breath. "Lead on, Macduff."

Lucky frowned, uncertain if the man's fever had made him think Lucky was this Macduff fellow or if he'd missed some joke. That made him uneasy, since Dalfon had always been quoting this and that text like he thought everyone in the world spent all their days reading books. And this man's voice sounded for all the world like his best old worst first love. But if it was Dalfon, wouldn't he have said? Or maybe he didn't even recognize him.

"Is your name…" Lucky lost his nerve and instead said, "I'm Lucky."

"You sure are—" The other man's voice caught, and he drew in several more quick, pained breaths.

Hell, this was no time to waste with talk.

Lucky strode quickly and quietly through the towering reeds into the deeper water. Slow-moving warm currents washed up around his thighs, and Lucky sensed fish scattering away from him. He heard his companion slogging behind him and felt the waves generated by the man ripple into his own body. He forced himself to focus on the land just ahead.

Lucky kept a quick pace, though every ten minutes or so he paused, allowing his struggling companion to catch up. Lucky didn't know how the man continued to move, hunched over and drawing in ragged breaths like that, but his will and stamina impressed Lucky plenty.

At last they reached the raft. It wasn't much more than driftwood and pine logs lashed together with reed ropes, but it floated like a cork and lay low enough to the water that none of the Swaims were likely to spot it moving through the overgrown marsh.

"Here," Lucky whispered to his companion. "Rest yourself against this cypress. And I'll have us out on the water in no time."

"I can't—" The man doubled over, clutching at his chest and pulling gasps of air through his clenched teeth.

Lucky didn't allow himself to think about his action—he'd have been too afraid to act if he'd paused even a moment. He placed his hand against the man's forehead. Damp locks brushed his fingers. The skin blazed hot as a soft-boiled egg.

Then he opened himself to the power of the cool waters rippling around his ankles. At once the illusion of a sluggish, lazy marsh shattered. Even here at just the edge of the Inland Sea, the sheer power of the ocean roared through Lucky. His ears rang and his entire body trembled. It felt like too much to bear—as if he was being swallowed by endless depths. His lungs filling with water. Brine pouring over his eyes and choking his throat.

But he fought against his rising panic. He could do this. He knew he could.

Three years ago he'd managed to control his fear long enough to relieve his sister Effie's suffering when she'd writhed in the grip of scarlet fever. For a few hours he'd even thought he'd saved her. But her fever had returned and he hadn't been strong enough to withstand an entire ocean flooding through his body a second time.

Now he imagined the waves calming, turning to ice.

Cold rushed up through Lucky, and he held it though it made his fingers ache.

He ran his hands over the man's brow and down the back of his head to the nape of his neck. With each motion he slowly released more and more of the frigid power pent up inside him. The skin beneath Lucky's fingers cooled, his shuddering limbs stilled. Again and again, Lucky caressed the other man and tried not to remember doing the same thing—uselessly—for Effie.

"Thank you," the fellow murmured. His voice sounded rough. "That's enough. We should get moving. You said you had your raft…I think."

Lucky felt his hands being pushed away, and he came back to his senses like he was breaking the surface of a frigid lake. He gulped in a breath of air, feeling groggy and embarrassed by the tremors that shook his hands.

"My raft…that's right." Lucky stepped away from him quick and scurried to his raft. He loosened the single mooring, then snatched up his pike pole. The other man moved much more slowly. He remained quiet as he knelt down on the raft. Lucky shoved it off the muddy bank and into the flowing water. They drifted. Lucky navigated the shallows between sandbars as the other man lay on his back gazing at the night sky through the opalescent lenses of his goggles. He didn't speak, and Lucky didn't know if he was sleeping or if he'd succumbed to the curse and lay dead.

Just now Lucky felt too spent to touch him and find out. He'd done as much as he dared for the other fellow. Now he allowed the powerful current of the Inland Sea to take them.

For nearly three hours Lucky and his silent companion drifted while the land gave way to a vast black sea and a river of stars filled the sky. Lucky set aside his pike pole, sat down to dangle his legs off the edge of the raft. Tentatively, he allowed his senses to skim the water. Waves rocked the raft and eddies grasped it, but Lucky carefully nudged and tugged his own path through.

Twice Lucky felt the sleek bodies of plesiosaurs pass beneath him. The huge creatures didn't frighten him nearly as much as the immense depths surrounding them. He'd already lost himself once tonight in all that vast water. And he didn't even know if it had been worth it. His companion lay still as a corpse.

At last Lucky caught sight of the black curve carved out from the midnight-blue sky.

Five miles from the muddy shores of Riverain County, Moreau Island rose from the Inland Sea's salty dark waters in three rolling hills. As they drifted closer, the weathered heads of submerged statues appeared to peep up over the waves, like stone mermaids observing their passage. If it had been light, Lucky could have peered down through the shallows and picked out the granite angels and bronze monuments that populated the sunken graveyard.

Before 1858 everything beneath the Inland Sea had been dry land: prairies, farms, plantations and vast estates like the one built by the Moreau family. Then earth mages had torn open an unnatural rift, and the waters of the ancient ocean had flooded through. Behind the floodwaters had come all those ancient creatures that had once existed only as rare fossils.

In the big eastern cities little changed, in fact, but in places like Moreau Island, the turbulent past was not buried deep. Wreckage from the first rush of floodwaters littered the shallows around the island with huge, opalescent boulders that Lucky liked to imagine as the remains of an ancient temple of the Illini people. They shone in the moonlight and piled up around the island like immense bones.

The raft's bottom scraped over a sandbar, and Lucky jumped off and tugged it onto the grassy shore. Two large crocodiles raised their heads to observe him but neither appeared interested enough to rouse themselves from their stretch of the banks. Lucky moored the raft to a weathered statue of a plump cherub. Then he slid his fishing basket from his shoulder, laid his rifle down and collapsed onto the wild grass.

At this his companion began to rise, which caused a burst of happiness through Lucky's chest.

"You're alive!" His voice sounded loud as an alarm bell in the darkness and woke a group of little pterosaurs who'd roosted in a tupelo tree above.

"That's me, coming back like the proverbial bad penny," the man mumbled.

Relieved, Lucky closed his eyes. Distantly he heard his companion stagger from the raft and make soft, awed noises about the moon-white rocks piled among the gravestones. "Do you know what these are?" The man sounded delirious, and Lucky wasn't certain if the question was rhetorical or not. Just now he felt too exhausted to care. His stomach grumbled, but it didn't keep him from dropping into sleep.

When he woke it was to the smell of wood smoke and frying fish. Tiny orange sparks drifted up from a fire and burned out against the night sky. Lucky rolled over.

His companion had obviously regained enough strength to build a fire in the lee of two nearby gravestones. The man leaned up against the taller of the stones, with his goggles shoved up on his head to hold his hair back from his face. He'd helped himself to the catfish from Lucky's basket, spitting them on a stake and setting them over the flames to cook.

With the light playing over his features and shining across the silver streaks in his blond hair, it became horribly obvious to Lucky that this man didn't just sound a lot like Dalfon Elias. There was no mistaking the white scar that cut through his left eyebrow like the tail of a comet or the hard lines around his mouth and brow that made him appear far older than his twenty-five years. That was him, in the flesh and looking rough—the front of his coat tattered and bloody, a bruise darkening his cheekbone. And of course, the smug bastard just gazed up at the stars as if he hadn't a care in the damn world.

Lucky wanted to knock that easy smile right off of his face. At the same time some part of him still longed to wrap his arms around Dalfon and tell him how much he'd missed him. If that didn't make Lucky a fool, he didn't know what did. Dalfon had promised a fine life for the two of them together in the west; then he'd left Lucky waiting at the Edgewater Coach Station.

And Lucky had waited.

He'd stood for hours on the muddy street, anticipating that wonderful moment when at last Dalfon might appear. He'd watched the sun rise as high as his hopes and then sink down into the dirt.

Now Dalfon had the gall to show up and trot alongside him like he didn't know Lucky from Adam. Despite all that, Lucky's heart pounded in his chest and as much joy as rage roused in him at the sight of the man. Lucky wasn't certain if he felt more angry at Dalfon or himself for harboring so much longing.

"You gonna lay there staring all night or come over and eat something?" Dalfon called.

Lucky glared at him thinking that, yes, he was more mad at Dalfon then he was at himself. Maybe madder than at anyone else he'd ever met.

"Seems a waste not to eat fish while they're fresh," Dalfon added. "If you aren't hungry, I don't suppose you'd mind me helping myself."

That was the last straw. Lucky jumped to his feet and stomped to the fireside. "Those are my fish."

"Don't think I said otherwise, did I?" Dalfon replied with a smile.

The man was infuriating! But Lucky couldn't think of a rejoinder that didn't make him sound like a foul-mouthed brat.

Lucky crouched down and glowered at the bright orange flames. The catfish smelled good. Dalfon must have gutted them and filled their bodies with tarragon, which grew wild all across the island. He'd probably been the one who'd strewn fern and licorice fronds across the large, flat rock near the fire. Lucky had taught him that trick during the six months Dalfon had tarried in Riverain County.

Dalfon lifted the spit from the fire and, using the flat of his hunting knife, slid all three big catfish onto the frond-covered rock in front of Lucky.

"Can't offer much in the way of silverware, but you're welcome to my knife, if you'd like." Dalfon turned the hilt to Lucky.

"I got my own." Lucky pulled his fishing knife from the sheath at his belt.

Dalfon nodded. He wiped the long blade of his hunting knife across the grass, cleaning it, and slipped it back into its sheath. Lucky stared at the blackened bodies of the catfish. Then he stole a glance up at Dalfon. The front of his coat looked nearly as scorched as the fish.

"Ain't you still dying of that curse Frank Swaim hit you with?" Not that Lucky wanted to give Dalfon the satisfaction of thinking he cared. He was simply curious and making conversation.

"I'm touched by your concern."

"Don't be." Lucky cut through charred fish skin to the steaming flesh beneath. "I just want to put my claim on your hunting knife and revolver once you drop."

"Well, I'm going to have to disappoint you, for today at least." Dalfon tossed a piece of pale driftwood into the fire.

Lucky ate a couple mouthfuls, waiting for Dalfon to explain himself, but instead the man leaned back against a gravestone and returned to gazing up at the stars. Lucky finished off one entire catfish and made a couple stabs at the second, but he didn't possess the appetite to choke down the rest. He entertained a petty urge to shove the remains into the fire and deprive Dalfon of any, but couldn't bring himself to do it. Dalfon might have hurt him, but he'd only be disappointing himself if he let heartbreak turn him so spiteful and mean.

"You want this?" Lucky gestured at the remaining fish.

"You had your fill already?" Dalfon asked.

Lucky nodded and shifted over as Dalfon moved closer to eat. Even using a hunting knife, he was real neat. When he reached inside his coat and fished out a kerchief to wipe his mouth, Lucky almost laughed. But he found himself gazing at Dalfon's expressive mouth and strong hands. The first time Dalfon had kissed him, it nearly bowled Lucky over. No one had ever kissed him so passionately—hell, no *man* had ever kissed him at all before then. Lucky could feel the heat rising in his face as he recollected the shocking sensations.

Dalfon glanced up, and for an instant his gaze held Lucky's. He smiled, all assured and knowing, and Lucky looked quickly away. He glowered at a big clump of wild grass and the velvety moss next to it. His eyes lit on the sprawled legs of a spider as big as his hand. Lucky nearly jumped, but something in the perfect stillness of the huge bug stopped him.

What he'd first taken for legs, he realized, were metallic spines splaying out from a cracked gray sphere. Black symbols of spells etched the surface of the silvery legs. The gray orb at the center flaked away like ash as a slight breeze rolled over the hill.

Lucky turned back to Dalfon. "Is that the curse Frank Swaim cast on you?"

"It is." Dalfon took a mouthful of fish and frowned at the curse. "A nasty thing, and not cheap. The Swaims did me that much honor, I suppose. That's made from electrum—silver-and-gold alloy. Quite a pretty sight when it was first made, I imagine. Before I burned it out, there was an orb of solid alchemic stone big as a plum at the heart of it."

Lucky didn't know much about spells or alchemic stone. They and holy books were the tools of learned theurgists, not mages. But he did know alchemic stone powered the mechanical spells theurgists crafted, and pure stone was more valuable than diamonds.

He extended his hand to touch the ash, wondering if there might still be a pure shard of the precious mineral within. Dalfon caught his arm.

"Don't," Dalfon said. "I burned out the curse's source of power, but the spells are still intact."

"But it's dead—"

"Not dead, just sleeping. Someone like you could bring it back to life with the touch of your finger." Dalfon frowned at the curse. With him leaning so close, Lucky smelled the soot and blood staining Dalfon's coat. "Back in the bad old days of castles and knights, theurgists used to wire mages up to their spells and burn through them instead of alchemic stone. Even now most spells come alive when they're touched by a mage. And a mage as handsome as you, well it might just fall in—"

"Who said I was a mage?" Lucky demanded.

"Nobody." Dalfon gave a laugh as he released Lucky's arm. "I'm just not a complete idiot."

"So you say." The instant Lucky got the words out, he regretted them. Not because they'd impact Dalfon one bit, but it was a childish response and so obviously untrue that it embarrassed him.

Dalfon didn't even dignify it with a rejoinder.

Lucky folded his arms over his crossed legs and glared into the fire. Gold flames devoured lengths of white driftwood like a funeral pyre consuming bare bones.

Hardly a foot away, Dalfon ate quietly and then cleared away the fern fronds and fish bones. A moment later, he returned to the fire and settled beside Lucky. Lucky felt intensely aware of Dalfon despite the fact he refused to look at him. Somewhere off in the wooded hills, a whip-poor-will sang out. It struck Lucky as somehow meaningful that the bird's courting song sounded so sad and lonely.

"You know what that is right up there?" Dalfon pointed to the twinkling light above the horizon.

"The evening star," Lucky replied.

"That's one name. It's also called Venus, after a goddess of love." Dalfon offered the bright star a fond smile, like they were old friends. "But I call it my Lucky star. Whenever I look at it, I think of you."

"Sure you do." Lucky rolled his eyes. "Every single night you just look up there and think of me, even when you're fucking sheep herders and miners."

Dalfon had the audacity to cast Lucky a reproachful glance, like Lucky owed it to him to lap up his sweet-talk after three years. Dalfon tossed a green twig into the fire, and the smell of searing sap filled the column of smoke. A few moments passed, and Dalfon's silence began to annoy Lucky, like a scab he knew he shouldn't scratch but couldn't keep from picking at.

"So what did you do to piss off the Swaims?" Lucky asked at last.

Dalfon rubbed the tattered front of his coat, then threw another twig onto the fire. It snapped and popped in the flames.

"I don't rightly know," Dalfon said. "Though I have a strong suspicion."

"How can you not know how you made someone want to murder you?"

"Well, I seem to have a talent for it." Dalfon glanced to him and held his gaze. "Because I don't know what I did to infuriate you aside from coming back like I promised I would."

"Promised? Like you promised?" Lucky actually sputtered in outrage. Then he jabbed Dalfon in the chest. "What you promised was to meet me at the Edgewater Station, first thing in the morning! And I went and I waited. I waited for you all damn day! You never bothered to show!"

Dalfon stared at Lucky, looking strangely surprised and confused. Then his expression turned bleak, and he shook his head.

"You never got my letter." He said it softly, almost like he was talking to himself. "Effie never gave you my letter…"

"You didn't write me no letter—" Lucky cut himself short as he looked into Dalfon's face. He read an absolute and mournful certainty—the kind of realization that seized a man like an undertow and drowned his hope in an instant. Lucky had worn that expression himself after he'd broken the seal on that beautiful golden envelope, expecting to find a precious missive from his mother. Hoping that he could at last go home to her.

Instead he'd read prim condolences from a nurse who'd tended her in the tuberculosis sanatorium. Lucky understood that stricken expression down to the very marrow of his bones.

All the righteous anger brewing in his gut went cold.

"I never got no letter," Lucky said quietly. "Effie came

down with scarlet fever. She was burning up when I got home, and she hardly recognized me and Molly. Five days later she was gone." The raw sorrow and feeling of failure washed over Lucky as he remembered holding his emaciated sister's body in his arms and weeping. Lucky's eyes stung but he pulled himself together. He wasn't about to break down crying in front of Dalfon.

"Lucky, I'm so sorry." For a rare moment Dalfon seemed truly at a loss. "She was such a bright little thing. I can hardly imagine her..."

"She hung on to me so hard. Maybe she was trying to tell me..." Lucky cleared his throat and wiped at his eyes. He couldn't keep thinking about it. "After that, Pa Spivey set fire to everything of hers to keep the fever from catching."

"So, all this time you thought..." Dalfon trailed off.

Lucky couldn't hold his gaze.

He'd thought the worst. It hadn't even crossed his mind that something might have happened to Dalfon or that messages between them might have gotten lost. He'd made fun of the lovers in Dalfon's story of Romeo and Juliet for such foolishness, and still he hadn't given it a moment's consideration. He'd just been so sure that a man like Dalfon couldn't really love a fellow like himself.

Dalfon had brought so much joy into his life. But somehow Lucky hadn't been able to believe it could last. And when he'd thought Dalfon had left him, he hadn't felt surprised but almost resigned to the heartbreak. He hadn't questioned it or looked for Dalfon, because what would have been the point? He'd only have roused his own hopes to have them inevitably crushed again.

He was always abandoned. That had been the only certainty in all his chaotic life.

Lucky scowled down at the dirty nails of his hands, a terrible guilt and frustration churning through him, twisting the grief of his sister's death with his heartbreak over

Dalfon. He hadn't been able to defeat the raging fire of her fever, and he'd wasted three years silently cursing Dalfon and hating himself for not being able to forget him. He wanted to howl at the sky, but what good would that do?

"What'd it say?" Lucky asked. "The letter, I mean?"

"I might have lifted a line from Mr. Whitman. 'I ate with you and slept with you, your body has become not yours only nor left my body mine only.'" Dalfon lay back in the wild grass. He gazed up at the stars like he'd done on the raft. "Of course I promised that I'd change my rambling, no-good ways if you would just trust me. Give me two weeks to recover and join me in Chicago at the Castle Hotel. I enclosed a twenty-dollar bill."

"Wait, what did you have to recover from?" Lucky thought of the scarlet fever that had taken Effie. It horrified him to think of Dalfon all alone burning up like that, waiting for him.

Dalfon looked a little self-conscious but then smiled.

"I don't much like admitting it, but I'd taken something of a beating. Though you can bet the bellhop at the Castle was pretty impressed when I claimed I'd come by my bruises and split lip wrestling a tornado out of my way."

Lucky felt sure Dalfon was right, but that still didn't answer his question. He couldn't have been roughed up by Killer Curtis. The outlaw hadn't even pulled his gun when Dalfon had shot him down. Everyone said so.

"Did Curtis's brother come after you?" Lucky asked.

"Jimmy? No. He took off the minute Curtis hit the ground, and as far as I know he's still running." Dalfon sighed. "It was Pa Spivey and two of his friends. They came after me behind the saloon."

"Pa?" Lucky couldn't imagine Pa Spivey had taken offense at seeing a murderer like Killer Curtis meet his end. "Why?"

"Why do you think? You followed me around like a second shadow and were always giving me those hungry looks—"

"I didn't!" Lucky felt a guilty flush spread across his face. Sure, he'd trailed Dalfon, but he hadn't been as obvious about it as a lot of the girls or even Mrs. Margot Swaim.

"Yes, you did." Oddly, Dalfon laughed. Then he rolled up onto one elbow. "And so did I, all right! I was just as caught up as you were. Probably more so, because what the hell was I doing hanging around a dismal swamp town for months for except to be with you?

"So of course Pa Spivey got suspicious and started spying on us. When he jumped me, I knew the only choices I had were either to shoot him dead or get the hell out of town. I wasn't about to murder your pa—adopted or not. So...so, I left you. But I gave Effie a letter for you first. I swear I did."

Lucky nodded. Three years he'd been so angry and hurt, and all that time Dalfon had probably been feeling the same for being stood up at the hotel.

"What did you do when I didn't show in Chicago?" Lucky asked.

"I waited. Kept hoping you'd come." Dalfon shook his head. "After three weeks I couldn't afford to stay any longer. I figured you feared that we wouldn't be able to make lives for ourselves. That I wasn't a reliable man to risk so much on. Then I reckoned that you were probably right."

"But I didn't think anything of the sort," Lucky protested.

"Well, I realize that now." Dalfon laughed, then went on. "But at the time it made me reconsider the life I'd been leading. Living by my gun, constantly on the road hunting bounties for anyone who could pay. I wasn't much better than the outlaws I took down, was I?"

Lucky thought he had been. Better than a lot of the respectable men of Edgewater too. Certainly better than the

Swaim brothers. But saying as much would just make him sound foolish, he supposed.

"What'd you decide then?" Lucky asked.

"I realized that I had to actually make good on those changes I'd promised to make in the letter you never read." Dalfon gave another dry laugh, then reached into his coat and drew out a star-shaped badge. "I had to find a lawful way to provide for and protect us both. Then come back and give you a better offer."

Dalfon handed the silver badge to Lucky. It felt heavy and warm in his hand. A halo of square letters surrounded the star and proclaimed the bearer to be a detective in the Pinkerton Agency as well as a licensed theurgist.

"I worked my ass off for that," Dalfon said. "Hunted train robbers across both halves of America, rescued a foreign prince from his abductor—which it turned out was his secret wife. That's not even counting all the studying I had to do for the theurgy test."

"Don't you have to be a Bible-thumper to get a license?" Lucky hadn't pegged Dalfon for the religious type, despite him being the son of a rabbi.

"Naw. There's plenty of holy books that aren't Christian and still contain powerful spells. In fact, being familiar with Hebrew gave me a leg up on most the other students when it came to the Tanakh."

Lucky nodded warily. The idea that Dalfon had become a theurgist filled him with misgivings. Dalfon knew he was a mage now, for certain.

"You ain't gonna put a collar on me, are you?" Lucky asked at last.

"What? Of course not. And neither is anyone else, for that matter. No one has the right to collar free mages unless they've committed a felony. The Mage Liberty Act passed five years ago." Dalfon just shook his head. "I suppose it didn't serve Pa Spivey to tell you that, did it? Not when he had you under his thumb, dowsing fresh-water wells for him."

"No. I guess it didn't," Lucky admitted. "Though I wouldn't have bet on him keeping abreast of the law himself. He never troubled himself too much with those sorts of details. Not once he'd convinced himself that his newest scheme was going to win him a fortune."

"There were a lot of schemes?" Dalfon asked.

"Oh, yes. And we never knew where he'd get his next bad idea," Lucky said. "Seemed like the more far-fetched or ill-advised, the better he liked a plan. Before he passed, he read a newspaper story about that millionaire, Louis Moreau, dying. Just like that, he dreamed up a harebrained scheme to lay claim to the Swaims' western property as well as this here island. It didn't matter to him that everyone for miles around knew he wasn't any long-lost grandson of Mr. Moreau's. He kept swearing that he could prove he had a closer relation to the Moreau family than the Swaims did. Nothing came of any of it. Pa Spivey died as poor as ever…"

Dalfon cocked his head and seemed to consider Lucky in an almost concerned manner. Lucky could all but see the wheels turning in his mind, but Dalfon just said, "Can't say I liked him, but I'm sorry for your loss."

Lucky shrugged. It wasn't that he hadn't felt a sort of sadness at Pa Spivey's passing, but it hadn't neared the anguish he'd suffered learning of his mother's death or the hell he'd felt when he'd fought so hard and still lost Effie. Pa Spivey's demise had only seemed sorrowful because neither he nor Molly had worked up two tears between them at the man's graveside.

"Thank you, but he wasn't…" Lucky tried to think of the words. "I suppose that if I hadn't been able to remember my real parents, it would have been easier to care about him."

Dalfon reached out and put his arm around Lucky. The weight and warmth of him felt comforting. Leaning up against Dalfon came as a relief, like drawing in a breath after too long underwater. He hadn't wanted to be mad at Dalfon before and was relieved for a reason to give it up.

"You never did tell me about your life before you were shipped out here," Dalfon commented.

"You didn't say much yourself either," Lucky replied, but with a smile. He knew Dalfon had left his family home when he was only fifteen and that he'd run with very rough company up in the wilds of the Rocky Mountains. But Dalfon always embroidered his stories with so many jokes and tall tales that Lucky wasn't quite certain of how much to believe—though he'd found it all charming.

"I poured out my whole sad story of growing up as the spoiled son of a California rabbi and then skipping town to ride with a troop of degenerate rangers." Dalfon's grin undermined his attempt to appear affronted. "Probably bored you too much for you to remember it."

"I remember everything you ever told me. I just didn't believe it all. It's hard to imagine you out riding the range with a yarmulke pinned under your cowboy hat and two sets of dishes in your saddlebags."

Dalfon laughed at that. "Well, perhaps I led you to believe I was a hair more devout than I might have been, but I promise I told you most everything just as it happened… more or less."

"You actually waited out a snowstorm playing checkers in a cave with a grizzly bear? And you rode a triceratops into Fort Arvada with two bandits tied across its back?"

"The bear was hibernating, and the triceratops had been raised and trained by a mountain mage, but yes, it's all true." Dalfon placed his hand over his heart. "I swear."

Lucky almost wished it wasn't, because compared to Dalfon, what had he done with his life? Dowsed about a hundred fresh-water wells to earn the Spiveys money, fished the salt marshes and tangled once with One-Eyed Pete. For the most part, he'd fought his own urge to run off on grand adventures, for fear of the price his sisters would pay for his freedom. By the time he'd been free of Ma and Pa Spivey, he'd felt too broken by loss and failure to aspire to anything but surviving in the same rut his life had already become.

Belatedly he realized how perverse he'd turned out, taking comfort in the reliable emptiness of his desolate existence.

"I ain't rightly done nothing compared to you. Anything I tell you will be dull as dirt."

"There isn't a thing about you that I find dull." Dalfon shook his head. "You just can't see how fascinating you are because you're used to being you. You're like that star up there. He's always flying in the glow of his own brilliance, so he can't even suspect how barren and black the rest of the sky is."

Lucky felt a flush rise through him. "You sure know how to butter a fellow up, don't you?"

"I know how and where to apply sweet oil to make things slide in nice, if that's what you mean." Dalfon grinned, and Lucky felt his face heat with embarrassment and excitement. He was quite aware of how skillfully Dalfon could administer oil and a massage before he eased himself inside a fellow's body.

"I don't suppose you got any of that sweet oil on you now?" Lucky asked in a whisper, despite there being no one but saltwater crocodiles to overhear him.

"Sadly, I was not quite so presumptuous as to bring it to confront the Swaim brothers. But I think we might be able to entertain ourselves in any case, don't you?"

Anticipation thrilled through Lucky as he quickly worked open the buttons of Dalfon's vest and shirt. But he pushed the fabric aside slowly, like he was spreading the curtains of a theater stage. Firelight glinted across Dalfon's blond chest hair and shone bright across the tender scar tissue and dark bruises at the center of his chest.

"Those from the curse?" Lucky asked.

"That curse wasn't quite a match for my Magen David." Dalfon lifted his hand to touch the silver star pendant that lay in the hollow of his collarbones. Tiny lines of foreign script decorated each of the six points, but only a charred crumb sat at the center of the star. "I used this to drain their curse and heal the worst of my hurt. It's burnt out now, but it did the trick."

"Those bruises and that scar..." Lucky could hardly look at them without thinking of how very close they lay to Dalfon's heart. "Don't they hurt?"

"Nah. You put all that out of my mind." Dalfon smiled at him and ran his fingers along Lucky's jaw and caressed the tender curve of the nape of his neck.

Then he bent and kissed Lucky so deep and sure that his lips and tongue seemed to send a thrill all through Lucky's body to the core of him.

Dalfon was so at ease with this, so experienced. Lucky felt like a greenhorn. But then he lifted his face and met Dalfon's desperate gaze. He felt Dalfon's heart hammering beneath his fingers. Knowing all the yearning was just for him sparked Lucky's confidence and made him feel entrancing.

When Lucky bowed his head and worked his tongue across Dalfon's nipples, Dalfon made soft, pleased sounds. But his entire body tensed when Lucky knelt lower. Dalfon couldn't seem to keep himself from helping Lucky remove his gun belt and work open the buttons of his denim trousers.

Dalfon's hot, flushed prick jutted up against Lucky's fingers. For a moment Lucky indulged himself in the sight.

Dalfon was the only man he'd ever known who was circumcised—it lent him a sleekness, a kind of defiance. Where other fellow's pricks hung sheltered and hooded, as if ashamed, Dalfon stood bare and brazen. Lucky kissed him once lightly for that.

A quiet gasp escaped Dalfon. He curled his hands through Lucky's hair and traced the back of his neck with restrained, gentle strokes. His touch grew more desperate as Lucky sank down taking Dalfon's taut shaft deep. Lucky savored how every lash of his tongue and vibration of his throat shot through Dalfon's body. At last he won a desperate cry and an exuberant splash of ecstasy.

Dalfon sagged there for a moment like he'd met his match. He lifted his head to gaze at Lucky through the loose curls of his sweat-damp hair.

"You look so pleased with yourself. So damn beautiful." Dalfon kissed Lucky's swollen lips. He pushed Lucky back onto the ground. "Let's see if you can take as good as you give."

Lucky did his best to last, but he was already hard and ready for release. And Dalfon surely knew his way around a fellow. Within a minute the pleasure grew too powerful for Lucky to contain. He came like a geyser. Dalfon grinned up at him and wiped his mouth as if he'd had himself a slice of the best cake in the bakery. He lay down beside Lucky and closed his eyes, still grinning.

They dozed briefly and woke together. Dalfon pulled his discarded coat over them. They gazed up at the night sky. The big yellow moon stared back down at them. The night air gusted off the Inland Sea, but the glowing embers of the fire continued to radiate warmth. Lucky felt almost afraid to admit how happy he was, as if the moment he actually gave himself up to bliss it would all fall apart.

"How did a treasure like you end up in a backwater like this?" Dalfon wondered aloud.

"Just lucky, I guess," Lucky replied, amused to make a pun of his own name before Dalfon could.

"I'm asking in all seriousness. How did you end up here?" Dalfon asked.

No one had concerned themselves with his history before. Generally, people simply nodded in a sad understanding way when Pa Spivey admitted they'd adopted Lucky because it had been cheaper to adopt as a son than to hire him on as paid labor. If he possessed a history before he'd come to the folks of Edgewater, they didn't care to hear about it.

"I lived in New York originally. *Ma mère* stitched leather gloves and *mon père* drove cabs for the Hansom Cab Company, at least until he went back west. Then it was just *ma mère* and me, though he sent letters. He and his brother were going to make their fortunes in the gold fields."

Lucky could still remember his mother holding one of his father's letters out to him so that he could smell the fragrant ponderosa pines saturating the pages. He didn't want to recollect beyond that, but Dalfon waited, watching him curiously.

"Just after my tenth birthday *ma mère* contracted consumption—tuberculosis, the doctor called it. We weren't wealthy. *Ma mère* had been when she was a little girl, but after she wed *mon père* most of her family wouldn't even speak to her. She eloped from these parts to New York before I was even born so I never met any of them. But when she fell ill, one of her aunts arranged for her to be treated in the sanatorium at Saranac Lake. *Ma mère* entrusted my care to a cousin of hers here in Riverain County." Lucky absently tugged up a blade of grass and folded it between his fingers. "Before the flood, *ma mère's* people owned property all across the county and some of them stayed, I suppose. Anyway, the woman never came for me."

Lucky hadn't cast his mind back to those early days for so long that now the memories seemed strangely dull and faded, like oil paper when it yellowed, and all he could see through it were the faintest shadows. He wasn't certain how long he must have stood, anticipating the arrival of his mother's cousin outside the coach station. Had it been two days or three? He'd been lightheaded from thirst and hunger by the end, he remembered that. And he'd tried not to cry but had failed when night fell and only stray dogs seemed to wander the streets.

Now he wondered if that hadn't somehow added to his sense of inevitability when he'd feared himself abandoned by Dalfon and once again waited under that creaking wooden sign and watching people come and go as the sun sank.

"Something wrong?" Dalfon's question brought him back to the moment.

"No. Not now." Lucky pressed his body closer to the heat of Dalfon's naked skin. "Eventually someone noticed that I was standing around the stagecoach station, and Mrs. Margot Swaim took it on herself to arrange for the Spiveys to adopt me."

Dalfon nodded like he'd guessed as much.

"And your father?" Dalfon asked.

"El Chino." Lucky supplied the nickname that his father had so proudly used and often teased his mother for mis-pronouncing with her strong French accent. "He was born out west and headed back there to win us a fortune from the gold fields. I don't know what happened to him. Maybe he's still out there panning for gold and thinking that *ma mère* and I are waiting for him in our apartment above the Gauntier Boutique."

"You remember either of your parents' legal names?" Dalfon asked the question casually enough, but that didn't make it any less odd.

"Why'd you ask that, of all things?" Lucky crushed the grass blade between his fingers. A sweet green scent drifted from it.

"Well, you have to have a name other than Spivey," Dalfon responded, though it didn't answer Lucky's question. "Is it so strange to wonder what it was?"

"Not exactly." Lucky studied Dalfon's face. He looked sly, but that was hardly new. "It's strange that you would ask about it when Pa Spivey was digging after the same information from my birth certificate just a few months before he passed."

"Maybe not so strange as you'd think. Did he tell you that he hired a detective from the Pinkertons to look into your mother's background, to see if she—or you—were entitled to property and money now that Louis Moreau has dropped dead?"

Lucky studied Dalfon in the embers' glow.

"Are you telling me that Pa Spivey hired *you* to find out about *ma mère*'s family?"

"Not me, no. Can you imagine how awkward that would have been?" Dalfon replied, with just a flash of a smile. "Jerry Buck took the case. I was working out in the Nevada territory at the time. But Buck knew that I'd been down here, and so he contacted me. I put him onto Margot Swaim, since I remembered old man Brewer once mentioning that Margot was distantly related to the Moreau family. I also asked Buck to look in on you for me when he made the trip down here."

Uneasiness passed over Lucky. Pa Spivey and Margot Swaim were both dead, and there had been those rumors about the Swaim brothers killing a Pinkerton. Had Pa Spivey actually convinced a bunch of folks that he was sitting on the heir to the Moreau lands—convinced the Swaims so well they committed murder to protect their claims? Lucky couldn't see how something like that could be possible. He didn't exactly resemble any of the old families from hereabouts.

"But my family name is Song-Garcia, not Moreau," Lucky objected. "Says so on my birth certificate."

"Yes, but digging back to your parents' marriage license clears the matter up. Moreau was your mother's maiden name before she eloped with your father." Dalfon rolled up on to his elbows, looking far more awake then Lucky felt. "It's all in Buck's notes. Including the fact that Louis Moreau had a change of heart on his deathbed and altered his will to favor his estranged daughter and her child over his deceased wife's relations—the Swaims."

"The Swaims?" Lucky asked. "That's not a coincidence, is it?"

"It's not. Louis's last wife was aunt to the Swaim brothers." Dalfon gave Lucky a particularly knowing look. "I think Margot was the cousin your Ma contacted to take you in."

Lucky had no idea what to make of all this. He couldn't imagine prim, condemning Margot Swaim as a relative much less summon any feeling of family for a stranger like Louis Moreau. Moreau was one of those names he'd read in papers and thought little of except that great riches hadn't seemed to bring the man much joy, judging by the arrogant, sour visage of his portraits. This talk about inheritance and a grandfather he'd never known—never could know—disturbed him. He'd felt so much more relaxed before, when it had just been him and Dalfon lying here together. An unwanted thought occurred to him.

"Is all of this really what you came back to Riverain County for?" Lucky asked.

"No. I was always coming back for you. But all of this, as you say, came along with me. Maybe solving it is something I'm supposed to do—maybe that's why I had to lose you for three years." Dalfon's gaze lifted again to the evening star. "Do you believe in destiny?"

Lucky glanced to the stars but returned his attention to Dalfon. All that light in the heavens moved steady as clockwork, but Dalfon? He presented a riddle with almost every word he said.

"You mean like when the preacher talks about the end times coming and how nobody can escape the lake of fire?" Lucky scowled. "I'm not inclined to believe in that. *Mon père* taught me that no matter how sinful we may be, we are always reborn with the opportunity to redeem ourselves. Life never ends, it simply takes on a new form."

"Maybe that's what makes you such a sympathetic and forgiving soul."

Lucky just laughed. "I was hardly forgiving when I thought you'd run out on me."

"I rode with a man who got himself hanged after shooting a woman on her wedding day all because she resembled the girl who threw him over years before," Dalfon said. "Trust me, vengeful you ain't. You might have been mad, but you still shared your food and heard me out. You're just the sort that old Shakespeare was chasing after when he wrote, 'Shall I compare thee to a summer's day? Thou art more lovely and more temperate.'"

"That ain't got a thing to do with believing in fate," Lucky said, though he felt oddly flattered by all the thees and thous Dalfon quoted.

"Sorry, you distracted me. And for the record, I don't hold with all that hell and eternal damnation either," Dalfon agreed. "But I do believe that some things—some people—are so important to each other's lives that they're drawn together over and over. I think that's how it is for me and you. No matter how far I wandered from you, I kept thinking of you, and everything I did always brought me back to you. You may think I'm spinning some far-fetched story, but I'm not. Hand to my heart, even I didn't believe it at first but now I'm sure. Dante got it right when he wrote, 'Do not be afraid; our fate cannot be taken from us; it is a gift.'"

Lucky scrutinized Dalfon with skepticism. Three years gone didn't strike him as being drawn back together by any inexorable pull. If it was fate, then it damn well took its time.

"I know I sound ridiculous, but just hear me out and you'll see." Dalfon sat up. "When this business with Pa Spivey started, I was working in Nevada for the Borax Brothers—"

"The owners of Three-horn Borax Company?" Lucky had a tin of the cleansing powder back at home. Pretty much everyone owned one of the big yellow cans with a snorting triceratops printed on the label. The Borax Brothers weren't celebrities, Lucky knew that, but it was exciting to imagine himself having any kind of personal connection—even if it was just that he knew Dalfon.

"The very ones," Dalfon informed him with a wry smile. "Anyway, they hired me to look for a missing person back east, and that's when I discovered that Jerry Buck and I were digging through the same records. It didn't take us long to work out that we were searching for the same person but in the hire of different men. That seemed like a weird coincidence, so Buck rode down here to check the situation out."

"I never saw any Pinkerton," Lucky felt obliged to say. "If I had, I'd have set him straight about Pa Spivey's whole scheme."

"I'm sure you would have. But he'd planned on approaching Margot Swaim first. She'd hinted that she was willing to disclose important information in exchange for funds that could secure her a divorce from Bernard. I don't imagine that plan worked out well for her or Buck." Dalfon's expression turned briefly sorrowful, but he shook his head. "When Buck didn't report back, I rode down after him, and I admit I wanted to see you even if it did mean trouble, so I went to your house first. And just my luck Frank and Harry Swaim mistook me for you and jumped me at your place."

"That's when Frank cast the curse on you?" Lucky asked. Dalfon nodded.

The full implication of that closed in on Lucky. The Swaims had been waiting for *him* with that curse. If Dalfon had arrived after Lucky had gotten home, he probably would have opened the door to discover Lucky's corpse sprawled on the dirt floor.

"I laid Frank out and took off," Dalfon went on. "About a minute later, I realized that I had to find you, because if two of the Swaims were waiting in ambush at your house that left one out in the marsh, hunting."

Lucky studied Dalfon. It had been such a near thing and at the same time no mere chance that Dalfon or the Swaims had been out at the edge of the marsh.

"That has to be fate," Dalfon said. "It can't just be pure chance that led me back to you exactly when it did. There's something uniting us—I don't have a word for it except fate. It feels like we were always meant to be together. As if my life is somehow yours." Dalfon's expression turned a little self-conscious. "Or at least that's how it feels for me."

Lucky wasn't certain he believed in fate, but he understood what Dalfon meant. He felt more alive, happier, and simply more himself with Dalfon. And yet the idea of giving in to it, of basking in so much joy only to lose it again terrified him. But he had to take that chance. He'd already lost three years of happiness with Dalfon to his own bleak expectations. That hadn't protected him from any pain only ensured it.

He leaned into Dalfon and wrapped an arm around him. Dalfon kissed him gently. The glow of the embers made the silver in Dalfon's hair appear golden. They were both still too spent to do more than kiss and caress one another, but even that felt lovely. They leaned into each other, at ease.

A curiosity occurred to Lucky. "What about the Borax Brothers? Didn't you start out looking for someone for them?"

"Yep. The same person Buck was looking for." Dalfon grinned at Lucky. "You. The Borax brothers are Juan Song-Garcia and Hector Song-Garcia. Hector hired me to find you, his lost son."

Lucky gaped at Dalfon. Excitement, disbelief and anxiety whirled through him like a cyclone. His father... As a child he'd dreamed and fantasized so much about his father finding him. But as the years passed, his hope had brought him only grinding disappointment. In the end he'd been almost relieved to abandon any thought of meeting his father ever again. Now Lucky grappled with the idea of reuniting with his father after twelve years. Would his father be delighted or disappointed in how he'd grown up? The fact he'd hired Pinkertons to find Lucky reassured him some. At least he knew his father had missed him.

"But what were the chances of him hiring you, of all people?" Lucky asked.

"You see what I mean about fate. Everywhere I searched, everything I wanted, every question I asked—the answer was always you, Lucky. Always."

That did seem like being dealt four aces twice in a row.

So much good fortune at once. Too much to believe it could be real. Lucky gazed at Dalfon and struggled with the impulse to crush the hopes that Dalfon's words had revived within him.

"So what do I do with this?" Lucky wondered.

Dalfon's smile faded a little and he cocked his head.

"Well, what is it you want to do?" Dalfon asked. "You want to meet your father?"

"I do but what if he—" Lucky didn't want to admit his fears aloud. But Dalfon simply continued to watch him, waiting. "What if it's all wrong somehow and he's not *mon père*? Or if he hates me—"

"I don't think either of those things are likely to happen. But if they do, well then we'll still be all right. If the man I met—who is the spitting image of you—turns out not to be your father, we'll keep looking. And if he has the poor judgment not to take to you, well, that's his loss, Lucky."

Lucky nodded. Hearing his fears voiced and answered so calmly didn't just reassure him, it reminded Lucky that he'd come through far worse already.

"Come back to Chicago with me and at least let the Moreau estate and Mr. Song-Garcia know that you're alive and well," Dalfon went on. "Beyond that, it's up to you. You know where things stand with me."

Did he? Reflexively, Lucky wanted to distrust all the sweetness and promise that Dalfon seemed to offer, but he stopped himself. When the world bent over backward to give him the joy he so desired, it would be utter cowardice and idiocy to turn it away for fear of it failing.

"Chicago it is, then," Lucky said.

Dalfon beamed at him and moved as if to kiss him again, but then a loud, low roar tore through night. Dalfon straightened and immediately drew his pistol from its holster. Lucky sat up and peered through the gloom.

"That was One-Eyed Pete's challenge roar," Lucky said. "Someone is coming too close to him."

There wasn't much that alarmed the giant saltwater crocodile, but sometimes sailboats set him off. Dalfon snatched up his discarded clothes and quickly pulled his moon goggles back over his eyes.

"It's a catboat," Dalfon whispered, "with a longhorn bull painted on the sail."

"The Swaims." Lucky had seen Frank take the small sailboat out a number of times in the past. He squinted into the dark and just made out the tall triangular sail. "How'd they find us here?"

"I don't—" Dalfon cut himself off and swore. "The curse. Bernard Swaim must have traced it."

"We need to get the thing away from us, then." Lucky noticed the metallic gleam of the curse's silvery spikes lying beyond the fire.

Dalfon stepped past Lucky and picked the thing up. "Or we use it to draw them into the woods, then circle back to set their boat adrift. That should strand them here while we make a clean getaway on your raft."

"You think that could work?" Lucky knew the hills of the island pretty well, but it would be tricky to lure the Swaims far enough from their boat they wouldn't notice it drifting. It would also mean outdistancing them to circle around without being seen on the way back.

Lucky buckled up his pants and snatched up his rifle.

"It'll work if we split the trouble between us." Dalfon shoved the curse into his coat pocket. "I'll draw them after me. You drop back to the beach and set their boat on its way across the sea. Then I'll loop back to you."

"I know the island better. I should be the one to lure them into the woods," Lucky argued.

"I've got moon lenses to show me were I'm stepping, and in the dark that could make all the difference—"

"But you don't know how to reach the beaches like I do."

"True, but I can carry this curse without awakening it," Dalfon responded. "And since I'm not a water mage, I'd have a hell of a time wading among all those crocodiles, much less moving a sailboat just where I pleased. You're the one who can do that, not me."

It took Lucky a moment to realize Dalfon was correct. He wasn't used to thinking of himself as powerful—certainly not compared to Dalfon. But he realized he would be the one who had to try to move the boat, especially with Dalfon being hurt.

Still, he couldn't see how Dalfon intended to circle back to the beach when he didn't know the island trails. Able to see in the dark or not, a place this overgrown presented all sorts of falls and tangles. Not to mention miles of beach.

Lucky considered for a moment. "Over the rise of this hill, there's an abandoned chapel. If you cut back behind it, you'll find a cobblestone path. It's overgrown and uneven, but it curves below a rocky overhang and leads to an old crypt in the side of the hill. Then it runs down to the water. I'll have the raft waiting on the beach where the path ends. You'll know the spot because there are two of those giant white rocks washed up against each other. They form an arch."

"The alchemic stones, you mean?" Dalfon asked.

"No. The white rocks, like the ones you were looking at when we first got here and you asked…" All at once Lucky realized why Dalfon had sounded so awed by the boulders. "Those are alchemic stone?"

"Yep." Dalfon nodded. "I'd wondered why the Swaims were willing to risk murdering a Pinkerton to get control of salt-flooded property. Then I saw this place and realized it has to be worth a fortune. You're gonna be rich as Croesus, Lucky."

"I'd be over the moon just now if I wasn't so worried that we aren't going to live past this hour."

"You're going to live, Lucky." Dalfon pulled him close in a hard embrace. Then he lifted his head, and Lucky felt his entire body tense. He released Lucky and adjusted the lenses of his goggles. "They're mooring, not too far from where you tied up your raft. Looks like it's just the three brothers, but they're all three lugging dinosaur guns. I'd better get going."

"Take care of yourself." Lucky kissed him quickly. "I won't forgive you if you don't come back to me this time."

"I wouldn't forgive myself," Dalfon replied with a grin. Then he dashed up the rise towards the thickets and woods that hid the crumbling chapel. Lucky dropped back, distancing himself from the dull embers of their fire and hiding in the shadows of the gravestones.

Only a few minutes later, he saw the Swaim brothers step into the light of the dying fire. All three men carried large-bore hunting rifles. Frank crouched down and warmed his hands while Harry swung his rifle up as a bat winged past him. The report of the rifle boomed like a cannon.

"For the love of God, Harry," Frank growled. "Stop shooting at every living thing. Save at least one round for the Pinkerton, will you?"

"Go catch a fart," Harry replied. "You're only complaining because you don't have the guts to do what needs doing."

Frank shot his brother a murderous look, and Lucky wondered if the brothers might simply kill each other, but then Bernard drew near.

"Hush, both of you," Bernard said, his words silencing his younger brothers. He stood at the edge of the fire with what looked like a compass in his hand. Something seemed off about the shape of his head. Lucky studied him, picking his form out from the surrounding shadows. Bernard turned towards his brothers and the firelight. Alarm shot through Lucky as he realized Bernard wore goggles with milky-white moon lenses. He'd be able to see Dalfon clear as day.

"He's headed up the hill," Bernard announced, and he looked again at the small device in his right hand. "He appears to be making very good time for someone in the grip of a curse."

"He must be dead by now. Probably just his remains being dragged up a tree by a cougar," Frank commented.

"Yes," Harry replied. "The catfish-catching cougar that rafted him across the strait. That seems likely."

"If it really was the Spivey kid's raft we can assume he's here too," Bernard said.

"Then we can take care of both our problems in one night," Harry commented.

Lucky didn't remain there to hear them further malign him. He crept on his hands and knees between the gravestones until he reached the salt sedge growing at the edge of the beach. There, the tall grasses and bulrushes disguised his silhouette.

Lucky raced along the beach. The surf lapped at his feet, coiling and pulling at him while One-Eyed Pete watched him pass in silence. He found the Swaims' catboat easily; its triangular white sail stood out from the dark water like the steeple on a church. Not far from where it drifted, several logs from Lucky's raft bobbed in a tangle of slashed reed ropes. The rest of his raft lay strewn on the beach destroyed beyond repair.

Lucky resisted the urge to swear and instead considered his options. Really there was only one: the Swaims' catboat. It sat, with its bow up on the sandbar while the stern bobbed in the surf. Bernard had moored it to a tree.

Lucky stood almost frozen with dread. No doubt Bernard Swaim had placed spells on the boat to keep it from being boarded by undesirables like himself. The only way he was going to get aboard it would be to reach into the drowning depths of the waters surrounding him. His throat tightened just at the memory of feeling salt water choking him. He'd endured it once already tonight. He didn't know that he could do it again.

But the thought of Dalfon waiting for him with the Swaims closing in behind spurred Lucky to act.

He waded out and laid his hands on the side of the catboat. It heaved against him. The surface seemed to bristle at his touch, and shocks of red light flicked up like needles, pricking his fingers. Lucky clenched his teeth against a cry. His hands burned like he gripped fistfuls of angry jellyfish. The pain brought tears to Lucky's eyes, but he didn't draw his hands back.

The surf crashed against his legs. He pushed against those agonizing red tongues with the cool and vast power of the sea. The water swelled into his senses and seemed to swallow him, blotting out the moon and stars overhead. Losing himself in the lightless depths and miles of rolling waves terrified him, but not so much as failing Dalfon did. His ears roared and his lungs burned for air. But Lucky held on and kept the ocean's power flowing through him and flooding into Bernard Swaim's poisonous curses. He drowned the spells and washed his will through the wood, steel, rope and canvas. At last he completely doused the fiery scarlet spells Bernard Swaim had carved all across the boat. Even the Swaim emblem washed from the sail.

Then he broke from the ocean's grip, gasping in lungfuls of warm, night air. He sagged against the boat, his whole frame shaking like he'd just emerged from an ice bath. He wanted to remain there, regaining his strength, but there was no time for him to rest. Dalfon needed him.

Lucky took up the catboat's mooring line, shoved the keel off the sand and clambered into the shallow boat. The tide gripped him immediately. He pulled himself onto the thwart and dangled one hand over the gunnel to touch the water.

This time he took in only brief sips from the vast sea surrounding him, just enough to catch a current. Then the water sped him around the island to the bay where two huge alchemic stones formed a ragged arch.

The stones gleamed—almost glowed—in the moonlight, as did several of the cobbles of the path winding up the steep cliff face. Most of the path lay obscured beneath brambles. Dogwood clung to the sheer rock face, while ivy spilled down from the overhang. Though the stone outcropping where the entry to the crypt stood remained relatively clear. A single magnolia tree spread its petals in the gloom.

As the catboat bobbed and rocked beneath him, Lucky searched for any sign of Dalfon. High on the cliff above, a flock of small pterosaurs startled from the foliage. Then the thunderous boom of rifle fire resounded over the water. Dalfon bolted across the open space near the crypt.

A second rifle shot sounded, and a hunk of stone splintered and tumbled down the cliff to the beach. Dalfon disappeared into the cover of brush. Moments later Frank and Harry Swaim pelted after him. Bernard followed at a more leisurely rate. He paused on the outcropping and surveyed the beach below him. Then he knelt and lifted his long rifle.

On the path, Harry whooped and hooted like a hound dog after a fox. Lucky couldn't discern Frank's commentary but felt certain it wasn't complimentary. Taking the situation in, Lucky could see what the Swaims planned. Harry and Frank would drive Dalfon out onto the open beach, and Bernard would pick him off from his high vantage point.

Lucky shouted but his warning didn't carry over the breaking surf and Harry Swaim's ecstatic howls. Then he caught sight of Dalfon edging down towards the archway of alchemic stone. Frank Swaim burst from the path behind Dalfon. He fired. Brilliant blue flames burst up from the archway where the spells in his ammunition struck the alchemic stone. Framed in eerie blue light, Dalfon fired his own pistol twice. Frank toppled to the ground, and Harry Swaim went silent. Dalfon peered up at the path behind him, then he turned, and Lucky knew from the way he straightened that he'd sighted the sail of the catboat.

Dalfon charged from the cover of the archway. Lucky shouted for him to turn back but already Bernard angled his rifle down, taking his time to aim. The moon lenses he wore gleamed.

Lucky swung his battered Sharps rifle down from his back. Only one shot, and he wasn't certain he'd make the distance. Dalfon pelted across the loose sand.

Lucky aimed for the milky-white lens covering Bernard's left eye, then drew in all the raging power he could contain and poured it into the bullet as he pulled the trigger. The Sharps kicked into Lucky's shoulder, and at the same moment he heard Bernard's rifle roar.

Bernard's bullet sent up a ribbon of red light exploding only inches from Dalfon. Dalfon fell to his knees but staggered up and kept running. Bernard's rifle dropped from his hands and clattered down the cliff.

Lucky set aside his rifle and reached out to Dalfon as he stumbled through the deep water and rolling waves. He lunged forward; Lucky caught his hand and hauled him aboard the boat. They held each other. Dalfon shivered and pressed his face into Lucky's shoulder.

"Are you all right?" Lucky asked. "They didn't hit you, did they?"

"Not nearly as often as they tried." Dalfon pulled a game smile, but he sagged in Lucky's arms, and his face looked as white as the sail. "Bernard may have winged my flank."

Lucky glanced down and horror gripped him. Blood streamed from Dalfon's left side. It pooled over the floor of the boat, and Lucky knew instantly that Dalfon was losing far too much, far too fast. Dalfon sank from Lucky's arms and sprawled against the thwart.

"No." Lucky crouched beside him. Hot tears filled his eyes. "No. You can't be hit. We're gonna get away together. It's our fate."

Dalfon stroked his cheek, and his fingers felt icy.

"It's your fate. It's always been you…" Dalfon's hand fell limply.

"No. No, you can't leave me again." Lucky tore open Dalfon's coat and shirt. The ragged gash in Dalfon's abdomen gaped jagged as a shark's maw. Bernard's cartridge had ripped straight through his back and punched a hole in his gut. Desperately, Lucky attempted to staunch the river of blood, but his hands couldn't even cover the open wound. Burning hot blood welled over his fingers. He couldn't stop it.

All the sea for him to call upon, but he couldn't stop this one red stream.

Dalfon's head dropped back at a terrible angle. A sob wrenched from Lucky. He couldn't lose Dalfon. He couldn't. The money, the land, even finding his father—none of it was worth Dalfon's life.

His eyes fell on the burnt-out charm hanging around Dalfon's neck. The dull star of Dalfon's Magen David. The charm had healed Dalfon before, but the alchemic stone that powered it was gone—burned through. But if what Dalfon said was true, Lucky could power the charm himself by touching it.

Without hesitation, Lucky grabbed it, clutching the cold metal hard in his fist. The six points bit into his palm, then a sickening vertigo swept over him and a burning sensation tightened his throat. The burn flared to scorching agony—as if his veins were blazing seams of coal igniting his whole body.

His hand jerked reflexively, but he forced himself to keep his grip on the charm. It didn't matter if it killed him, not anymore. He clenched his eyes closed and let the power of the surrounding sea surge through him as the charm burned him away.

He didn't fight the flood of darkness and cold water that engulfed him. Instead he welcomed the strength it brought him to fight for Dalfon's life. As briny water filled his lungs and burned his eyes he opened himself to the immensity of the ocean. He drank in vast waves as if they were air. He reached down into black depths, lit only by flickering strange creatures and pulled power from the dark currents. Lucky's senses rose across miles of open water and coastlines of crashing surf, drawing up swells of immense force.

In the midst of roaring storms and cresting waves a strange calm filled him. He was beyond drowning. Nothing could harm him here.

In a cool, distant way he knew his body lay, small and shaking, stretched across Dalfon's. The tiny hull of a fragile boat held them both. He was there and at the same time miles away, twirling through waterspouts and racing beneath howling gales.

"Lucky." Dalfon's voice sounded soft and far away, but it drew him like a siren song.

"Lucky. Darling, please don't..." The pain in Dalfon's words reverberated through him. He recognized that hurt—that broken-hearted loss—too well.

Lucky's senses flew across the vast leagues. He threw himself from the grasp of the surrounding waters and fell like a cresting wave back into his own cold flesh.

Strong, warm hands caught his fingers and pulled them

free of the charm. Lucky opened his eyes to see Dalfon sitting up on the thwart and holding his hand. Dry blood streaked his abdomen, and Lucky could see fine hair and smooth skin beneath.

He threw his arms around Dalfon, hugging him hard, and Dalfon returned his embrace, pressing his face into the curve of Lucky's neck.

"I thought you were…" Lucky couldn't bring himself to say the word.

"Me too, darling." Dalfon sounded almost surprised. "I felt sure I was a goner, but then there you were." He lifted his head and grinned. "Shining over me just like my Lucky star."

Epilogue

Above the Inland Sea 1900

Dalfon studied the view beyond the airship portal. Fat white clouds drifted over the dark waters of the Inland Sea like islands released from their earthly bonds. Gulls and pterosaurs swooped past, and the setting sun gilded them to the luster of 24-carat gold. Then the airship breezed into the icy, white mass of a cloudbank, and the view turned uniform and pale as a blizzard. Delicate patterns of frost limned the edges of the portal.

Inside the airship, heat generated by the humming alchemic engines whirled through overhead fans, producing the feeling of a tropical evening breeze wafting through the lounge. Glancing around at the well-heeled travelers, a man would never have suspected that they soared through driving February winds or that only hours earlier they'd raced to outdistance the dark winter storm that had seized Chicago.

No, here in the lounge an atmosphere of relaxed luxury reigned.

Heiresses, socialites, robber-barons and captains of industry gathered around the mahogany tables, sipping cocktails and chatting.

In the midst of the well-heeled crowd, Dalfon picked out Jim Miller, a ham-fisted son-of-a-bitch whose leptoceratops herds had grown at the same fast rate that other ranchers turned up dead. The five weathered men playing poker at the table next to Miller had stripped down to their waistcoats and shirtsleeves, and judging by the revolvers hanging from their hips, Dalfon guessed they numbered among Miller's army of hired guns.

Two tables farther down, looking overdressed and uneasy, Miller's scrawny wife sat among a group of laughing women. They'd all worn feather stoles up to the lounge. But unlike the others who merely draped their wraps over the backs of their silk chairs, Mrs. Miller made a show of summoning her maid. She berated the girl for her tired appearance and handed her iridescent stole over while remarking that the authentic ridingbird feathers were more valuable than the maid would ever be. The women surrounding Mrs. Miller appeared aghast but Mr. Miller beamed at his wife's mean display.

Charles Dickens had penned a few condescending remarks about the coarse quality of certain newly rich folks, and Dalfon thought those sardonic sentiments applied pretty well to the Millers. Except where Mr. Dickens's characters were tacky with furniture polish, the Millers struck Dalfon as rank with the stench of human degradation and murder.

Feeling his mood sinking, Dalfon turned his attention away from Miller and his party. He sipped his gin gimlet and opened up the memoir he'd purchased just before Lucky had booked their flight to Fort Arvada.

At once his mood lifted.

The biography was the second in a series and followed the scandalous adventuress, H. Astor, on her journeys deep into India as the country threw off the rule of the East India Company and England. Only fifty pages in, and already Dalfon was riveted. The author's disgust with her fellow countrymen, coupled with her growing friendships with native merchants, scholars and beggars, filled Dalfon with a thrilling anticipation for the bold acts of treason that now made H. Astor infamous. (And got her books banned in the new British capitol of Toronto, in Canada.)

But beyond that the text itself was permeated with fragrance and poetry. Butter lamps and camphor incense perfumed the pages while thunder transformed into the eerie roars of tigers prowling the dark night. The fragment of one poem in particular held Dalfon's attention.

The stars will be watching us, and we will show them what it is to be a thin crescent moon. You and I unselfed, will be together, indifferent to idle speculation, you and I. The parrots of heaven will be cracking sugar as we laugh together, you and I.

He'd never heard of the Persian poet, Jalāl ad-Dīn Muhammad Rūmī, who'd penned the verses, but he wished he could know more of the man's work. It made him think of lying in the moonlight with Lucky, and he smiled as he read the lines again.

Dalfon rushed further into the memoir while around him soft conversation drifted through the room, not quite drowning the melody plucked out by the latest player piano. At the end of a chapter Dalfon looked up just as the airship broke through the cloudbank. A spectacular sunset blazed between the towering peaks of a snowy mountain range, while below a vast dark sea crashed and rolled.

Dalfon frowned. How damn long could it take an engineer to give Lucky and a prospective buyer a tour of the bridge and engine rooms? Then, remembering the wide-eyed exuberance of the weedy engineer who'd designed this newest airship, Dalfon reckoned he still had a good half-hour to wait. The man had rhapsodized over the newly installed wireless telegraph and something he called the *radio spectrum* for nearly the whole hour he'd shared the carriage ride to the airfield with Dalfon and Lucky. Dalfon sighed and resigned himself to a little more time of solitude in the bustling lounge.

Black-suited waiters cruised the lounge, surveying the pampered, wealthy passengers and furnishing them with drinks, exotic fruits and other extravagances when called upon. Dalfon remembered his gin and applied himself to it.

Across the room he could see that either not enough whiskey or too much had gone down Miller's belly. The man glowered out at the sunset and slumped in his chair with the petulant expression of a bulldog grown too fat to lick its own balls. Miller kicked the chair of one of the men playing poker. The fellow, who'd had his back to Dalfon, turned.

Dalfon scowled. He hadn't laid eyes on Tom Horn in eight years, and if it had been eighty it wouldn't have been long enough. Back then Tom had been the one with a Pinkerton's badge, and Dalfon had idolized him more than a little. He'd been the sort of imposing, hard man of the world that, at eighteen, Dalfon had longed to become. Quiet, sardonic and already famous all across Colorado, it was said there wasn't a man he couldn't track or a firearm he couldn't handle with deadly accuracy.

To Dalfon's displeasure Miller jabbed his thumb in Dalfon's direction and leaned forward to mutter something to Tom. At once, Tom's attention snapped to Dalfon.

Both of them reflexively dropped their right hands to their revolvers. Dalfon reckoned he could draw a hair faster then Tom, but he knew for a fact he didn't have it in him to open fire in a room full of innocent folk. Tom on the other hand had already proven himself perfectly willing to gun down any number of unarmed, uninvolved bystanders. He'd slaughtered two of Dalfon's associates whose only offense had been to witness him and his men murder the upstart ranchers, Nate Champion and Nick Ray.

Tom had lost his badge and his job over the incident, but to Dalfon's mind he should have been strung up. It wasn't as if the minor rebukes had kept Tom from going on to assassinate countless other innocent men and boys at the behest of wealthy ranchers like Miller.

Dalfon lifted his right hand from his gun belt and took another sip of his gin. Tom smiled and he too released the grip of his revolver. Then he stood and sauntered to Dalfon's table. He didn't ask to join Dalfon but simply pulled out the chair intended for Lucky and dropped his big frame down.

"Well, it's been a coon's age since I last laid eyes on you, Dalfon. But you know I never forgot your face. Last I heard you were throwing down for Pinkerton."

Dalfon nodded.

Studying Tom, he took a little pleasure in recognizing that the years had not treated him kindly. Gin blossoms flowered beneath the deep tan of his weathered skin, and most of his thick black hair had retreated leaving an isolated oily tuft to sit over his forehead like an abandoned outpost. The whites of his eyes had turned as yellow as his teeth, and though he remained as tall and straight as ever, his muscles looked withered.

"You'll forgive me for not recognizing you right away, Tom." Dalfon forced one of his sharp, bright smiles. "You've gotten so damn old, I mistook you for my granddaddy at first. What are you now, a hundred?"

Tom's eyes narrowed, and Dalfon could see him considering taking a swing. Dalfon stared right back at him, ready to take Tom down to the floor and beat the life out of him. But Tom just barked out a dry laugh. His gaze remained cold and assessing.

Dalfon realized that Tom hadn't survived to forty by taking on younger, stronger men in fair fights. It wasn't surprising that as he grew older he'd become less notable for his fast draw and brawling nature and more notorious for shooting men in the back from a safe distance.

"Sometimes I do feel like old man Methuselah, considering how many of you green boys I've outlived." Tom gestured to one of the waiters and the young man blanched. He slunk to the table and all but shot away from them after Tom ordered pisco and fresh oysters for himself and Dalfon.

"Miller don't mind footing your tab as well as mine. He can afford about anything you might want," Tom told Dalfon.

"I had no idea that the man was so sweet on me," Dalfon replied.

"You have a reputation." Tom shrugged. He didn't appear particularly impressed but he wouldn't be. In all the years Dalfon had hunted other men, he'd never gone after a fellow who hadn't taken a life.

"His dance card looks full enough already." Dalfon inclined his head towards the four other men seated to Miller's left. In fact, now that he considered it, the number of armed men Miller had brought with him for a flight aboard a secure, luxury airship struck Dalfon as so far outside normal that it seemed less indicative of a need to display his wealth to the other passengers and more of an act of paranoia.

"If I didn't know better I'd say he's looking as haunted as Macbeth after Banquo's ghost dropped in on his banquet," Dalfon commented.

Tom frowned and the lines in his face became deep as canyons.

"No Banquos in our parts, but there was a rancher who had an accident near Miller's place a few months back." A smile twitched across Tom's lips, giving away the part he no doubt played in the man's murder. Then his scowl returned. "Turns out the widow is one of them damn wind mages and has about a thousand blood relatives up north in Sovereign Tribes Lands. Miller thinks they're on the warpath for him."

Dalfon almost laughed because if anything would serve bastards like Jim Miller and Tom Horn right it would be the Sovereign Tribes turning the might of their mages against them. The last bastard who'd merited such wrath had been Captain Edward S. Godfrey, who had given the command to open fire and sparked the massacre at Wounded Knee. (Ironically, Godfrey's attempt to end the Ghost Dance had woken immense power in the Black Hills and united hundreds of bands into the independent nation that now controlled much of the northwest.)

Dalfon shook his head. "Miller's done a hell of a lot more than have one rancher killed if he's managed to provoke the Sovereign Tribes."

"What Mr. Miller's done in the whole of his life isn't my business and I don't figure it's yours either," Tom replied, and Dalfon felt certain that Miller wasn't the only one up to his neck in shit. Likely Tom stood just as deep.

"The man's paying good money," Tom went on. "And there's bound to be one hell of a ride ahead for any man tough enough to sign on with him. So are you in or not?"

For an instant Dalfon felt that old drive for action and adventure rise in his blood. Maybe if Tom had made the offer to him when he'd been a fifteen-year-old runaway, he'd have accepted just to feel excited and alive. But now he'd seen more than his share of action and learned that the measure of a man's character could be taken not only by the battles he won but also by those he refused to fight.

As Dalfon formulated his response, seemingly every person in the lounge went quiet, turning rapt attention upon the doorway. Both Tom and Dalfon looked as well. And

Dalfon's heart swelled with a strange mix of joy and pride.

There stood the now-famous heir of the immense Moreau fortune, Luc Song-Garcia. Dalfon's own Lucky.

With his shaggy dark hair fashionably shorn and slicked back, the fine angles of his face stood out clearly. All the world could see the expressive quality of his dark eyes and appreciate his handsome, full mouth. When he smiled, his whole face lit up, and he appeared somehow both young and worldly at once.

The increase in his income hadn't done his wardrobe any harm either. Gone were the loose sack overalls and the shapeless shirt that had hidden the hard lines and dexterity of his body. Now a black jacket cut from supple pterodactyl leather and a vest embroidered with gold silk emphasized his corded shoulders and long waist. Fine gold threads glinted from the dark cloth of his fitted trousers, and his boots gleamed like obsidian.

Gazing at him, Dalfon was reminded of a description he'd read of a deity carved into a Hindu temple: grace and power playing through lithe limbs and a seductive smile. Dalfon guessed he wasn't alone in the thought, when he heard one of the nearby women whisper, "He looks like an Indian prince."

For his part, Lucky appeared oblivious to the stir he caused. His attention remained on the statuesque Black woman standing beside him. She too drew stares and inspired whispered speculation. Most people knew of the deadly amazons of the African kingdom of Dahomey. They'd become renowned after crushing Napoleon III's attempt to drag his sunken French empire up onto West African shores. However, very few Americans had actually laid eyes upon one of the famed warrior women—at least not and lived to tell about it. But the cerulean-striped uniform just visible beneath the woman's long leopard-skin coat combined with the beaded emerald crocodile emblazoned across the woman's tall white cap were legendary.

At sixty-six, Seh-Dong-Hong-Beh was drawn and white-haired but still looked like she could run a man through with the sword that hung from her bejeweled belt. Though in truth, she'd come at the behest of her young king, to negotiate the import of custom-made Moreau airship engines. She and Lucky smiled at each other, exchanged a few words and then both laughed. Three younger Dahomey guardswomen, all with revolvers holstered at their hips, appeared amused as well.

Dalfon turned his attention back to Tom, who scowled at Lucky and Seh-Dong-Hong-Beh, making a show of appearing unimpressed. "Some people get it easy from the time they're born till the day they die," Tom muttered.

Dalfon almost laughed at the idea that either Lucky or Seh-Dong-Hong-Beh had numbered among the pampered few who navigated life without knowing a single hardship.

"When there's bitterness inside you, not even a mouthful of sugar will taste sweet," Dalfon replied, not that he expected Tom to recognize the proverb. It had been one of many that Dalfon's mother had repeated, though only recently had he actually realized the wisdom in it. Men like Tom were bitter every inch of their beings. No amount of good fortune or kindness would ever be enough for them.

Dalfon looked away from the man to see their waiter approaching the table with the glasses of golden pisco and dishes of oysters that Tom had ordered.

"You might as well take them over to the table there." Dalfon gestured to the poker players slumped in their seats near Miller. Tom scowled at Dalfon, and the waiter stood, looking uncertain.

"I got company on the way. So you'll just have to scoot on back to Miller and tell him I don't care what bait he puts on his hook I'm not biting," Dalfon told Tom.

Tom didn't budge. They both knew Tom had divulged a little too much to him for this all to end amiably. But Dalfon wasn't willing to fight here and now. He suspected that even Tom didn't relish the prospect of attempting to silence this many witnesses.

"Look," Dalfon said, "if you and Miller can't take no for an answer, then I'll be more than happy to settle this at forty paces after this airship sets down."

For a moment Tom just sat there, and Dalfon could almost feel resentment and hate rising off the man like steam wafting up from a boiling pot. Tom's right hand twitched and Dalfon's fingers curled around the grip of his gun. The waiter tottered back, and somehow managed not to spill either drinks or dishes.

Tom held up both his hands and pulled a grimace of a smile, then he stood.

"We'll finish this on the ground. Only decent to give you time to write your final will." Tom strode back to Miller and rejoined the other men playing cards. Oddly, the waiter offered Dalfon an almost conspiratorial little wink while Tom's back was turned and quickly followed the man to serve the table.

Dalfon scowled at the twilight gloom and the growing black silhouettes of the mountains outside the portal. At best he had an hour to figure a way out of this mess. Chances that Tom would fight fair, or even alone, were slimmer than an onionskin. Not that Dalfon wanted to engage in some idiot duel. Winning would only make him an outlaw and losing… Well, a corpse wouldn't have much of a future traveling the world and making love to Lucky.

"Mind if I join you?" Lucky's voice pulled Dalfon back from his grim contemplation of the twilight.

"Of course!" Dalfon almost cringed at his own far-too-hearty response.

Lucky sank down into the seat Tom had vacated seconds before and cocked his head, considering Dalfon.

"Your friend didn't run off on my account, did he?" Lucky asked.

"Tom Horn is *no* friend of mine. And across the room isn't nearly far enough away."

Lucky's expression shifted from concerned to surprised, and then settled into a look Dalfon didn't think he'd seen before—almost a guilty excitement.

"Tom Horn." Lucky stole a sidelong glance to where Tom sat slugging back his pisco. Dalfon could hardly stand to look at the man.

"Is Seh-Dong-Hong-Beh going to join us?" Dalfon asked, to get his mind off the heap of trouble Tom Horn would doubtless cause. He was going to have to explain it all to Lucky but he felt too riled up to keep his voice low and restrain himself from hurling something at that son-of-a-bitch Miller. Of all the flights why did the bastard have to be on this one? When had riding the rail become too common for him and his gang?

"No, she wanted to talk more with the security chief up on the bridge," Lucky replied. For no reason that Dalfon could understand, he flicked another quick glance over to Miller's party, and a sly little smile lit his face.

Dalfon considered Lucky for a moment then leaned a little nearer to him.

"Is there a reason you're looking so smug and sneaky?" Lucky nodded.

"Do you recall any of that conversation in the carriage concerning the radio spectrum?" Lucky asked.

"Only that the newest airships have been fitted with wireless telegraphs, or something of that nature," Dalfon replied.

"Well, we decided to test the range of ours out, for Seh-Dong-Hong-Beh's benefit. And we were able to pick up signals all the way from the Lakota Island station to Fort Arvada…"

"And?" Dalfon prompted.

"It turns out lawmen are tearing through every train leaving Chicago, trying to lay hands on a Mr. Miller and a fellow traveling with him called *Tom Horn*." Lucky lowered his voice. "They're wanted for desecrating sacred ground and five counts of murder. They even shot a fourteen-year-old boy in the back."

Dalfon was not surprised. Though he did feel a little more resolved to do all he could to put Tom in a grave. He supposed he ought to describe his own encounter with the man to Lucky since they were already on the subject. But Lucky got that sly look again and went on.

"As it happened, the chief steward was on the bridge when we picked up the transmission, and he recognized the description of Miller and Tom Horn as well as four other felons in Miller's pay. Then the boson shows us a note that a maid slipped to him when they passed in the hall. It just said 'Miller is here'. He couldn't make heads nor tails of it till that instant."

Dalfon thought again of the worn-looking maid and felt a surge of admiration for her audacity. Surrounded by cold-blooded killers and still she'd done what she could to stymie them. Fist and pistols weren't the only weapons that could kill a man, sometimes it only took a girl who kept her wits.

Though considering the situation, he and the ship's crew would need firepower to take Miller and his boys before they could flee back to the fortifications of Miller's ranch.

"Of course, right off, Seh-Dong-Hong-Beh offered to bring her women down here and blow the criminals' brains out. The ship's engineer almost fainted and started talking a mile a minute about cabin pressure and ricocheting bullets." Lucky shook his head, his expression wry. "Then the wireless telegraph operator informs us that she's contacted the airstrip in Fort Arvada and that they'll have the sheriff and his deputies waiting for our arrival."

Dalfon nodded. That was good, better than he could have hoped for.

"Having the sheriff at the airstrip will make things easier," he said softly. "But it's going to be tricky to keep all of these other passengers out of the crossfire if Tom or any of the others decide they aren't going to be taken alive." Dalfon felt certain no one would think anything of it if Lucky stayed back, safe, aboard the airship. But he wasn't certain Lucky would accept the proposition. Dalfon glanced across the room at the men and women gathered around them. There had to be some way to protect them.

"I reckoned it would be best if nobody fired off a shot at all." Lucky smiled. "So I had the ship doctor spike their drinks."

"Their drinks." Dalfon's thoughts had been so occupied anticipating the inevitability of a gunfight—and trying to work a safe way through the gunsmoke and searing lead whistling through the air—that it took him a moment to grasp the full implication of Lucky's words and put that together with the wink he'd received from the jumpy waiter.

He stole a glance over to Miller's party. Three of the poker players were already dozing in their chairs. Tom and the man across from him both studied their cards with half-lidded eyes and seemed to nod off as Dalfon watched, laying their heads down on the tabletop.

Miller still sat slumped, staring out at the night, but now Dalfon recognized the slack, glazed quality of his expression as that of a man deep in a stupor. Then with the timing that would have done a seasoned comic proud, Mrs. Miller began to snore.

The women near her lifted their chins, sniffed and moved to another table.

Dalfon laughed and Lucky grinned at him.

"You think it's safe for me to fetch Seh-Dong-Hong-Beh and the ship's officers to tie these scoundrels up and lock them in the brig?" Lucky asked.

"I think so." Dalfon stood along with Lucky. "I'd be delighted to lend a hand, in fact."

In less than a quarter of an hour they'd disarmed, roped and incarcerated Tom Horn, the Millers and their four gunmen. The greatest hardship was lugging Tom's deadweight into a cold cell in the brig. The man weighed nearly two hundred pounds. But when they were done, Dalfon felt exuberant with relief and also more taken with his lover than he would have thought imaginable.

"The battle, sir, is not to the strong alone," Dalfon quoted once they were alone in their adjoining rooms. "It is to the vigilant, the active, the brave."

"I suppose someone fancy said that." Lucky kicked off his glossy shoes and sat down on the big bed.

"Patrick Henry," Dalfon supplied. He sat beside Lucky. He wished he had words—his own words—to express just how vastly Lucky had enriched his life. How caring about Lucky had awakened ideals in him he'd thought long lost to a lifetime of rapacious self-interest. He could have so easily become a man like Tom Horn, or worse, because Dalfon knew how to sweet-talk and hide lies beneath the dazzle of a silver-tongue. His capacity for brutality and treachery could have made him a true monster.

One may smile and smile and be a villain, wasn't that how Shakespeare had put it?

Instead he was beginning to see ways of winning his fights without ever raising his fists. And he was learning that the most powerful words were often disarmingly simple—honesty laid bare. The idea frightened him some, but what was courage other than confronting fear?

"You know what I say?" Dalfon asked.

"What?"

"I love you." There it was, simple as salt and awaiting an answer.

Lucky flushed and put his arms around Dalfon. He said nothing but his kiss was beyond eloquence, while outside the night sky lit up with countless stars.

ACKNOWLEDGMENTS

I've been very fortunate to receive historical pointers, feedback, encouragement, editorial insights and cup after cup of black coffee just when I needed them from many generous and talented people.

In particular I want to give thanks to Nicole Kimberling, Tenea D. Johnson, Anne Scott, Carl Cipra and Gwen Toevs.

I also owe a debt to Tracy Timmons-Gray of Read With Pride for inspiring me to publish *The Hollow History of Professor Perfectus* as well as to Elizabeth North and Tricia Kristufek at Dreamspinner Press for taking on *Get Lucky* in its first incarnation.

Last but not least, thanks to The Team and my family for just being here with me. And to Alexarc Mastema. (Alex's Maniac Coffee has played a vital role in the generation of many of my projects and I hope it will continue to fuel inspiration for many more to come.)

ABOUT THE AUTHOR

Award-winning author, Ginn Hale lives in the Pacific Northwest with her lovely wife and their ancient, evil cat. She spends the rainy days observing local fungi. During the stormy nights she writes science-fiction and fantasy stories featuring LGBT protagonists. (Attempts to convince the cat to be less evil have been largely abandoned.)

Ginn Hale's publications include:

Maze-Born Trouble
Swift and the Black Dog
Wicked Gentlemen

The Rifter Trilogy
The Shattered Gates
The Holy Road
His Sacred Bones

The Cadeleonian Series
Lord of the White Hell Book One
Lord of the White Hell Book Two
Champion of the Scarlet Wolf Book One
Champion of the Scarlet Wolf Book Two

Anthologies
Irregulars
Charmed & Dangerous
Magic & Mayhem
Once Upon A Time in the Weird West
Hell Cop
Hell Cop2

9 781935 560517